THE ANGELIC GAME

ANIA MALINA
PARIS DREAMBOOK

The
Angelic Game

LAWRENCE OSBORNE

BLOOMSBURY

First published 1990
Copyright © 1990 by Lawrence Osborne

The moral right of the author has been asserted.

Bloomsbury Publishing Ltd, 2 Soho Square, London WIV 5DE

A CIP catalogue record for this book
is available from the British Library

ISBN 0 7475 0573 X

10 9 8 7 6 5 4 3 2 1

I am indebted to F. Gonzalez-Crussi, *On the Nature of Things Erotic*
for details of the life of the Marquis de Sade, to Oliver Sacks's paper
'Cupid's Disease' in *The Man Who Mistook His Wife for a Hat*
(Duckworth, 1985) for information on dormant syphilis, and to Denis
Mack Smith, *Mussolini* (Weidenfeld & Nicholson, 1981).

Typeset by Hewer Text Composition Services, Edinburgh
Printed in Great Britain by Butler & Tanner Ltd, Frome and London

From the beginning of childhood the mouth of Lili Dorziat was a source of scandal. It did not belong on a child's face. There was something irredeemably licentious about this mouth — a provocation to butcher and baker, and even to Lili's unlucky father, the master horologer whose celebrated clocks began to take on a libidinous aspect which propriety could not condone.

A convent could muster no defence against the mouth's charming vulgarity. Nor could the five men in Lili's life who each betrayed himself through his own peculiar weakness while Lili almost passively incited his doom. A clotheswear industrialist succumbed to an obsession with mutilation. An armaments tycoon fatally sampled the world of humiliation in which he dealt. A Catalan communist turned bestselling pornographer and suicidal gambler. A fascist image-maker developed a carbuncle so grotesque it was deemed intolerable to Il Duce's empire. A bastion of the old order of rural paternalism yielded to a profound confusion which ultimately rendered him transvestite. Never had the insolence of one mouth undone so many.

Swinging between Gothic irony and the moralizing farce of Preston Sturges, slapstick metaphysics and digressionary speculation, Osborne's satire intoxicates the reader — and lends startling new meaning to the term oral history.

TO MY FATHER AND MOTHER

I

1

Her name on the Prussian birth certificate was Lili Dorziat, but
for some years, following the simple evidence of the eyes, she
was called 'the clockmaker's copper brat'.

True, her horologer father ennobled her with sublime crea-
tions. Mahogany pendulum clocks, glass-bell clocks with silver
figurines, tooled pocket watches with rotating calendars and maps
of the skies, 'Moorish' pieces with brass-riveted chains and ara-
besques inset with sandalwood. But nothing he made for her could
wipe away the malaise that floated like a cloud of flies around her
mouth. Even his most haunting fantasies could not rectify its oral
vulgarity, a vulgarity which was enveloped in charm . . .

At the end of his career, in 1897, Bruno Dorziat decided to
dedicate a clock of Copernican complexity to his teenage daughter.
On its sides he painted moorhens, bowls of cherries and a portrait
of his pink *devochka* dressed as Diana.

It has survived along with other Dorziat mechanical timepieces,
in one of the provincial museums of East Germany. Its lozenge-
shaped machicolations, carved pine-cones and brilliant colours
make it the star attraction. But it is not the perforated gable and
lacquered panels that hypnotize: it is the models that pop out of
the two-door hatch on the hour – a shepherd and a milkmaid
dancing a rustic polka.

Wherever in the world the clocks have landed, the same charisma
singles them out. The brass example in the Topkapi, called 'The
Flying Fish' because of its fishing scenes containing the infant
Lili armed with a salmon net, attracts large crowds of 'voyeurs'
who cannot help feeling soiled by its 'libidinous construction'
(the remark of an enraged janitor). A chiming cuckoo clock in
San Francisco has the same effect upon schoolboys. But it is the

last clock, the bell-ringing house of the dancing shepherd and his subversive escort, that attracts the largest audiences. The museum which houses it has acquired an unwanted sexual reputation. Yet it is difficult to say what it is in the clock that stimulates the observer: the way the shepherd's finger touches the milkmaid's chin . . . the flirting hips . . . the eyes filled with painted blue china performing their polka . . . the red fingernails painted the colour of fire-engines . . . the details build up relentlessly to a shy sexual insult.

Master Dorziat's last work also has a history different from its tamer neighbours. It was acquired in New York by a representative of the DDR, who had been authorized to spend up to five hundred thousand marks at the auction for the effects of the clothes' hanger magnate Enzo Topolo from his house at Southampton, Long Island. At that remarkable sale, which was held in Topolo's former private rooms at the Waldorf, a crocodile portmanteau locked by the tycoon himself was put up for sale as lot 68 and opened – on his instructions – only ten minutes beforehand. The assessors and adjudicators were therefore obliged to take out the articles inside one by one as they came, without the benefits of examination or notes.

On that cold morning in 1974, the four rooms of Topolo's winter suite were full. The bidding for lot 68 began when the demonstrator, immaculately dressed in a frock coat, pulled out a small grey funerary urn of speckled marble containing a folded square of linen, in which could be seen a vaguely glutinous smear of decayed animal tissue.

The announcement of the contents caused a stir of disgust, then enlightened amusement. Evidently one of Signor Topolo's little practical jokes!

Anxious not to be outflanked, the bidders raised a thousand dollars for the urn and the smear. But the objects that followed it inflicted upon them even greater confusion.

A pair of industrial scissors, encrusted with black tar.

A steel bullet with a conical gold tip inscribed with the word 'Antofagasta'.

A fan smeared with *sang-de bœuf* lipstick from another age, an age of China porcelain mouths.

A handkerchief with the same colour lipstick printed on one corner in the exact shape of one of the aforementioned mouths.

A yellowed two-franc Swiss paperback with the title *The Dictionary of Secret Fruits* and a cover illustration of a man eating a palmful of pistachio nuts.

A copy of the fascist women's magazine *Clara* with a photograph of a model in a cut-away bathing suit posing on a Roman beach under the words, 'Di giovinezza il bel purpureo lume' – 'The Purple Light of Youth'.

But it was the last exhibit to be salvaged from the crocodile bag that finally aroused a genuine financial interest uncontaminated by confusion and embarrassment. The man in the frock coat, expressing surprise at its weight and bulk, hauled out into the glare of the lights a large carved clock with a gable pierced by lozenge-shaped holes.

The assessor announced: 'Mechanical timepiece from the workshop of . . .', he squinted at a plate fixed to the side, '. . . Master B. F. Stettin.'

The clock was paraded before the bidders.

Its brass points sparkled.

The adjudicator then remembered that with a mechanical timepiece it was preferable to show the working of the mechanism, the models and the tune of the bells, if there was one. The hands were pushed round to precipitate the sounding of a full hour and to the enrapturement of the assembled millionaires a series of bells arranged in the Dorian mode sang a Bavarian folk tune while a shepherd and a milkmaid shot out of the inlaid hatch and performed a simple but elegant dance.

The small dogs in the audience began barking, but the onlookers were charmed. A repeat performance was demanded.

The auction officials resumed their smiles.

The dancing couple were brought out six times to a crescendo of encores. Something so simple in so cynical a metropolis!

'And now', the adjudicator sang, 'shall we begin for this fine and exceptional piece, a unique example of the Pomeranian school . . .'

At this point the small man in a green felt hat from the East German embassy rose and laid down the first offer of ten thousand dollars.

The room was electrified.

The bids rose as the officials, cunningly affecting naivety, declared themselves unable to stop the carved shepherd and milkmaid from making their sorties and, propelled by their charm, quickly reached the threshold of fifty thousand. The man from the DDR wiped his forehead.

His principal opponent was Harold S. Ensenberg, the curtain-rail man.

Ensenberg raised the bid to fifty-five. The DDR man outdid him at sixty. The curtain-rail magnate raised him to seventy and then once again found himself surpassed at eighty. He began to fidget with his ear-lobe.

But by now the audience, having watched the clock being exhibited before them for the best part of half an hour, had begun to appreciate it in more subtle and personal ways. The erotic stimulation of the shepherd's finger, for example, made itself felt. A few other bidders entered the race. The officials, too, noticed the stimulation of the finger, the light and evasive sexuality of the wooden lips and eyelashes, the sly muscles in the milkmaid's thighs. They felt their faces growing hot. The bidding rose to ninety-five thousand and then a hundred thousand. The clock was becoming more attractive by the minute.

The eighty-year-old Ensenberg felt his face sliding into lechery.

'A hundred and forty thousand!' he muttered as he raised his hand to corroborate the bid, 'for a Pomeranian clock . . .'

But as soon as he had said it, the man in the green felt hat passed him with one fifty. The hammer was poised.

The dogs barked hysterically.

The sexually excited audience expressed its irritation at not possessing the source of its titillation.

And to think that a Communist in a green felt hat . . . it was unbearable!

As the hammer fell and the adjudicator pointed to the felt hat and said 'Sold to Herr Ingel!', the bidders erupted into a roar of disapproval. The little embassy man was jostled by his neighbours and felt himself unable to rise. The officials attempted to intervene. It was not fitting in such circumstances, the tragic death of Mr Topolo, a poor refugee from Europe made good, on his own premises . . . and the DDR man had brought a suitcase filled with dollars wrapped in yellow elastic bands!

But nothing could stop the bitterly disappointed Ensenberg. Striding over to the DDR chair, his flabby lips shaking with rage and the pale flap of his collapsed thyroid wagging above his collar, he spat into the embassy official's face: 'So there are dirty old men in Commie-land, too!'

A shout of support and approval. The officials waved their arms. Herr Ingel, ashen-faced, demanded an apology. The curtain-rail man clenched his fists. The ladies screamed their encouragement, the dogs yapped frantically, the adjudicator cooed soothing admonitions, the clock bells sang in the background and the canteen girl called the precinct police.

By the time the wailing squad cars arrived the guests were sprawled on the pavement outside, the German clinging to his clock, the furious Ensenberg pulling his ear and the assembled auction officials apologizing to everyone simultaneously.

A collective arrest and booking left the clock safely in the possession of the government of the People's Republic, who did not delay in placing it exactly where it belonged in the collection housed in the small town of K—— B——.

They were aware that history had merely repeated itself.

The clock that had found its way into the crocodile portmanteau of Enzo Topolo of Southampton, Long Island (who shall be met later), was only one insignificant fragment of the machinery of a secret history which began in the year 1884, when the clockmaker Bruno Dorziat, a Pole by the look of his round face and sloping eyes, arrived in the city of Stettin . . .

2

In the year 1884 the clockmaker Bruno Dorziat, a Pole by the look of his round face and sloping eyes, arrived in the city of Stettin with numerous rolls of paper in his possession proving a long and arduous apprenticeship in the horological workshops of Nuremberg. He arrived with nothing but a leather portmanteau filled with strange screwdrivers and dainty hammers, but within six months he had set up his own shop, the Dorziat Mechanical Clock Company, on Panienska Street. Almost immediately his order books were filled, a steady stream of customers filed through his atelier and showroom and he was able to marry a peasant girl from the small hamlet of Golub near Toruń whom he had hired to sweep his floors. Her name was Maryla and she prayed to the Black Madonna every four hours around the clock.

The small, shy Dorziat, barely thirty years old, having passed an apprenticeship of exemplary innocence, could not long resist his suppressed desire to reproduce. On the last day of that eventful year, as the hundred fancy clocks on the ground floor rang in the new year, he manœuvred the holy Maryla – undernourished gums, yellow teeth, elongated thighs – into the necessary position of uxorial submission on their four-poster bed and surrendered up his virginity with a soft but vulgar sigh.

During her pregnancy, which began at once, Dorziat con-structed his first self-automated cuckoo clock using a design in an Austrian magazine which he had acquired by accident on a trip to Prague. The design was unusual in several ways, every quarter-hour being marked by a metal whistle placed with scientific dexterity in the mouth of a lead squirrel, which was painted with the technique used to colour toy soldiers. Not only did the squirrel dash out of its 'cage' with perfect timing, it also lifted itself on its hind legs and performed a rough hemispherical dance, like a bee. The inspiration for the mechanism needed to make this squirrel work had come to him during the night his wife had conceived. A hundred obscure intellectual obstacles – which had prevented him from creating clocks with a character of their own, owing little to existing models – dissolved overnight and although he had certainly copied the basic design from *The Clockmaker's Almanac* of Vienna, the substitution of the robin redbreast in the magazine for a squirrel that could not only sing but move as well was entirely his own. And the movement of the mechanical animals was so fluid, so lifelike, that his Stettin customers declared they had never seen anything like it – blink your eyes and you'd think it was alive, about to jump out of the clock and into your arms. He doubled his prices for the new pieces immediately.

As he developed his fresh technique further, he found that he was able not only to construct single figures, which could be made to move with lightning speed and precision while making all kinds of melodic and time-keeping noises, but whole groups of these beasts and scaled-down humans that could shake hands, kiss, embrace and perform rudimentary waltzes. Not only this, with time he found he was able to make the hands and legs move with an expressiveness not yet seen even in the designs of *The Clockmaker's Almanac*. The figurines of his 'talking clocks' walked directly out of his daydreams into the flesh and blood world of money.

His reputation spread to Poznan and to Leipzig. When Maryla was six months into her pregnancy, a lone order arrived by post from Vienna. He had made his mark in the clock fraternity.

But as the Dorziat Mechanical Clock Company flourished in Panienska Street, the pregnancy was taking unusual turns. To begin with, the foetus grew with surprising speed and puffed Maryla's belly out to a size that provoked muffled feelings of irritation among the burghers of Stettin. She was too big for her stage of gestation. And the grotesque size of her stomach was complemented by a sudden degeneration in her day-to-day behaviour. For the first time in her life she found a stick of carmine-tinted lip salve and plastered her mouth with it until the lips were messily red all over and smudged in the corners like the mouths of the tarts of the metropolises. But worse than this was

9

the shape of the mouth itself. Wherever it appeared in public it solicited members of the opposite sex. It 'loitered' in the street, sneering at everything around it, and this quite independently of any of the facial features that surrounded it. It could not behave itself. Although Maryla was unaware of what her mouth was doing behind her back, and could not detect anything untoward by looking in the mirror, she could hardly fail to notice the reactions of disapproval and distaste that the cavortings of her mouth were eliciting, as it were, behind her back. A mouth like that on a pregnant woman, and smudged at the corners . . . why didn't the spineless clock-maker take matters in hand, deliver a bit of discipline and bring it back into line? A woman who is pregnant shouldn't have a tart's mouth. She should have a mouth that is pregnant, too. And yet the possessor of this mouth was unaware of the cause of her growing isolation. She had no idea that her own mouth was making her vulgar.

The child was born on the first day of October 1885. And as soon as the foetus put its head through the opening the mouth that had been displaying itself so shamelessly for nine months disappeared. Observers noted that the mouth had never belonged to Maryla Dorziat in the first place. It had belonged to the unborn child. Just as the mother had had to carry her child inside her for the period of gestation, she had had to carry its mouth as well, the only part of the baby that could manifest itself outside. Nor should this subtle and remarkable thesis be dismissed. As soon as the head of the infant, dribbling blood and vernix, pushed its crushed face between the pair of elongated thighs, every witness present saw the mouth instantly transfer itself from the mother to the daughter.

Her mouth yelled insults.

It was as red as the skin of a tomato and shaped in an elusive attitude of irremediable vulgarity.

3

The birth was registered in a respectable German newspaper, the *Stettiner Tageblatt*: 'To Bruno Andrej and Maryla Dorziat, Panienska Street, a daughter, Lili Natasha Helena, at 4.30 am, October 1st.

The christening was at St James, after which ceremony a wealthy customer who had commissioned a lantern clock for his country house in Pomerania donated a rocking cot garlanded with loops of sky-blue silk and covered over with a hood of French lace. The child lay embedded in a mound of initialled sheets and shining flounces and looked out into the world with the unfocused but unnerving gaze of a mathematician imagining Euclidean shapes. The eyes were blue – in fact, for some reason they matched the surrounding blue of the silk trimmings exactly. If she were lifted out of the cot, they changed colour immediately.

For her first year, the domestic life of the Dorziat family ran smoothly and sweetly. Orders poured into the Dorziat Mechanical Clock Company from all over Germany and Prussia, and Maryla continued her reading lessons so that by the middle of 1886 she could read a whole page of the Psalms without faltering. Bruno grew fatter and richer. New folds of flesh appeared around his neck and a wide gold moustache sprouted in the middle of a luminous and agnostic face. His standing both with the Stettin commercial fraternity and the local Eastern German Union Bank improved as rapidly as his baby daughter. And best of all, the blonde roots of Lili's hair, as much as the sloping eyes tapering into elegant and unusual canthi, proved her genetic connection both to her native podzolic plains and to the mysterious Tartar ancestor of whom – in a spirit of sentimental orientalism – he was so proud.

As she grew older, however, the mouth she had inherited as a baby effected a strange miracle upon her face.

By the time she was five, displaying the combinations of soft nose and chin, blue eyes, bulging cheeks, puffy neck and dimpled knee-caps upon which the adult usually latches all its latent tremble-lipped tenderness, her mouth was capable of provocations that had nothing to do with childhood. When the inhabitants of Panienska Street gave her packets of powder sherbet with a liquorice straw or linzer hearts wrapped in paper, they could not help staring at her mouth for it was unquestionably her mouth that made her unchildish. The men in particular were sensitive to its 'vibrating'. As with her mother before her, her mouth pulled her face out of its context. Incredible as it seems, it pulled her features out of order and made them slope to one side, sometimes so far that they floated in mid-air dancing to some tune executed in an inaudible frequency, the kind that is heard only by dogs.

'They say she has a lovely mouth,' Bruno reported back. 'But why do they never mention her hair, or her legs or her chin or her eyebrows? They can't say what they like about it, either. They blurt it out without wanting to: lovely mouth. I sometimes wonder if they're under hypnosis.'

'They're perverts,' Maryla spat. 'They looked at my mouth, too. It gives them ideas. You shouldn't let her out with . . .'

She was about to say 'with her mouth', but stopped herself.

'Anyway,' she went on bitterly, 'she hasn't got a lovely mouth. She has a mouth like the idiot in Golub. Blasphemous.'

The tradesmen thought otherwise. For long years they kept their secret to themselves. The baker Koffler, who dealt every day with the Dorziat girl, who skipped with sticky lips into his cream and orange shop for her *schwarzbrot* and *strudel* slices dusted with confectioner's sugar, felt an illegal attraction towards her mouth just as she said the words 'Thank you', as she did – punctually at half-past four. The lips were wide and elastic. Too big for a tiny face like that, but excellent taken on their own. The tongue never came out as far as the lips, but hovered above the bottom row of outsized canine milk teeth which were rooted in the healthy gums of a chimpanzee. Stuffed with pastry hearts, chocolate mice, molasses cakes and cinnamon apples, it still refused to be an object of tenderness and provoked him just as it provoked Goszinski the butcher, Stott the paper-maker, Rymkiewiecze the grocer with his rows of spice jars that drew her in in the afternoons and Zeromski the dentist, who stood behind a net screen in his surgery window to watch her go by. Watching her dance in and out of their respective orbits, they watched not the pair of white ankles in tan-coloured leather boots, the Leghorn straw hat the prosperous horologer had bought her in Strasbourg or the mulberry watered-silk ribbons laid diagonally across one shoulder if it was summer (a miniature wool bolero if it was winter) – it was the mouth, always just out of range of the shadow cast by the straw hat, an aperture filled with glistening unknown materials, which opened up unexpectedly in the middle of an ordinary face when they were least expecting it and sent everything around it into a crazy, prolonged tango which they couldn't help enjoying. So Zeromski, pecking at a schnapps in the Dancing Pig, would say to Goszinski: 'The mouth came by today. It was sore – it had white spots on it.'

And Goszinski would comment to Zeromski: 'Chapped by the cold. It's Abisch grease cream. Smells like tar.'

'You smelt it on the mouth?'

'She gave me a kiss. I gave her some stuffed chops. When I give her stuffed chops she gives me a kiss. It smells different every time. Sometimes it's orange blossom. Sometimes it's figs. In winter it is hazelnuts and coal. In spring it is bayleaves and turpentine.'

Overcome with anguished envy: 'And what about summer. What does it smell like in summer?'

Stretching his legs: 'In summer . . . ah, in summer it comes into its own. It's sweet and dry. It smells of nutmeg and cinnamon sticks. She gets them from Rymkiewiecze and sucks them on the way home. That's when I like it best. It leaves a smell of spice jars on your face. No, there's nothing to touch the mouth in summer. Even if in autumn it has a fantastic taste of chestnuts and liquorice. But there is, as I'm sure you'll agree, a mouth for every season . . .'

As she grew older, this mysterious organ grew accordingly in independence. By her tenth birthday, in defiance of a strict upbringing riddled with murmured Ave Marias and reinforced underwear, it had developed into an orifice so far removed from its natural functions that even without cosmetic decoration it was capable of insurrection on an alarming scale. Presents showered down upon her from avuncular shopkeepers desiring a kiss from it. Just one kiss, and a whiff of seasonal scent. And behind the lips, as before, lay treasures of teeth, gums, tonsils and a tongue which no one had touched. Lili Dorziat had already entered the weightless world of lust. Her mouth was the carrier of a lascivious germ, a germ which the clockmaker, with his superior sensitivity and understanding (and his occasional habit of delving in Viennese newspapers) would have called desire, but which the cruder tradesmen would have called filth. For Mr Zeromski and Mr Goszinski, like the majority of ordinary people, clearly understood – by means of sound and virile common sense – that vulgarity is only the part of the human soul which prefers to stay in hiding like a vagrant thug but which is unfortunately (though, thank God, only rarely) dragged kicking and screaming into the light of day through the action of irresistible forces.

And one such force was the mouth of Lili Dorziat.

A painting of a naked woman, a mistimed fart at dinner or the sudden appearance of a secret part of the anatomy might have produced the same effect, but Lili's mouth was always there, a constant presence, and in addition it was shaped like a marzipan cookie and smelt of a handful of fresh hay . . . and, yes, worst of all it was planted right there in the middle of the face of a ten-year-old girl, a face speckled with freckles, stained with raspberry jam, flushed with the first primrose pimples of incipient acne!

The precarious world of adulthood took a step back in disorder and then gradually, without looking for dangerous adventures, fell under the spell of a single adolescent mouth. It was 1895, the century of decency was coming to a hesitant end, and above all in that place once described by a Jarry stage direction as 'En Pologne, c'est à dire nulle part.'

4

In the secrecy of the two back rooms of his workshop, that sacred precinct with pages of magazine lithographs pinned to the walls where he worked late at night on a bench fitted with two vices and a drawer of paints, Bruno sat until past midnight drawing on large sheets of sugar paper his dreams of future clocks. Using only blue and magenta crayons, he mapped out the outer structure in a matter of minutes, then set to work filling in the increasingly dense flurries of details and mechanical apparatus which he considered the heart of the machine.

At about one o'clock, when he wound up the assembled mechanism of his latest creation so that he could hear its musical hum in absolute silence, Lili would wake up, jolted out of her sleep by the virtually inaudible high-pitched singing and creep down the stairs in her socks to the workshop. It was agreed between them that she was allowed to do this. Her mother was never awakened. Having reached the inner sanctum whose door was purposely left half open, she crouched behind the crack and watched her father in silence with her ear placed an inch from the turning cogs, biting his lip in concentration. His theory of machines was that their souls could not be harmonious without emitting the correct musical note. It didn't matter that the note could not be heard from behind the heavy wooden façade he would place over it: if the note was right, the clock would 'sing' to the heart. His face, contorted by this striving for perfection, implanted itself in her memory as the face of a priest listening to a horrifying confession. And yet underneath his narrowed eyes and squashed nose a beatific smile floated in the lamplight. When she went up to him and put her head on his lap she watched the skin above her relax and melt into long, melancholy lines. His head was a clock, and inside it an angelic machinery ticked over until dawn. During the day he was a completely different man.

But when he was truly alone, before the machinery was set in motion and he was carving his figures or tracing lines over the sugar paper – and especially at around midnight, when his imagination accelerated its erratic revolutions – he found his head filled not with harmoniously co-ordinated cogs but with a dreamlike cacophony which, by an uncontrollable process of contagion, spread to his hands. It was less easy to dominate their movements. For instance, if he was tooling the head of a small deer, concentrating perhaps on one of its ears with a pencil chisel, he found that his control over where the bevelled cutting edge went would begin to elude him. If he wanted the chisel to go a centimetre to the left, it would go a centimetre to the right. If he wanted it to slip gently downwards into the hollow of the ear it would rise instead and slip over the top, or make a cut he had never intended in a place where no cut had been planned. At first, the vacillations of his most favoured tool, an instrument he was intimately familiar with, were minute, mistakes and wanderings measured in centimetres. But their cumulative effect began eventually to take a toll on the overall effect of the figures. For whereas his earliest work had been characterized by an easy, vernacular innocence, the latest sculptures exhibited a different character altogether. They had lost their innocence. Their vitality had taken a new direction. Even in the deer's ear an unnerving insolence could be seen. It was not an ear any more. It was something more lewd. It grew out of the deer's head with a weird disrespect.

Having noticed this unquantifiable alteration in his treasured works, he examined the offending parts with a magnifying glass but could not see any one thing that could be blamed. His loss of control over the material was the cause, but however much he tried to intellectualize his chisel and bend it to his intentions, it followed a path of its own. Something latent within him was poking itself out of his fingers and into his chisel, making it carve against the grain of his calm, moralizing, equilibrious psyche and map out unforeseen configurations of his own shame. The heads of all his cute and familiar woodland animals, the cuddly rabbits, stoats and foxes that had formerly hogged the limelight of his family clocks, from now on sat uneasily on their bodies and when they were looked at from a very slight distance they burned with a soft lechery that was as fantastic as it was improbable.

'I struggle', he complained to his wife, 'to complete a blue tit or an otter for a scene of perfect innocence destined for family consumption, but the chisel won't go in the right direction . . . I'm being sucked into smut!'

In despair he gave himself a holiday and concentrated on the mechanical side of things for several weeks. But his hand itched to hold a chisel again. To be deprived of it even for three weeks was a loss tantamount to torture. He tried to escape from his depression by taking his daughter on expeditions to toy shops and Bukowa Forest, but wherever she went her mouth went with her, and – try as he might to deny the suggestion – something related her mouth to the ears of the deer which initiated the observer into obscure rites of vulgarity. A self-effacing witchcraft united them.

Finally he could withhold himself from his own gift no longer and descended excitedly to the atelier resolved to banish forthwith any trace of pornography from his delicate scene of pastoral happiness. He took a Bible down with him and intoned some verses before sitting down to work for the first time in twenty-seven days. Now he locked the door and told Lili that it disturbed her mother when she crept down the stairs to join him. He wanted to be alone. He wanted her mouth as far away from him as possible.

To begin with, he discarded everything he had been working on over the previous six months. He ordered some new wood, mahogany and ash, and bought a new chisel. He decided to abandon the representation of animals and concentrate on a human group instead. It was going to be something wholesome and appropriately bucolic. A grand and complex clock garnished all over with arboreal themes, pine-cones, autumn leaves, tendrils of ivy, minutely articulated cobwebs and a gable dripping with illusionistic raindrops. And at the centre, hidden from view until the moment when the bells rang in the half-hour, a shepherd and a milkmaid in folksy Teutonic dress, holding hands perhaps, or lifting their clogs to the sound of the bell, but at any rate doing nothing more than flinging a gaze of innocence into the outside world.

He had completed the front gable of the clock and painted the sides (where he was going to put two portraits of his daughter and wife on either side) by the time he came to the wooden couple. He began with the female. He started with the feet, naked in the grass, and worked his way slowly up the legs until he reached the thighs. But at the thighs he paused. To his satisfaction, the chisel had been obeying him up to the thighs, and the legs, from the knees down, were straight, pure and moral. But at the thighs, things began to go awry. The chisel started its old tricks, vacillating left and right, running away with itself, mapping a pair of thighs that were inadmissible. They curved outwards at mid-point, as if the femur had been warped by an imaginary lust. And by the time he reached the hips he knew that he was no longer himself, that he was an element manipulated within a force field.

In a panic he finished the figure as quickly as he could, knowing in advance that it was doomed, and started on the male figure, hoping that if he was innocent the obscenity of the female would be obscured or forgiven. But the male figure was even worse. It gleamed with exaggerated debasement.

In the shop window, where he placed it in an arbour of mistletoe and fresh convolvulus, it attracted the hushed and anguished silence of scandal. The flow of window-lickers that passed the clockmaker's to look into the display window was stopped in its tracks. A clock like any other clock, but with the difference that the finger of the shepherd was pointing directly, and waggishly, and sluttishly, towards the mouth of the milkmaid, yes, and the mouth of the milkmaid was co-operating, it was flirting with the finger. It moved when you watched it, but moved where and for what reason? A mouth like that on one of Herr Dorziat's milkmaids, and for home consumption, too! A mouth on view to all our children and our household dogs as well.

In the space of a few hours the clock provoked a ripple of disapproval. Herrs Goszinski, Stott, Rymkiewiecze and Zeromski rushed to the window to see what the uproar was about and immediately they remembered the mouth of Dorziat's lovely and seemingly innocent daughter. There was certainly a connection. They rubbed their chins.

Yes, the finger. It was up to something with that mouth of hers. Something was lurking in the undergrowth. Of course, he was a foreigner, he went to Vienna and Prague 'for his clocks'. And how had he managed to produce that licentious mouth of his daughter without being suspicious himself? How had he succeeded in filling the mouth of his carved dairymaid with exactly the same balance of purity and libido?

They were not equipped with ready answers.

The enigma of the milkmaid's mouth was as attractive and repulsive as that of the little Lili who used it to suck cinnamon sticks.

They were sure only of the necessity of collective civic responsibility and solidarity in the face of subversion from the mouth. If this dangerous and unlikely proliferation of mouths was not halted in its early stages, who knew what calamitous destiny it would drag them towards?

They protested.

And the unfortunate maker of the offending mouth was as unable to understand his brilliant invention of his milkmaid's orifice as they were. He blurted out to his wife when she furiously demanded an explanation: 'It's my *doppelgänger*!'

The Union of Artisans, that guild of craftsmen responsible for the trading success of their quarter, reported his pornographic fantasies to the Prussian police, who turned up at the doors of the Dorziat Mechanical Clock Company in blue uniforms armed with curved sabres slung from the hip. They stared for half an hour at the shepherd and the milkmaid. The libidinous intent of the master horologer was incontestible, although the descriptions of the mechanical figures which appeared in the notes they took during the inspection revealed nothing specific about their erotic content. They verified the open purveying of 'obscene clocks', possibly for export to the rest of Greater Germany. An order was signed against Dorziat and the clock was removed without delay.

'I always intended to please the customer,' the Pole protested. 'It wasn't my fault . . . we all have *doppelgängers*. In Vienna they're saying now . . .'

But Zeromski, who worked only three doors down, stepped forward with an ugly bubble of saliva on his lip.

'You don't have the right to speak, Dorziat. We all saw what you did, and so did our children. A shepherd . . . a milkmaid . . . that mouth . . . ugh!'

And Rymkiewiecze bolted forward with ugly and prurient stains on his forehead and cheeks.

'You thought we wouldn't see. You thought you'd get dirty old men coming in under the cover of clocks. Well, it didn't work, did it? You didn't count on the sensibility and the nose of your old friend Albert Stott! A very costly mistake, Herr Pole-Pornographer!'

Only one person enjoyed the spectacle of the effect produced by the clock on the hard-working city of Stettin. Lili lay in her room at night considering the straight line that could be traced literally in space between her mouth and the finger of the shepherd. His finger, like her mouth, possessed the dazzling vulgarity of reality. And as she imagined the trace bending away from her teeth out of the window and down towards the disgraced showroom, her mouth felt lighter and lighter, and after her mouth the rest of her body.

5

Visitors to the clock museum of K—— B—— might well also notice, if their eyesight is in excellent order and their spirit of curiosity has not been dampened by the excesses of Herr Dorziat's milkmaid, that this same timepiece, the very one that the boys in blue removed by force from the windows of the Dorziat Mechanical Clock Company that summer, bears on its left side two faces painted within crude escutcheons stylistically out of place with the Alpine imagery of the rest of the clock. They are Maryla and Lili, wife and daughter, affectionately immortalized, just as the clock itself is dedicated to them in writing by means of a brass plate on the underside invisible to the general public. The mother, it is true, is bloated and flushed, with visions of the Black Madonna locked into her porcine little eyes even in Bruno's sentimentalizing portrait. But the daughter . . . yes, the observers who have taken the trouble to stick their noses against the glass and bend their necks to get a closer look at her have all been affected by the daughter, a real Velázquez princess they mutter to themselves, look at the dimples, the refusal to sit still, the anthracite pupils dotted on with a single swoop of the brush, the mouth. There is something in her that makes them lick their lips. They feel soiled. The image of Lili on her father's last publicly displayed clock fouls them in a way that is incomprehensible. Her face appears to be moving.

She is definitely moving – in almost imperceptible steps – to the left. She slides to the left and they feel obliged to lick their lips. And still the police have not intervened! They feel they are looking at something *naked*.

But Bruno had only painted what he had seen.

As his order books emptied and the shop lapsed into semi-darkness, the coin-sized depressions in her elbows grew more elliptical and unusual in shape, the deltoid and sterno-mastoid muscles were defined, her flexors thinned out into elegant and aristocratic stems at the end of which pale, kiln-fired hands tapered into ovals and at the top end of the flute that divided her upper lip a zone of blue shade appeared that could not be removed even by sunlight.

She blossomed in the shadow of his catastrophe.

And by a cruel process of genetic retribution, the parents became more stooped, rucked and discoloured the more the daughter exfoliated. They shrank as she grew. Their mouths shrivelled into accidental openings in their faces as Lili's mouth inflated into the lycopene-coloured organ of a Winterhalt countess or a *trompe-l'œil* goddess tumbling in a chariot out of a ceiling filled with airborne unicorns and fluttering putti. The Dorziat Mechanical Clock Company was reduced to manufacturing two clocks a year for the Pomeranian noble and a German composer named Genova von Criminel, who demanded his clock should sound the glockenspiel tunes from *The Magic Flute*. The showroom was boarded up and Dorziat retired like an injured snail to his sanctuary, where his clocks continued to take shape in a spirit of half-suppressed pornomania. As the years passed they accumulated uselessly in the back rooms, stored with futile hope in unclosed boxwood crates, their pointed gables providing dynasties of spiders with the skeleton of a system of cobwebs that stretched from one end of the atelier to the other. Finally, in 1897, the Pomeranian died of an infarction of the myocardium and Dorziat went into an eclipse which could not be reversed. The age of the industrial clock was arriving. The epoch of cuckoos and milkmaids was drawing to an end. A soft twilight stole into the disgraced house on Holy Ghost Street.

'It's all because of her,' Dorziat *mère*, now thoroughly stuffed with cabbages and *apfel strudel*, complained. 'She's a tart and she's made you think like one. Why couldn't you have gone on making those nice clocks with deer and robin redbreasts in them? Why did you have to start taking that mouth of hers so seriously?' She stopped herself violently, as she always did when the subject of that thing came up, and let her embarrassment show. 'I'm not saying it was your fault, but you always gave in to her. What she needed was a hard whack in the face but you wouldn't let me. You worship her, don't you, you won't have Little Miss Tart whacked

22

in the face, will you, you let her lord it over both of us, and here we are with the Pomeranian dead of a heart attack and the mad German asking for half *The Magic Flute*. It's all come to nothing because of her and her . . .'

'I've never understood', the clockmaker interrupted wearily, 'why everyone hates her so much and why there's such a panic about her face. She has a human face and nothing else. Her mouth is the mouth of a twelve-year-old. I don't see any difference between it and any other mouth. It has lips, saliva, tongue . . . teeth . . .'

'You never had any instinct, Dorziat, and you don't know nothing about women, neither. She's got a tart's mouth and the whole town sees it. And furthermore,' her lip wobbled and a greenish oily tear began to materialize in the corner of her eye, 'furthermore she's out to eat us . . . there's something greedy in her. She looks at us as if she's going to digest us one day. She's slippery. I've always known there was something nasty in her, something opposed, you know, to the Holy Black Madonna, I . . .'

'Yes, the *digest*!'

'I swear I've been communicating with Her. She's told me all about the mouth! She says she was put in my belly by a suc . . . a suc . . . a . . .'

'A succubus.'

'Don't make fun of me, Dorziat.'

'A demon.'

'That's what She says. And to think it was in me, in me like a piece of my own shit!'

'Maybe the Madonna was exaggerating – or having one of Her little fits.'

'You can mock Her as much as you want, *shmendrik*, but there's one thing I'm insisting on – I swear before God and that is that she's got to go – we can't afford it any more, and a convent is what she needs. Maybe she could still be saved. They know how to whack faces in convents.'

The clockmaker turned out the scarred palms of his hands so that they faced his wife's wagging finger, thereby expressing simultaneous resignation and despair. The fire of mechanical dreams that had once twinkled at the centres of his pupils had been extinguished. The fat woman was going to lie next to him for years to come, the systole–diastole of her heart thumping out the last rhythms of his life, and his pride and joy, his cinnamon-scented Lili, was going into the abysmal seclusion of Our Lady of the Lilies, the convent selected by the vigorous and forward-thinking fat cow with black lips; and where would it leave him, after he had exchanged her for the blubber and milky armpits of Maryla Dorziat, née Golub, and the one hundred and thirty-five unfinished clocks in the ground-floor workrooms whose farcical and misunderstood delicacy would only prove, if any proof were needed, that smut is in the eye of the beholder and that a clock is never safe from the philistinism of the masses?

He thought about throwing himself off the roof of his house with the biggest clock tied round his neck.

He considered running away to Brazil and panning for gold, enough to buy a slave and a frock coat.

But he never dared to set foot outside the door.

The fat peasant watched him night and day.

He knew that he was doomed to perpetual domestic seclusion.

No more trips to the clocks of Prague. No more newspaper reading in the cafés of Königstrasse or boat trips down the Rhine with secretaries and seamstresses in straw hats. No more sloppy and heart-rending flirtations with printers' wives in Kuhn's rent-by-the-hour private rooms or adulterous winkings through restaurant windows accompanied by crafy insinuations made with his moustaches, no more froth, busts, contraceptives, electric candles, iced oranges and railway compartments. His masculinity was curtailed. He was tamed by his own *Torschlusspanik* – the terror of life's closing doors.

On 3 November 1897, he took his daughter to the railway station in a hired brougham following a long correspondence with Our Lady of the Lilies, Wahlstatt. The portmanteau contained two muslin dresses folded over a crucifix and a bunch of dried lavender. It rained over the grey houses. Bruno sat with his head naked under the rain, his eyes registering only the horses' steam and the miles of sulphur-coloured pavements. His hands did not move, folded neatly in his lap. Only occasionally his eyeball slipped unconsciously to the right and caught a glimpse of the white face next to him with its belladonna eyes and blueish lips.

As they were standing by the train his corpse-like hand reached out and, fitting itself uncomfortably into her hand, gripped her thumb and index finger in an awkward digital embrace. It was half-past two in the afternoon and a vaporized sun shone through the sinister twigs of November. Forlorn anonymous birds twittered in the trees. Lili Dorziat closed her eyes and when they opened she found herself in the papier-mâché realm of maturity. She swayed and tried to vomit but kissed her dead father's cheek instead. She was falling through empty air as she kissed him, with the mechanical birds whistling in the chestnut trees and the cardboard clouds scudding through absurd black spaces. As she walked away along the platform, even the station clocks assumed the insolent thinness of paper cards. A lugubrious and arrogant empire of paper! She was walking not on asphalt but on a long decrepit carpet that could easily be pulled from under her feet. And beyond the childish bits and pieces of fences, houses, tracks and stairways, the sky which was rapidly clearing contained a nightmarish menagerie of clockwork objects revolving louchely to a sound of cogs and spindles, while down below a zoo of tick-tock faces whirred and clanked around her to a fraudulent music of mechanical keys. The world was in motion and she was an enslaved part of its amateur machinery.

Everything shone and glittered. The sun came out.

And the worst of it was that the sky was blue.

II

6

The convent of Our Lady of the Lilies, founded in 1678 on the
site of a manifestation of the Virgin ensconced in martagon
lilies, stood near the small town of Wahlstatt until a hazy
day in 1945 when a Soviet tank, pursuing a herd of cows
by mistake through a field religiously planted with *Lilium
martagon*, opened fire on the ochre-yellow walls which suddenly
appeared out of the mist and sent a handful of shells through
the octagonal spire of the chapel, the lancet windows of the
refectory and the empty dormitories, burning everything to
the ground in twenty minutes. But a mere forty-eight years
previously, before history had cracked one of her characteristic
jokes and sent tank-tracks across a herbarium still modelled
squarely on the *materia medica*, the Middle Ages persisted and
in the deep fingernails of the Abbess Ausubel who greeted
the clockmaker's daughter from Stettin stale flecks of blood
could be seen, the blood that escaped from her own flagellated
arms.

Thunder and lightning accompanied Lili Dorziat's arrival,
and with it the faint sound of an organ. The bare apricot
trees in the orchards and the yellow walls surrounding the
cluster of original buildings were lit electric blue. The niche
above the preserved gatehouse boasted its Virgin made from
the translucent alabaster of Volterra, lily in hand, but as a
precaution against the possible attractions of the spiritual life
Lili had already searched through her portmanteau, dragged
out the silver crucifix put there by her father and thrown it
out of the window. When Ausubel saw her, she was struck
by her empty blue eyes and the neat trough at the front base
of her neck, outlined by two taut tendons. The skin at the

bottom was oily and silvery. The Abbess was unprepared for it.

The dormitory cells looked out over the orchards to the left and, to the right, a reservoir in the shape of an ear. In the distance, a strip of blue hills. Discoloured moons blazed over further expanses of cereal crops. Pheasants plodded and pecked among cornflowers and stooks.

Suddenly confronted with the solid empire of nature, Lili recoiled. Day after day, month after month, birds flirting with bees, seeds flirting with soil nutrients, solstices flirting with equinoxes.

Instead of the pliable material of God's childish creativity infantilely celebrated in the hymns of Our Lady of the Lilies, there was a machinery gleaming under various atmospheric lights like a four-ton Krupps cannon in a copy of the *Vienna Military Gazette*. The machinery squeaked and purred softly. It enacted incessant Philistine rituals. Hawks darted out of the blue and tortured miserable little ornithids with their beaks. Foxes bolted across patches of mowed corn in time to eviscerate prancing rodents without a trace of an apology. Why did crocuses appear out of nowhere at the same time as the red noses of alcoholic poachers? Why did bursts of idiotic music soar out of silence in her direction just as an owl was sending insolent pellets through the air?

'Don't talk to me about nature,' she said in the confessional. 'When I look at nature I feel a desire to empty the contents of my stomach. It's clear to me, father, that nature's days are numbered.'

And the priest would splutter: 'But, my child, the little birds . . . the little flowers . . . the rippling streams . . . the bubbling brooks . . . God's pliable material!'

'I can't help it, father. It makes me spew!'

'How can it be? You, a little girl? And you aren't moved to joy and tears by the sight of the rabbits and the newts, the sunsets and the blue tits, the marigolds and the Jenny Wrens? It can't be . . .'

'It all makes me sick, father, I swear it does.'

'Well we can't have it, do you hear, we can't have you spitting in the Creator's face. And to think of all the stoats and butterflies and lily pads and ears of corn and dewy cobwebs you're rejecting. It's nothing short of disturbing. Have you been dreaming normally of late? Have you felt unwell? I'm sure, my child, that when spring comes, bearing with it all the glories of God's feisty temperament, all of His – so to speak – fireworks, you'll look around you and you'll change your mind, you'll wonder why you ever said such things. Yes, you'll feel thoroughly ashamed. You'll come back and make your apologies!'

But she had told the truth the first time. She was finished with animals and sunsets. Solitude in the cell confirmed the ever-increasing sensation of weightlessness and the particularity that went with it. Her fingers, her toes, even her nose, were the centre of everything. Nothing beyond them – nothing beyond what she had decided was the angelic – mattered more than the see-saw cogwork of a clock.

The Abbess Ausubel maintained a vigilant watch over the pagan from Stettin, but more than anything she was softened by the trough of skin at the base of the girl's throat. It invited kisses which she had long since learned to suppress. The priest had come directly to her after hearing Lili's confessions.

'You will have to act,' he counselled and bit his lip. 'She refuses to be enticed by the glories of nature and . . .'

Ausubel interrupted.

'I know. She eats like a horse as well.'

'Does she?'

The priest was astounded. But it was true: rumours had begun to fly around the Sisterhood concerning the prodigious eating power of the Dorziat girl and, as soon as Ausubel learned of her rejection of nature, she was intrigued. She had never seen such heresy combined with such gourmandise.

The truth was that Lili had begun eating in a different way as soon as she had realized the depth of her disgust with Creation. At first it was the damp cornbread and hard-boiled eggs served after vespers with a glass of chalky water and enough rough salt to cover the pad of a thumb. She stuffed them all into her mouth at the same time, earning rebukes which could not restrain her, swallowed them with the sound of a split drainpipe and burped without a hand in front of her mouth. But as soon as she had mastered this simple meal, she progressed to Friday fish,

Sunday milk and Tuesday's raw spring onions. She piled them all into her mouth, which not only accommodated them but accentuated their proletarian crudity as well. Her cheeks puffed out, milk dribbling down her chin, and her mouth turned livid with strain. And as soon as she had emptied the buccal cavity and swallowed everything down, she began again, cramming every ingestible object in reach between her gums with the soft grunts of a starved cow while the eaters at the other tables looked on with fear mingled with sniggers. After two weeks' ceaseless stuffing of edibles into the Dorziat mouth, its owner had been given the alarming and poetic sobriquet of the ant-eater.

She snuffled her food in the same way as this semi-legendary animal.

Hidden behind a screened window in the refectory, the Abbess watched her fill her mouth again and again with lightning speed. The doctor from Wahlstatt was in attendance.

'It is evidently', he diagnosed, 'an incipient form of hysteria.'

But it was not the right thing to say to Ausubel.

'The desire to eat has nothing to do with the womb.'

Doctor Reiner adjusted a monocle and pouted.

'No, no,' he said, 'excessive eating, like excessive dieting, is, I assure you a symptom of hysteria among adolescent females. In cloistered conditions, the womb . . .'

Herr Doktor Reiner, then, a member of the *avant-garde*?

'Or aren't you feeding them enough?' he added with a smirk.

'It's only one of them,' Ausubel countered. 'The Dorziat girl. There's something abnormal about her . . . her . . .'

'Come now, Abbess, you weren't going to say her mouth? To say the least, that is a little childish of you.'

'Let us just say that Satan has certain ways of manifesting himself.'

'Oh, so Old Nick is a voracious eater and likes to descend upon the mouths and digestive systems of pubescent pensioners? You are clearly not *au courant* with the latest work of Esterhazy and . . .'

'What Esterhazy says has nothing to do with us here, Herr Reiner. I was hoping you would be able to point to some more obviously medical factor, some schoolgirl factor, something to do with their ovaries, perhaps, their enzymes . . . ah . . . their cycles . . .'

'Enzymes?'

Reiner tittered and wiped his mouth.

'She is a hysteric and I wouldn't be surprised in the least if she was subject to visitations, voices in the head, split personality, sudden weeping, violent alternations between gluttony and self-starving . . . in short, the entire complex of symptoms which hysteric subjects display.'

'Doctor Reiner,' Ausubel said calmly, 'I have no intention of letting you examine her in the light of Esterhazy. I won't permit Jewish psychology. I think theology has more to tell us about Miss Dorziat than anything the Jews can provide. You don't think that I'd let any of them be *inverted* in that way, do you?'

'Ah well, maybe you're right,' Reiner said with all the squirming irony he could squeeze into the word. 'She does have a funny mouth. They don't all have funny mouths like that!'

Ausubel stared at her mouth, now dribbling with mammaglia. Although Lili could not see her through the screen, the mouth seemed as if it could. The Abbess shivered with revulsion. The doctor looked at it through his monocle and a fiery smile made its way on to his own lips. They were both transfixed.

As the weeks passed, Lili's gluttony intensified. Whole carrots and beets disappeared down her gullet, followed by Friday biscuits, bowls of *Kugel*, radishes and quartered quinces, round slabs of black bread and tepid cholent, slivered turnips and raw button mushrooms. Beefbones, patioka and fried lamb's kidneys vanished into her mouth as quickly as Balkan-style carp and crude blueberry tarts. But her weight did not increase. On the contrary, her body became more streamlined. Her hips became more slender, her adolescent fat evaporated. The insatiable eating machine took on the form of a pared-down Venetian courtesan.

Abbess Ausubel began to sweat in her sleep.

Her latent sapphism was floating uncontrollably to the surface.

The axis of her world was sloping to one side, gently and crazily.

When Lili smiled at her, the ferocious little teeth spattered with sodden crumbs and flecks of lamb detached themselves, and her, from Our Lady of the Lilies and carried them both forcibly into the nightmarish world of nature. Ausubel crossed herself and when she was alone in bed she was careful to keep her hands as far as possible from her body.

7

At the beginning of 1898, with the figures of poachers drawn black against parallel lines of snow clearly visible from Lili's windows, the virus of gourmandise which had manifested itself up to now only in the mouth of one girl spread to four or five others. Aping the unpopular Lili, they began ransacking the dinner tables without regard to the reprimands that rained down upon them. They ate and ate until they felt sick and vomited up the contents of their stomachs during the night. But this did not deter them from continuing the following day. They stuffed their mouths full of food during the day and ejected it with faultless regularity as soon as the sun had gone down. They could not be made to stop. They craved satiety and their mouths would not leave them alone.

At the end of the week, a dozen of them were vomiting at night and the echoes of their retching prevented normal sleep. After a second week, the number had doubled. Their soft and plump bodies, however, did not increase in sophistication as Lili's had done. On the contrary, the Abbess was relieved to see that their thighs were definitely getting larger, as were their necks and bellies. Confronted with this medical anomaly, she was forced to call in further outside opinion, though the sarcastic Reiner would not do. The priest who travelled from the town to give confession was consulted instead.

'But', the Abbess said, 'why are they so tubby after all the vomiting? Why are they not getting thinner not fatter, like the Dorziat girl?'

'If I ever smelled devils, it's now, Sister Ausubel. As you say, most rightly, they should be getting thinner and now, what's happening to them – they're exploding, getting fatter as you say, Sister Ausubel, *inflating*. That's what devils like to do!'

'And they're still vomiting, without a pause . . .'

'Inflating and vomiting!'

'You think . . .'

'The Book, Sister, the Book always stuns them.'

'We've never performed an exorcism here. I've never agreed to it. But now', she bit her lip so violently it began to bleed slightly, 'I have to stop them throwing up. I can't have them throwing up in my convent. And I've noticed that all this throwing up makes them look nastier . . . yes, their mouths have all become twisted.'

The priest peered at her to make sure he had heard correctly.

'Why, that's also a sign,' he muttered. 'Twisted mouths.'

Ausubel went back to her room. She didn't want the priest to perform the exorcism. It was a duel between herself and Lili's mouth. She waited an hour in silence, preparing herself inwardly and even taking out her private whip to run her fingers along the thongs. She was feeling an increasing excitement. The oily patch of skin at the bottom of Lili's neck was coming nearer. She had only to ring the bell and it would appear before her in an attitude of submission. The mouth . . . the oily patch . . . what would they feel like when she touched them? If only she was eating voraciously. If only she didn't have to carry out exorcism on that very same mouth, to change it, to bring it back to goodness. She would be simultaneously exorcising her own titillation. Which was why she had to have the cross, with the sharp metal patellas of Christ biting into her palm. At length she sent the priest away and rang the bell for her secretary. Lili was to come up at once. As she waited, she felt the creases under her breasts fill with sweat. Her own mouth was trembling. She held the crucifix in her left hand.

Lili was called from the garden. She arrived with grass in her hair. The Abbess saw the oily patch between the two tendons immediately and then the mouth, chapped as it always was, large and unstable.

She took a step forward, as if to crush the girl with her authority or at least make her lie down humiliatingly on the floor, and the first words of her rehearsed accusation were actually on her lips when she was arrested by the oily patch. It shimmered in front of her and the mouth . . . the mouth wavered, slid about and swam in and out of view. It was brilliant red. It shone in the sunlight pouring into the Abbess's study with the colour of the blood it contained. One movement left or right and she felt it would destabilize the entire convent. She had to be careful with it. And at the same time she wanted finally to lunge forward and kiss it with her own.

'You know why you're here,' Ausubel said, squeezing the brass shins in her hand. 'You're making the girls eat against their will. I know you're making them.'

'Are you going to punish me?'

A voice like a musical box!

For a moment Ausubel almost relented.

'It's not a question of punishment,' she said more gently. 'Something is possessing you and it has to be withdrawn from you. It isn't unusual. The Church even has rules for times like these.'

'Sister Malkowitz says the air is filled with devils and you can breathe them in.'

'Sister Malkowitz is right about the breathing, Lili. And when they get breathed in . . .'

'They have to be breathed out?'

'I always knew you were an intelligent girl. What we have to do is pray and breathe. But first you have to take off your shirt. I need to see your stomach.'

Lili took off her shirt.

Around the rim of her stomach lay a zone of softness like the flabby hem of an oyster. Ausubel paused with the cross in her hand, hesitating before laying it across the navel. Like the patch of oily skin in her neck and the vibrating lips of the mouth, it militated against the order around it, emitting the lecherous signals ordinarily associated with winks and crooked fingers. She felt her mouth gravitating downwards towards it – a disgusting feast of adolescent tissue! – but stopped her vertigo in time to replace it with the cross. The girl was looking over her pubescent breasts at the feet of the Saviour and sneering at them, although it seemed at the same time as if she was merely smiling. The Abbess began her recitations.

As she incanted, moving her right index finger crosswise across the infernal abdomen, she watched the three areas of the body that attracted her. She had her cup of holy water ready and from time to time flicked it across the white skin, where it landed and formed brilliant little globules. She had to stop after only a few lines and wipe her face. The mouth was beckoning her, though it was closed and obedient. The navel had grown deeper. The oily patch in the throat was pulsating to the movement of a large artery. Accidentally, she let one of her fingers touch Lili's ribs. And before she knew why she was allowing her fingers such unprecedented freedom of action, the thumb had followed the little finger which had already touched and then the whole palm laid itself out across the stomach.

'Why are you smiling?' she blurted out coldly. 'You shouldn't be smiling at a time like this.'

But the mouth was not smiling. It was moving in a way she could not identify.

'I'm not smiling, Sister Ausubel,' Lili protested. 'I'm not smiling at all.'

Suddenly uneasy, the Abbess attempted to continue the recitation and the flicking of the water, but she could not take her eyes away from Lili's mouth.

'You don't think I'm stupid, do you?' she hissed. 'I can see exactly what you're doing. Or can't you control yourself? I suppose your mouth is something separate from you? The expulsion of demons is not a joke. Or do you think it's a joke? Obviously you think it's a joke or you wouldn't be . . . you wouldn't be doing what you're doing!'

'I'm not doing anything at all, Sister.'

'Yes, you are. You're pretending not to be doing anything. But you are, you are . . .'

She took away the crucifix.

'You're playing games with your lips!'

The Abbess stood and told Lili to do the same. They faced each other in the streams of sunlight. Ausubel had no idea what to say. She felt her hand itch. She wanted to hit the mouth in front of her, which had not stopped its minute cavortings. A red and vulgar mouth, the mouth of a tart in her convent, aborting her plans for sanctity, nobility and nature worship! Of course, the mouth was possessed. It was inhabited by something vile. She had seen something identical in her youth on a gargoyle in a French church. It is not, Ausubel knew, the eyes which are the windows of the soul, but the mouth.

Of all the orifices the mouth was the one of which she was most afraid. And as the mouth of Lili swung before her performing a cancan with its lips and teeth, she wanted to tear it off the face and extinguish it. Her hand braced itself. The girl was smiling, though she protested that she was not. If she drew blood from the mouth, she would at least destroy its capacity to dance in front of her. And yet, just as she was curling up her fist, her own mouth, no doubt responding to a call to conspire with another mouth, was preparing to go and meet it, to plunge headlong in the most horrible of organs.

She dropped the crucifix on to the floor and let out a coarse and inarticulate cry of fear.

Bringing back her arm as far as it would go, she punched the mouth as hard as she could, sending the child sprawling and cutting one of her knuckles on an incisor.

A spot of blood hit her on the cheek.

Lili tumbled backwards and sat up holding her mouth, from which a stream of pink fluid poured down with the slowness of saliva over her forearm. A look of astonishment . . . a broken molar . . . a gurgle at the back of the throat, suppressed laughter, a titter of infantile triumph.

The Abbess heard it and stepped away, humiliated. She forgot to nurse the knuckle and her own blood dripped into the teak floorboards.

All she could say was: 'It was you.'

Lili burst out laughing.

Her mouth had not been severed from her face.

8

'There is nothing to do, in the circumstances', wrote Abbess Ausubel to Bruno Dorziat, 'but follow the advice of the doctors and return her to you, if you would kindly forward the fare from Wahlstatt. I realize that, though this may come as some surprise to you, I have no need to emphasize the unpleasant, not to say pathological consequences of permitting, under any circumstances whatsoever the . . .'

The clockmaker, unravelling her false arguments, threw up his hands with fury and enclosed a banker's draft for the rail-fare in an envelope which also contained a letter defending his daughter's mental health. It was written with sloping characters, indicating an incipient attack of *Globus hystericus*. When the Abbess received it she breathed a sigh of relief and signed the expulsion order along with the standard release papers. But her hand was trembling violently. Even as she moved the pen across the provided line, it swerved about as if to form an O, as it had been doing for some days. In fact, whenever the Abbess put pen to paper it did the same. Was she drawing mouths over those odds and ends of papers and manuscripts, abstract and incomplete mouths instead of her normally linear doodles? She had no idea, but the tension in her wrist that made the Os appear all around her was going to last as long as Lili was with her under the same roof, and the punching of the mouth haunted her. The circular form of the mouth had entered her by force. Her corruption took the shape that a wet mouth leaves when it is pressed against a sheet of paper . . .

But in the loneliness of her cell Lili was packing her bags with pleasure. Her own mouth had healed completely, except for a pale notch in the upper lip. She woke from her frequent dreams with composure, with dry palms and refreshing memories. Her face, in particular, felt elastic and energetic when compared to the rotting fragments of nature visible from the window, and above all her teeth, her lips and gums, which had completely recovered their perfection.

There was no question of her superiority to nature.

One day she was sifting through the wrapping paper which her father had used for her religious objects. One of them was a page of a Riviera newspaper with a lithograph of a woman in a plumed toque eating what looked like a sparrow under the headline: The Princesse de Brancovan tastes the *Poulardes Granvilles à la russe* at Cannes!

Under this, at the bottom, outraged complaints about the profits of prostitutes using the hotel foyers in Monaco.

Propelled by a sudden disturbance in the area of her mouth, she knew where she wanted to be: with the Princesse de Brancovan and her *Poulardes Granville à la russe*.

In that moment she decided to mis-spend her father's advanced rail-fare.

On the day of her expulsion, as she walked across the courtyard to the gate, Ausubel (hidden in an upstairs window) watched with fascination the porters recoil from her with the minute reflex actions of instinct. The whole of nature recoiled from her. When she paused and turned to scan the wall and windows, the poisonous flash of her mouth made the Abbess step back. And then it was gone. Ausubel wiped her throat and forehead dry. The disease was passing, as surely as the plagues of the past burnt themselves out with time.

Her body could return to its normal state: a cardboard construct punctured with empty holes posing as sexual orifices.

The vomiting eased. The vulgarity passed and faded away.

Once again, the birds twittered, the sun shone, etc.

Buried carefully inside her ribcage, and invisible to the faces in the windows, Lili Dorziat's heart measured out the tempo of a musically organized, disciplined but irresistibly crescendoing pornographic excitement.

III

III

9

Just as Lili was leaving Our Lady of the Lilies, that is on 14 August 1898, not far away in a lecture hall in the academic city of Heidelberg the distinguished pathologist and criminologist Dr Eberhart Disher-Klebb was beginning a lecture before an audience of three hundred peers and undergraduates on the physiognomy of criminals which was to be deeply influential in the first twenty years of the following century.

'Whereas it is noticeable', the Doctor pronounced, tapping a diagram of a sectioned human head on the blackboard behind him, 'that the cranium of Jews is at least between three and five centimetres smaller in circumference than that of the average Caucasian (and we will leave discussion of the nasal structure to a later date), it has equally been found in recent research that members of the criminal fraternity, too, are structurally distinguishable from others. For example, it has been suggested, and to some extent verified, that the jaws of murderers are somewhat elongated with prominence given to the molars and upper incisors. And then again it has been suggested by a large amount of pathological evidence that the mouths of prostitutes are larger than those of ordinary women, being both wider from cheek to cheek and deeper in terms of labial thickness. In many cases, as you will have noticed, science merely confirms what common sense has always infallibly dictated. Judges, for instance, have always been able to classify the mouths of women set before them for sentencing, and the mouth of the prostitute, in particular, has always been relatively easy to identify. It has simply needed time to amass the weight of physiological evidence and arrange it into serviceable theory. Some pathologists, particularly those working in Germany and Switzerland, have even given the ratio of variation between the normal and abnormal female mouth as one-sixteenth to one. A large difference when one considers the implications. Henceforth, we confront the possibility of a pathological and forensic science in which all elements of doubt and chance have been removed, in which morality will be technically legible in the physiognomy of the human face and in which it will be possible to create a complete and reliable taxonomy of vice. We are embarking, then, on the first steps of a bold new age of certainty and justice, an age, gentlemen, in which the book of woman and the book of the Jew will no longer have to be read in darkness, with the aid of a magnifying glass and a cross . . .'

The Disher-Klebb hypothesis must have travelled southwards as fast as the train that carried Lili Dorziat and her mouth (extended by one-sixteenth to the side) to Nice, for within six weeks of her arrival a series of hand-distributed photographs had appeared among the city's archons bearing – juxtaposed among the muscular thugs in striped shirts and carnival masks – the unmistakable form of her oral organ.

Her liaisons were rapid and diverse.

A photographer found her soliciting in the foyer of the Italiens, at that time filled with orange trees and people like the Prince d'Albufera. The commercial possibilities of her mouth were immediately apparent. In a photographic studio in the hilltop suburb of Cimiez he shot her alone on pile rugs with grapes in her navel. The resulting images were made into hard-backed cards and sold by whispering touts near the station, and the superior sales figures of her poses compared to those of other models could not be denied. It was the mouth that was selling them. More sessions in the Cimiez studio resulted in her being paraded in animal skins and chic boleros cut away to reveal her nipples. Four hundred were sold in one afternoon.

Rumours of Bolero Lili in the Riviera newspapers . . .

Leaving the photographer, she found her way into imbroglios with building developers, customs officers, theatre managers, members of the élite crew of the yacht *Princesse Alice*, strollers picked up at the Circle de la Méditerranée, bellboys and *sommeliers*, shipping clerks and mineral-water specialists (assistants of the great Professor Dieulafoy lecturing in Monaco), Russian poker experts, moustachioed gamblers in nankeen pants and travelling sellers of homeopathic hair restorers.

The Côte d'Azur's cosmopolitan lust began to revolve around the corners of her mouth, so proving once and for all the validity and inherent nobility of the Disher-Klebb theory of mouths.

The golden age of the child prostitute had been ushered in, bearing with it thousands of pubescent anatomies ready to propel a whole civilization into a worship of chins, elbows, knees, navels and mouths, a lust for youth which had not been seen before.

By the end of 1898, our thirteen-year-old cocodette could afford baths of Montebello mineral water and a daily intake of jaborandi and iridin.

Six months later, in the spring of 1899, she rented a room at the Hôtel des Palmiers and filled its hand-painted cupboards with *faux canezous* and tarlatan dresses.

She could be seen on the Promenade in a pair of fur-edged *bottines* and crêpe de Chine parasol, her disturbing child's face turned against the sun to preserve its whiteness.

After a year of work, she met the director of the Orphée theatre, Achilles Besançon, who fell in love with the unusual wideness of her mouth.

When he saw it at a performance by the tenor Tamango in his own theatre, he felt the inner softness that characterizes enslavement.

For five months she went every night to his rooms at the Orphée filled with bronze lustres in the shape of Rhine maidens and signed photo-portraits of Isidore de Lara and Zambelli. The director wrote a number of songs as a result, the most famous of which was 'Shopping, shopping there's nothing but shopping!' put to a tune which reminded him of a pair of female knees.

However much he played it to himself, it reminded him of adolescent knees.

When it was performed at the Orphée on 23 October 1899 by Isabelle Rouche dressed as a seventeenth-century barmaid bearing a tray of apples held just under the line of her breasts (and inscribed with the word 'pommes') the public shared this impression.

The working class got to its feet and began shouting, 'Knees! Knees!'

She bared her knees: hysteria.

A man was knocked out by a flying shoe.

A woman's knee was bitten in the chaos.

Within three weeks other words had been added by popular demand.

Salty Maria
Has little white knees
She pees in her bed,
An abominable tease! . . .

Who would have thought that the golden-hearted, pure-lunged proletarians of Europe's 'translucent garden' would have permitted themselves to be 'raped by vulgarity'? Who would have guessed that the aristocrats who left scented cards behind them would have so readily abandoned the exquisite *avant-garde* melodies of Debussy for a greasy musical meditation on the theme of patellas?

By the end of the winter the whole coast was singing it in its sleep.

The prurience of portable bathing machines was jeopardized by a tendency to exhibit knees.

Everywhere, the pagan force of the knee was in evidence; when a knee was revealed it excited admiration. It seemed as if, just for a moment . . .

But by the beginning of the new year the anonymous subject of 'Salty Maria' was ready to change direction and move elsewhere. Both her body and her mouth had become light, detached and colonialist in spirit, flushed as they were with success. They were bored. They were weightless in a world of weight.

10

History moves not in straightforward lines but by means of sudden and unexpected detours, ambushes and corridors of mirrors, louche coincidences and parallel events. In 1938, for example, a mere thirty-eight years later, the great director Ernst Lubitsch began his film *The Eighth Wife of Bluebeard* in the pyjama department of a Riviera clothes store, where an American millionaire attempting to buy only the top half of a pyjama disputes patterns and colours with an impoverished French heiress who wants to buy only the bottom half. The director may or may not have heard stories of encounters of the past from his local baker or the man who brought orange juice on to the set, but this scene had occurred before in a hat shop, where the Jewish industrialist Adolphe Heym, owner of the Heym Metal Shoe-Eye Consortium, disputed his right to buy a lamé toque with a fifteen-year-old prostitute equipped with a pair of chalcedony earrings set in gilt metal.

As in the film, there was a notice stencilled on to the glass of the shop front ('English Spoken, American Understood'), and as in the film the salesmen were small and aggressive with strong accents. But where the Gable/Colbert encounter differed from the Heym/Dorziat was in the prominence of Lili's exposed anatomical parts in the creation of erotic complexities. For whereas Lubitsch navigates the characters through the genteel storms of farce, we are following the history not of a character but of a mouth. And so from time to time our story will turn to knees and then to elbows and then again to noses and so on, until the entire machinery of vulgarity has been described from top to bottom, or rather from head to foot. It is only the pornography of an age which surrenders unknown secrets and it is the discrete parts of

49

the bodies of its stars which determine the lives and deaths of millions.

Lili Dorziat, having sheathed herself in an exoskeleton of clichés, walked one day into the millinery department of the Hambly clothes store. Choosing her moment, she jumped on to a toque with a bird of paradise feather at exactly the same moment as the owner of the Heym Metal Shoe-Eye Consortium. The 56-year-old businessman was trapped by the inexplicable charm of her elongated mouth.

He was tall and grey and wore a Froment-Meurice ring with a table-cut stone on one hand.

Lili looked carefully at his Redfern tie and clipped fingernails. And as she did so the industrialist felt his left ear softly vibrating. He put his hand to it as if to steady it, without knowing what nerve had been touched. When he realized that he had put his hand to his ear unconsciously to prevent it from leaving his head, he smiled uneasily at himself.

'I'll tell you what,' he said. 'I'll buy the hat for you, yes I will, I'll certainly buy the hat for you!'

His painful gallantry was a success.

And reality separates from fiction at this point, for in *The Eighth Wife of Bluebeard* the litigants divide the bill 70/30.

Seduction took place between the mouths with the female mouth clearly in the ascendant, and before blame can be apportioned one way or another, another chapter has suddenly opened in the tortuous and varied adventures of Mlle Dorziat's oral organ.

11

The shoe-eye manufacturer was housed at the Martinez. Every morning he scanned the newspapers for traces of his shares in Royal Dutch and the Rio Negro Logging Company and every evening, drawing the curtains of his room, he went to sleep with the *Roeder's Almanac* open at the page of the relevant ascendant planets.

Heym's designs for metal shoe-eyes were exhibited at the Palais de l'Industrie in the summer of 1898 under the title 'Oeillets en Délire' and his ingenious conceptions in the form of triangles, stars of David and assorted Tantric geometries excited the interest of crowds of foot connoisseurs who declared that his bold experiments had changed the meaning of the human shoe. But the factory in Ivry-sur-Seine never produced his daring drawings and his account at the Banque de France was kept inflated by the infallible mass production of Model 162: the standard tin slot for the sixteen-hole female *bottine*.

As Lili had read in a biographical article in *Le Pilori*, half a century before the Heym family had branched out from their small banking concern on the rue Chaussée d'Antin and invaded large sections of the Seillère bank, Worms et Cie the coal merchants and the PLM Railway. By the turn of the 1880s they were investing in the zinc mines of the Congo. Adolphe's father had commissioned Mauguin to build the family house on the rue Taitbout in Paris and filled it with antiques procured from an agent in Macau. Péreire and Fould came to dinner. The Heyms ramified into military képis, umbrellas, sewing machines, corsets and . . . metal shoe-eyes. Bronze caryatids appeared in the breakfast room.

After his father's death the solitary Adolphe lived as a recluse whose only after hours' pleasure was to smoke a narghile while dressed in a quilted banjan and to take a cab to the Chabannais brothel on Friday afternoons. In the late autumn, he went to Nice for the climate. During the rest of the year he rose at dawn, covered his face with rice powder and painted flushes on to each cheek with a hare's foot brush. In the evenings, after lonely dinners on the boulevards, he took the preparations of henbane and nitro-glycerine that his doctor made up for him in unmarked paper sachets and which complemented his firmly established habit of cocaine.

But Heym had one weakness that lay below the surface of his semi-mechanical daily life: a taste for adolescent girls.

At the Chabannais, they were able to cater to it. They had teenage Creoles and fourteen-year-old provincials. But his hoarding instincts kept him away from that outrageously expensive establishment apart from his Friday reservation, and he was forced instead to hire decrepit villas in the suburbs where he could take the child prostitutes he picked up in the Batignolles. Cutting up a bag of plums into halves, he had his *trôleurs* trample them to a pulp on his stomach, after which he ate them with a silver fork. It was not that he was attracted to the girls' feet. If anything, it was the incomplete development of their noses and breasts that warmed him. His attachment to the eating of the plums was connected with his own mouth.

As soon as he discovered Lili, he was sure that he could do away with the others. Without delay, he insisted that they go back to Paris. In the couchettes going northward, he sank his teeth hard into her knees and thighs and then, not knowing why his passion was increasing, he went for her ears, biting the lobes so savagely that they began to bleed.

Mortified, he apologized profusely.

But when she was asleep he tried again, nibbling them more gently this time, yet still giving vent to a desire to assault them. And as before, feeling his own ear moving slightly, he reached up and steadied it with his hand.

When they were in Paris, he lost no time in renting her an apartment on the rue de Navarin. He filled it with little luxuries, bibelots and a stove of Dresden china, and then turned up at the door punctually at seven o'clock on three nights of the week.

Standing immobile and silent by the bed, he undid his collar, the buttons of his shirt and, with puritan weariness, the sides of his spats. He was methodical and unhurried. A slight quivering in his neck made him human. He snapped open the buttons with phlegmatic irritation. His features during this undressing were invulnerable to expressions of desire and his fingers did not fumble as they undid her clasps.

As his teeth bit into her lobes, his mouth became tender and hypocritical.

And as it did so, she saw, his hand always went up to his own.

His grey and scrawny body momentarily lost its repulsiveness.

A childishness entered his voice.

The master of the Heym Metal Shoe-Eye Consortium lost his maturity as he mauled the ear-lobes of his kept adolescent.

12

Unexpectedly, she had found exactly what she wanted. She hired an abigail. She had the *Gazette Anecdotique* read to her in the shuttered dressing-room aromatized with jasmine and orange blossom while a hairdresser from the adjacent street made up her hair. Chocolate and marmalade followed a mild emetic of jalap. After breakfast she dressed either in plaid taffeta for lunch or a redingote for a drive through the Bois. On four evenings of the week they went together to the Folies-Marigny or the Variétés. On Tuesdays they ate a six-course dinner at the Maison d'Or and on Mondays they went to the Alcazar.

Although he did not reveal anything to her, Heym had been feeling for some months the growing pressure of instability. On the ground floor of his building on the rue Taitbout, the *concierge*, though employed by his family, did not desist from shamelessly posting a page torn out of the *La France Juive* in the glass panes of his door. As they passed through the vestibule oblivious to his tenants but always aware of the rhythms and intonations of misanthropy, the voice of the *concierge* boomed out,

The Yids, the Yids
It's always the Yids

and then after a pregnant pause:

That sodomize the Fatherland!

The southerner was a subscriber to *La Libre Parole*, which occasionally published recipes for 'cooking Jews in garlic sauce'. His eyes peered through the glass as the proprietor stepped past and caught Heym's white face in its greatest moment of vulnerability.

The industrialist had seen him once during a riot near the Boulevard Magenta among meat workers from La Villette who had gathered to watch the siege of the Ligue Antisémite on the rue Chabrol. Their faces had collided in the crowd, the *concierge* sneering and winking, his furious little eyes filled with bile. If he met Heym in the courtyard as he was scrubbing the flagstones with a wet broom covered with suds, he would shake his head and say, 'They don't take Guérin out of Fort Chabrol except on a stretcher!'

For weeks after the Fort Chabrol affair Heym had felt himself being watched. From time to time envelopes filled with excrement came through his letter-box, scrupulously delivered by the *concierge*, and once a politely worded letter asking him if he would consider donating his skin to the Union of Apprentice Drummer-Boys.

The dry and ascetic Heym, brought up in an equilibrious universe of Pleyel pianos and discreet mazurkas, felt the empire of reason cracking beneath him.

He took out his chequebook and bought his lover gifts: a chrysoprase Fabergé telephone, an agate elephant with a sexual wash-basin hidden in its back and an hour-glass with minute pearls instead of grains of sand.

His money was freeing itself from him.

And in the same way, he abandoned himself to his teeth when he undressed Lili, ambushing her body in the hope of drawing little specks of blood.

'It's not that I want to hurt you,' he explained guiltily, 'but there are things that are difficult to question. I know they're looking at me – they're watching me all the time. I can even feel them watching me when I'm here, in the bedroom. When I bite you, they know all about it . . .'

He remembered the stare of homicidal anguish in the *concierge*'s face when he had first seen the white-faced Caucasian girl climbing his stairs.

What if he saw the spots of blood on the sheets he carried down for him? Yes, it wasn't Jewish blood. It was the blood of the Fatherland! The blood of virgins! He had created a rite of blood at which the muscular barbarian downstairs could only be an impotent spectator.

★

On weekends he took Lili to the Restaurant de France at Asnières, where they stayed in rooms overlooking the Seine. He rowed her up and down the river. In the evenings they sat on the veranda leading down to the punts. She didn't look like a child: her mouth 'invaded' everything around it and set it in motion. When he was alone with her he was timidly afraid to touch it . . . the residual fear of the small boy bitten in the face by a lhasa apso.

In the calm sound of rushes and water he forgot the riots and the recipes for Jews in garlic sauce.

In the bedroom filled with aquatic reflections, he marvelled at the neat cohesion of her ear with her head. The skin ran in a smooth continuous line from the web under the lobe to the corner of her mouth. And though the whorls of cartilage inside the organ were of only technical interest to him, the lobe itself seemed to wink at him, to incite and soil him.

He took it hesitantly between his teeth and felt it infecting his mouth.

13

For Lili's sixteenth birthday in 1901, Heym took her to the spa at Ems. Finding, however, that she liked to spend fifty thousand thalers a week at the roulette tables, he brought her back to Paris.

When they returned they lost themselves gratefully in the crowds at Longchamps and the Tir aux Pigeons.

At Ems her mouth had been the object of displays of abjection.

The whiff of abasement had shaken Heym badly.

He could not understand this excess of body.

And yet, as it increasingly entered his own body, he felt freed by it – just as he had always been by the taste of crushed plums.

'I can't think what it is,' he confessed. 'As if someone were performing an operation on parts of my body without my knowing it. Sometimes, if you want to know, I think it's you!'

His infatuation with her ears intensified so that by the end of the year her collection of earrings was unrivalled.

The scars on the lobes healed quickly and before they did he was careful not to open them unnecessarily. The skin had to be white and unruffled, a virginal envelope of tissue. But nevertheless, following the logic of his fetish, he could not do anything but increase the pressure of his bites, tearing the tissue with greater controlled force. If there was no increase on the last time, he felt as if they had not made love at all. His passion was measured by the weight-to-surface ratio exerted by his teeth. And before he knew it, he was dreaming not of mere laceration, the patterns left by incisions, but of complete detachment altogether . . . a severing of ear from head.

Incredulous before his own fantasy, he held his teeth in check.

But for the first time he began to feel the need for a pair of scissors.

★

Heym's reaction to the unknown was a short course of physo-stigmine and an increased daily quota of phosphoric acid. At the Ivry factory, he paced among the machines looking at the ears of the female operators, which he could observe at leisure. He was the master of ninety-two pairs of ears. In one of the warehouses, where thin sheets of tin were stored in bales, he found the scissors he had been looking for, heavy industrial tools used for slicing the metal leaves. But why had he gone to look for them in the first place? Why was he stuffing them under his waistcoat and walking out of the warehouse with the blades cold against his navel? When he was alone in his office overlooking the machine-rooms, he took the scissors out and felt the edges of the blades against his thumb. They weren't sharp enough. He would have to sharpen them himself. Only when the factory was empty could he descend to one of the turning lathes on the floor and begin sharpening them with slow and thoughtful turns of the hand . . . and still he had not discovered why he was using the lathe in the first place. He needed the scissors to complement his growing vulgarity.

When they were razor sharp, he hid them in his portmanteau and brought them home.

He locked them in his study desk, wrapped in a square of green felt. A secret joy came with them. They signalled the beginnings of an unprecedented revolt in his body.

Since his childhood, his miserable little body had been regulated and disciplined. It had been made to obey orders from the head. When the head said 'Sit!' it sat. When the head said 'Stand!' it stood. At first, the head in question was his father's. Then, quite suddenly, it was his own that imitated and took over the functions of the paternal head. What were inheritance and duty if not this imitation of one head by another, this tradition of heads barking orders to bodies? Head succeeded head until the dominance of heads was taken for granted. The family was tolerant and civilized. His aunts played mazurkas on Sunday afternoons. They drank tea out of Chinese cups. The values of the head dominated effortlessly. Through many generations the heads had held sway.

As a boy he had felt the first stirrings of rebellion against the tyranny of heads. His hands had always longed to disobey the head that so monarchically gave them orders. Other parts of his body had also wanted to break the hold of heads over the realm of physiognomy. While his father's head had sat at the 'head' of the family

58

commercial imperium he naturally had not dared to challenge its authority. But as soon as it had disappeared the old desire was resurgent. His hands wanted to form fists. The very same fingers that joined the aunts on the Pleyel for an afternoon's Mozart were prepared to skulk around on street corners looking for heads to smash! They were longing for his body to break out into open rebellion, for his feet to dance away with him, for his hands to run riot in the wild vacuum of the natural world, where knives, hammers and knuckle-dusters, as well as the cruel blades of scissors, lay ready for action, and for his ears gradually to detach themselves from that head whose despotism he had so come to detest.

All he lacked was a form. Hitherto, his only escape from the slavery of heads had come in the brothels or in the suburban villas, where he experienced the first glimmers of disorder in his limbs. The girls set him free. But only Lili set his ears free from the chains of his head. A fidgeting thug was sprawling hidden within the geometric confines of the elegant industrialist of the rue Taitbout. His head was separating, with increased velocity, from his body.

Nevertheless, he kept his dinner dates with the *arrivistes* who played cards with him: the Schwob d'Héricourts and Deutsh de la Meurthes. Why did they send him invitations? Because they had seen him with a carnation in his buttonhole at the Alcazar with a blue-mouthed woman. Yes blue, potentially an unattractive colour but in this context . . . and the more they looked into him, the more they appreciated the rising stock of Royal Dutch and the amalgamations of South American assets collected in a portfolio of cunning and elegance. But Heym had forgotten about his shares. He appeared as usual in his *breloques* and tie-pins, walked in the park with a cane, took off his hat to Bernheim de Villiers on the rue de Rivoli . . . but alone with his head, that disastrous hysterical organ, he dreamt of the *concierge* and the detachable ears of the fair sex.

He had marginalized the *concierge* at the beginning of his affair with Lili. Now the *concierge* was back, this time inside his head, a difficult place from which to eject him. And as Heym walked through the streets of the city by himself he felt something following him, a vibration behind his back shadowing his movements. When he turned and looked he saw nothing. But it was there: a repulsive displacement, like a cup that has not been correctly replaced on a saucer. And the pulsation, this minute derangement on the edge of his field of vision, was not a cool and natural phenomenon – it made his finger-pads sweat. He suddenly became a stickler for trivial correctness in all things. The sight of a napkin unfolded or lying in the wrong way threw him into rages. And with every rage he felt he was correcting the moving warp behind him, the zone of shadow which he decided was the Yid-hating *concierge* on his tail.

'He waits until I've gone by,' he explained, 'then he picks up the kitchen knife and follows me. He keeps his distance. Yes, he's a cunning little bastard. I mean, he's a cunning big bastard! He's reporting my movements to the Grand Occidental de France. He's a spy for the Ligue Antisémite, as if . . . as if that couldn't be read all over his face. You can see it in the mouth. A butcher's mouth. And the cleft in his chin. Oh, no laughing, please. He has a recipe for Jew Casserole. And they've decided to track the Yid bankers, because, as you know, we're taking over the world, yes, we're a giant human octopus in a top hat . . . how do I know he takes the knife with him? How could he not take the kitchen knife? That's his orders. Take the kitchen knife and slit his throat if he puts you in a jam. They have their orders. It's organized. I was there at the Fort Chabrol. I saw him in the street. He was carrying a rolling pin. Yes, a rolling pin! He was going to smash a few Yids in. And what a piece of luck he's the *concierge* at Adolphe Heym's! The perfect strategic position. He knows what I'm dreaming about, but I know what he's dreaming about as well. He's dreaming about what my ears would taste like in *bouillabaisses* of theirs, squid and Jew's ear together with a bit of lobster . . . their fantasy is to consume us in heroic acts of cannibalism!'

Although Lili began to smile behind her hand, the thought that had suddenly entered Heym's head, with its heady mixture of gastronomy and amputations, was more true to life, more inspired by the actual life of the street, than he could ever have guessed. For at that very moment, only a few streets away, in the street adjacent to the rue de Navarin where the hairdresser lived, Heym's own dreams were coming to life in the form of that very same person, the coiffeur Nino and his wife Florina . . . coming to life in a drama which it is worth interrupting our narrative to relate since – through daily contact with Lili – it was the doomed Nino who first contracted, as easily as if it had been the plague bacillus *Pasteurella pestis*, the violent and unpredictable vulgarity of the ear.

60

14

For several weeks, the coiffeur had ploughed his fingers through Lili's hair and passed them within centimetres of her ears. Every morning in the half-lit bedroom he looked at her face reflected in the mirror in front of her. If she caught him staring too hard at her mouth, as he could not help himself doing, she asked him a question about his wife. Was she eating enough? Was her weight stable? Did she like chignons or tresses? And the coiffeur, letting the backs of his hands trail unnecessarily against her nape – so much that the balls of his thumbs rested sometimes against her top vertebra – blinked and turned his gaze back to the ears, which filled him with the acupunctural sweetness of imagined adultery.

What he could not understand was why she kept asking him about eating, and in particular the diet of his wife. Maybe she's a compulsive eater, he said to himself. Look at her mouth. Looks like it. A gastromaniac.

He went home once a month with his linen hair-bag full of her curls, perhaps infatuated with them, and puzzled by the enigma of the mouth. Why did he feel 'exposed' to it, as if to a chip of uranium? He had no idea.

But one night in November, as he was cutting his own hair in front of a mirror, he was overwhelmed by a sudden desire to start feeding his wife. Yes, he said to himself, I want to stuff her, force her, fatten her, fill her up. And immediately he ran out to a restaurant and came back with a basket of crayfish. He ran up to his wife, who was sitting in bed.

'If you don't eat these crayfish right now,' he shouted at her, 'I'll smash your face in!'

Yet there was a clumsy tenderness in his voice.

The wife began eating. She was terrified. She tore the crayfish up herself and stuffed the pieces into her mouth with small, dull grunts.

'And what's more, I forbid, I absolutely forbid you to vomit them up!'

In the morning he brought her eleven croissants and forced her to eat every one. At lunch it was a tray of terrine and goose liver paté followed by an *œuf cocotte* and a bar of chocolate. She was nearly sick but his look was homicidal. She began to fatten. At dinner he prepared himself a *roti de veau farci aux pruneaux* served with potatoes braised in milk and finished with a complete Diplomate filled with glacé cherries and covered with *crème anglaise*. Her hips swelled until by midnight her former thinness had begun to give way before incipient plumpness. And if she had regurgitated everything he had given her he would have forced her to eat it again, as well as breaking her nose.

The regime was maintained for a week.

At the beginning of the second week he plied her with cheeses. Her breakfasts were enlarged with slices of ham served with sweet pickles and eggs. At midday he sent a roast capon and a dish of *dauphinoise* potatoes down her throat; at five, *tartelettes* with coffee, at seven snails, poached bass with white butter sauce, jellied beef decorated with aspic triangles, sweetbreads in brown butter sauce, sautéed kidneys in mustard, calf's liver with cherry tomatoes and peas and stuffed mushrooms with a casserole of tripe.

Before long she was definitely fat.

Her shoulders accumulated rolls of subcutaneous tissue which then spread to her elbows and on to her fingers. In despair she tried to vomit in secret, but when the barber caught the sour smell on her breath he hit her forty times across the thighs. In between meals he enticed her with walnuts, raisins, sugar hearts and moulded jellies. She had to eat. Even when she slept he tried to drop currants into her mouth. His savings were halved in a single month in order to satisfy his craving to fill her up and the money spent was metamorphosed into rings of fat on his victim.

And still it wasn't enough.

For there was one part of her that remained stubbornly thin. Her ears would not respond to the regime. However much he stuffed her with food, however much her face puffed up and her belly swelled, her ears would not put on weight. The barber was incensed. Was this a trick of hers to evade her wifely duties?

Overlook her ears? Forgive the thinness of her ears? There was not a chance. Her ears would not escape. He would make them fat, too. They could resist his plan if they liked but if they did . . . they would have to come off! Yes, they would have to come off, if the worst came to the worst.

He fed her for three months. Her weight doubled, then trebled. It was such a shame in a petite woman. The customers agreed. A monster for a husband. Shouldn't she see a doctor? But then maybe he liked her fat. Why shouldn't he fatten her up if she was his wife? He had his reasons.

One night at the end of February he found he could feed his wife no more. And in addition the ears were not getting fatter at all. Suddenly enraged, and not knowing where to go from here, he gave himself up to a husbandly rage.

'I've given you everything,' he screamed while the fat woman cowered under the bed, 'but you abuse my abundance! You think this food can go on for ever! You've overstepped yourself. You're a pig ready for slaughter! What other use is there for all that fat? You think it's all been for nothing? I'm going to sell you to the butcher! Piece by piece!'

Bestial noises were heard through the walls. The barber swearing, the wife unable to move because of her weight clawing the floorboards, digging her nails in as he dragged her out from under the bed. The zing of a knife sawed across a sharpener. He carried out all his threats meticulously. Laying her across the bedroom table, he split open her belly and rhetorically reclaimed all he had put into her. But then an even more secretive sound came from the ground-floor kitchen which adjoined the bedroom: the sizzling of a frying pan. When the forces of order broke into the flat at ten thirty they found the barber seated at table, a napkin stuffed tidily into his shirt. His eyes were round with surprise and indignation. Before him lay the frying pan and a plate bearing a neat circle of small red beets, artichoke hearts and assorted pickles. And in the centre was an ear sautéed in garlic and salted butter with a pinch of pepper. One was already lying snugly at the bottom of his stomach. The other had been carefully divided into four and was about to join it on its mysterious journey. After all, he had fattened her up – why shouldn't he reap the rewards, as anyone else would? What did the police think? Did they think food grew on trees?

At the lunatic asylum near Dieppe where his family sent him, the barber could later remember nothing about the three months in which he had fattened up his wife and then bitten her ear. He refused to believe that he was not the victim of a plot by the State against immigrant barbers. As for the ear, he could not even remember how it had tasted. Only sometimes, when he was dreaming about it, did he wake suddenly and say, half asleep, with no one present, 'A taste of pork fried in lemon, but without the suggestion of human flesh.' The wife was buried with her extant ear and her coffin was in no way out of the ordinary as far as size was concerned. The whole story is still repeated in the *quartier* and the great silent film-maker Anton Pek made a forty-two minute feature from it in which the lead actor – a strapping Hungarian with a false nose – instead of graphically removing his ear with a razor, falls down instead with an attack of *le petit mal* foaming toothpaste at the mouth and mouthing dumbly into the camera the famous quip of Talleyrand: 'Messieurs, surtout pas de zèle!'

15

Reading the reports in the *Mercure*, Heym unlocked the drawer where he had planted the scissors and took them out. They were beautiful. The edges of the blades were finely honed. How had the hairdresser done it so neatly? Had he been in practice? The newspaper stories didn't scare him. On the contrary, the hairdresser had given him a sign. He returned to the Batignolles with the scissors in his pocket.

His favourite age group was the fifteen to seventeen year olds, because the ears of these semi-adults were at the same time delicate and mature. Was it possible that an ear alone could make overtures to him? But it was undeniable that they pouted at him, causing him to suffer a growing weakness, as if they were capable of molesting him.

On the Boulevard Bessières he followed the street-walkers from a safe distance, his thumb and fore-finger sliding gingerly up and down the blades hidden in his pocket. He might follow for hours, until the lights went out and it was safe to get closer, to come within touching distance of the ear. At other times, he hung around the cabarets waiting for the *femmes interlopes* to make their appearance on the street. When he returned home, Lili saw him wiping his fingers in small sugar bowls filled with alcohol solutions, as if the fingernails had to be cleared of debris, and then dipping the tips in rosewater to hide the odour.

In the winter of 1901, on a small street near the Boulevard Bessières, a sixteen-year-old prostitute was found unconscious near the railway tracks with the lobe of her left ear cut off. It had been sliced off diagonally and so severed cleanly in two. The fragment of flesh lost was less than half the size of a postage stamp. From the slightly staggered wound it was clear that a pair of scissors had been used. The attacker had not raped or tried to kill her. He had simply taken the bottom part of the ear-lobe and run off with it. The right ear was untouched. Had one ear been enough or had the ear thief been surprised during the operation? The blood around the face had also been carefully mopped as if not to disturb the harmony of the face. And though she had passed out the girl had not been hit. Too drunk to resist she had parted with half her immature charm without knowing it.

Nor was she the last victim of that winter . . .

On 28 February a draper's daughter was found half frozen in an abandoned house in Bobigny. She had met a gentleman at a beer hall on the Boulevard de Rochechouart and had spent the night with him at his villa. He had pestered her ear all night. In the end he had demanded it jokingly, then taken her into the kitchen, held her down at knife-point and taken the lobe while she was still unconscious from a blow to the back of the neck. The house was rented from a Russian chemist. The renter, under a false name, could not be traced . . .

For years after the mutilation of Bobigny, the newspapers and periodicals were filled with ear-orientated scandal. Women covered their ears in public in deference to the intimidation of such bizarre and impudent robbery. Diagrams of the halved lobes fed a voyeuristic demand for details. Heym, looking at them, raised his eyebrows and tutted: they made it look clumsier than it was. It was possible to perfect a technique of surgical detachment that would enable the anatomical thief to get what he wanted without the victim being aware until it was too late. Didn't they suspect the antics of a diseased doctor, as in the Whitechapel murders? It was insulting that they hadn't even raised this possibility. The robbery of lobes might provoke outraged editorials complaining of the decadence evident in such snide disrespect for the holy, the sacrosanct female anatomy – taking a lady's ear-lobe was even worse than killing her outright with a hammer – but in the end they were only the lobes of street girls, socially insignificant lobes, degraded lobes, lobes marginal to the canon of Human Form. What he needed was a mainstream lobe, one imbued with the majesty of the male sex. He needed a lobe charged with the authority of the Nation.

Returning from a night at the Folies, after first plying her with flatteries, he opened his thoughts just as they were getting out of the cab within sight of the *concierge*'s window.

'I've had an inspiration,' he said calmly. 'I would say that if we were to cut off that troll's ear he'd think twice about following me around for the Ligue.'

'But . . . you've never hurt a fly in your life!'

'Well yes . . . that's true of course . . . but sometimes it is necessary to act . . . to avert catastrophe. And what if I don't cut his nasty little ear off? He'll get bold. He'll get ideas. Oh no. We can't have a pogrom on the rue Taitbout!'

'But the police . . .'

But Heym didn't hear.

'He thinks I won't touch his ear, he thinks I'll give it a miss . . . whatever has got into his head? He thinks we all lie down and take it in the face. Well, he's not a Cossack!'

They went up the stairs in silence. Heym's hands shook as he held the banister.

'It's true', he continued slowly, 'that he's big. You see, it will have to be you. He'll only fall for a woman. You have to go down and get him drunk. When he's on his back, I'll slip in and . . . snip-snap!'

'You're insane.'

'I'm not insane at all. This is defence of the race!'

'He won't buy it.'

'What? All you do is move your mouth. I've watched him watching your mouth. Doesn't everyone watch your mouth? What can he do against an assault from your mouth?'

In the apartment, he took out a bottle of Yquem, then changed his mind. 'On second thoughts, give him the stuff in the kitchen.'

While she was finding the right *décolletage*, he trimmed his nails patiently with a pair of clippers. He had taken the scissors with him to the Folies, as he always did now, and they were ready in his pocket.

As Lili went down the stairs, he leant over the banister and hissed: 'Remember . . . your mouth!'

The bottom of the stairs was dark. The *concierge*'s oil lamp was lit and standing on his table, however. She could see him through the glass door, hunched shirtless over one of his clandestine broadsheets. His arms were covered with tattoos. When she knocked he turned round suddenly and squinted through the panes, frozen with surprise. The Jew's tart – covered in diamonds from head to foot, and her mouth pressed close to the glass! He rubbed his eyes with his knuckles. She wanted him to get up . . . open the door! Forgetting his bare chest, he did what she wanted. Out of a freezing night came her Pinaud perfume, a smack of violets right in the nose!

He smiled stupidly and then, remembering his sex, slyly.

So she wants to come in . . .

Difficult to believe his luck.

'What's that?'

He pointed at the bottle.

'I stole it from the Jew,' she said. 'I'm sick of his bullying so I stole it.'

'So he hits you, does he? Quite right you stole the bottle.'

'I thought you . . .'

'Why not? They steal from us, why not take it back from them? It gives me pleasure, it really does. If he comes down the stairs, sweetheart, I'll kick his balls in!'

'Oh you wouldn't, would you? Thank God you can defend me.'

'You were frightened, weren't you? You were frightened old Shylock would cut off his pound of flesh. Well, it could've been worse than that. You did the right thing. Thought I was lonely, didn't you, needed a bit of . . .'

'I saw you once before. Such big arms!'

'Oh you saw them, did you? It's the weights that do it. See.'

And he flexed his biceps. She squealed, then poured him a drink. He drank it with one swallow.

A few minutes later his mouth, encased in wet hairs, was swooping down towards her shoulder. He swayed, teetered on his right foot, then shifted violently to his left.

'You won't stay still,' he complained. 'Did the Jew make you dance about?'

'You're so thirsty! I would never have believed it if I hadn't seen those arms.'

'The arms . . . the arms, that's nothing, I've got other things than arms, arms is the least of it, sweetie.'

His hand landed with a thud on her buttock. The hairs smelt of cooking wine and the suckling lips between them opened to reveal a thick ox tongue covered with white pimples. He was clucking deep in his throat. When his tongue met her breast, which had popped out into the rarefied world of rape, he passed out with a fetid expulsion of air.

He landed on his back under the table.

She opened the door and found Heym waiting in the vestibule. He had seen and heard everything.

His eyes were crazed.

'Did you see him?' he gasped pathetically. 'Did you see him?'

'He's asleep.'

'For the first and last time in the presence of a Jew!'

'You didn't mean it about the scissors?'

He had taken them out and was testing them on air. They made a rasping shearing sound, the enormous blades gleaming in the oil light.

'This is not a joke,' he said. 'I came here, as he says, in the spirit of Shylock. I want less than a pound, a few milligrammes will do, but he's going to wake up lighter . . . I've decided.'

'They'll catch you.'

'And charge me with what? I'll say it was self-defence. Drunken *concierge* versus the Heym Metal Shoe-Eye Consortium.'

The *concierge* made a noise under the table. If he woke up, he would go mad with his rolling pin. Heym pushed her aside and knelt down by his head. The features were blunted, flushed and stinking. The ears themselves were repulsive, loaded with unnecessary fat. Taking hold of the left one, he placed the blades of the scissors carefully against them in a clean diagonal line and brought the handles together with superhuman force.

The bottom half of the lobe dropped off with one cut.

Heym caught it with his other hand and held it up to the light. It turned blue immediately and dripped blood on to his shirt.

'Well, now,' he muttered. 'Look at that. The lobe of a bigot!'

But Lili had run out into the street, where a band of children with candles was passing. Snow fell softly into the top of the lamps. The *concierge*'s room was silent. Feeling a rising vertigo in his ears, the industrialist was waltzing gleefully around it, with hushed titters, his feet shuffling in the silence. Raising her arms as if she had nothing to do with it, knew nothing about the vulgarity he had just discharged, Lili let out a scream which caused the children on their way to a chapel to drop their candles, turn on their heels and run in a flutter of white frocks in the opposite direction.

16

But the police were not called, the industrialist retreated upstairs with his severed ear and the *concierge*, waking in the middle of the night in agony, could accuse nobody of theft except the teenage prostitute whose mouth had danced around him to a sound of ringing bells.

Nursing his ear with formaldehyde, he remembered that he didn't even know her name.

Meanwhile, the manufacturer of shoe-eyes had locked his doors and sat down with the ear-lobe at his salon table. Had he examined the contents of his apartment he could have seen that missing were: a pair of Staffordshire shoes, his ivory shoe-horns, his cabinet of tropical barks and pharmaceutical products, his tortoiseshell reading glasses, his gold-plated fruit knife, his inlaid snuff/cocaine appliance, his heated curling tongs, his silver pen engraved with the coat of arms of Lübeck, his glass lilies and his mother's semi-automated sewing machine.

But Heym was unaware of anything but the ear. It sat on his table, in a glass fruit bowl. He was elated. Unable to sleep, he kept guard over the ear for several nights, unable to move from his chair by the glass bowl though he knew he would have to explain everything to the forces of order. And what was it that rooted him to the spot through so many nights if not that the ear itself, like its possessor before it, seemed to pulsate, as if it had a life of its own, as if it were about to follow him if he left the room?

The employees of the Ivry factory, suspicious at his absence and needing to have their salary cheques cleared, decided unanimously to call a doctor and a priest to his apartment. The managing director, though, sat transfixed by the table, his chair, the glass fruit bowl and the gently decomposing ear. The room filled with a sweet and floral odour. The lobe turned on to its side, easing itself into a dignified position, and turned green. He could not take his eyes from it: it moved and turned colour as slowly as the hour of the pendulum clock. He was dreaming it, he was asleep without knowing it, or else the laws of nature had become witty in their old age. He tried to move, first his left foot and then his hands, but could not. The piece of ear paralysed every part of his body.

From green it turned to vinegar-brown, shifting in its cradle of glass. A *concierge*'s ear . . . large, but certainly human. The scissors lay near by on the same table, but unlike the lobe they did not move at all. Nothing moved but the dark triangle of flesh in the bowl.

Nights and days passed. Knocks on the door, footsteps, a few whispers reached him. One minute he was sure it was on the move again, the next that it had never moved in the first place. And yet its position was not what it had been the day before. It grew softer then harder, distended and contracted, grew shiny and then dull. If only he could have reached out for a grape, stuck out his tongue or at least enjoyed any of the expensive objects in the room, his Cuban cigars or English marmalades. But he could not move a muscle. The lobe turned over again and again, turning pink, violet, magenta, blue. It took on the glaze of a majolica tile, sweated, palpitated and refused to remain fixed in any definite chemical condition.

The employees, massed outside the door now, called the forces of law to break the locks and effect immediate entry into the tomb-like apartment. But as soon as the burly officers wielding hammers had forced their way in they were obliged to hold their fingers to their noses. The lobe had degenerated into a ball of mould from which a massive, concentrated aroma of rotting fruit assaulted the senses.

Le Flaneur, for the weekly edition ending 3 March 1902, recorded the case of the clotheswear industrialist and reclusive Jew Adolphe Heym: 'Procuring forcible entry into the defendant's home by means of crow-bars and assorted hammers, Officers Deladier and Joffroy discovered him alone in the company of part of a severed ear. Not only was the once brilliant, though solitary, proprietor of the Heym Metal Shoe-Eye Consortium registered at Ivry-sur-Seine in a state of abject and gruesome mesmerization before this ear of an uncertain victim, but the contents of his drawers being examined by the police yielded a whole array of such organs, necrophile mementoes of unknown crimes, in varying degrees of decomposition – for the most part apparently the lobes of young girls, the sex and age of each specimen having been determined by the latest forensic techniques. Informed of his arrest the entrepreneur responsible for keeping our shoes on our feet, waved his hands in the air and demanded that he be permitted instantly to kiss a copy of the Torah, a demand which demonstrates, if no other demonstration were needed, the extreme and bloodthirsty fanaticism to which the Semitic temperament is prone.'

The businessman was sent, like the hairdresser, to an asylum near Mulhouse. A month later he carved off a tiny sliver of his own ear and asked for it to be sealed in an envelope. The Metal Shoe-Eye Consortium was sold off to a Belgian hosier and the apartment on the rue Taitbout claimed by his German cousins.

How many years did he sit before the grille window on the seventh floor of the converted silk factory on the outskirts of Mulhouse fingering the missing edge of his right ear?

How many times did he declare that nothing was more obvious than the innocence that shone from his eyes?

How many astronomical objects did he observe and note down in his notebook, in which were also written garbled love letters to a child prostitute whose name could not be found on the register of inmates at the Mazas and Saint Lazare prisons?

The abigail employed at the rue de Navarin had been dismissed. Her employer had disappeared without trace. But at the beginning of the summer a letter arrived at the Mount Alban Sanatorium asking if it would be possible, for reasons which they might find grotesque but which the writer assured them were purely sentimental, to procure the slice of poor patient no. 123's ear, the removal of which had deepened his confusion.

The director of Mount Alban took pity on the pathetic request and sent her the ear wrapped in linen and placed in a funerary urn. The address was in Berlin.

The urn, the linen and the slice of ear arrived at a small apartment in the Charlottenburg district under the name of Dorziat. And who does not believe that a soul can be imprisoned within the tragi-comic form of an ear?

IV

17

There was once a hotel in Berlin called the Renoma, though even its location, now that all trace of it has vanished, is a subject of controversy. It is certain, however, that it once stood on a small street between the Tiergarten and Alexanderplatz and that its bathrooms of pink marble, English mahogany furniture and cast-iron 'Egyptian' columns attracted a clientèle happy to eat every night in a rose and walnut dining-room in the general shape of a lung.

It is possible that the Renoma was financed by its occupants, the itinerant arms manufacturers and negotiators who favoured its secluded discretion and privacy, and who included the wandering Goliaths of the magical realm of weapons: Sir Hiram Stevens Maxim, Sir Basil Zaharoff, the agents of Krupps and the redoubtable and secretive Gustave Hauser.

The last name is the most likely candidate, since the Danish munitions chief was a permanent resident at the Renoma for a period of three years, occupying the Barbarossa Suite between nos 67 and 72.

The Register of Companies for the years 1899 to 1904 makes no mention of the company which the dominant archon of the Renoma – and a figure of fun to the shoe-blacks on the street because of his mammoth belly – claimed to have bought in the latter part of 1900: Suger-Sarfati, 'philosophical instrument makers', designers and manufacturers of high-velocity artillery shells. Neither does the Internationale Biographische Archiv of Berlin, in which Hauser does appear under three pseudonyms, make any mention of the orders placed with this firm by, among others, the governments of Paraguay and Mexico. What is ascertainable is that, driven by the relentless and predictable logic of international competition, Hauser's newly acquired company came into conflict with two of the above-mentioned armaments personalities, Maxim and Zaharoff. The latter was the unscrupulous former agent of the Nordenfeldt firm responsible, among other exploits, for the First World War, for which he was later knighted.

A dark duel broke out between these three antagonists over the selling of machine guns to the Austrian army, in the course of which Hauser himself was wounded in the hand when Maxim's sabotaged machine mis-fired at the Steinfeld firing range in Vienna in the presence of Archduke William. Hauser later obtained satisfaction for his aggrieved honour with his procurement of an order for detonating incendiary shells from the Portuguese. With the proceeds of this sale, combined with earlier profits from the Chacos war in South America, it is possible that Hauser entered the development cartel responsible for the Renoma hotel as a majority share holder.

He set up his Berlin office in the Barbarossa Suite and had the walls hung with maps, drawings from his engineers and pictures of rose-lipped Christs which he mischievously turned upside down.

A globe was placed in his rooms, where he worked with a German secretary. On it were pinned yellow flags representing the presence of his agents and clients around the world. The globe was thick with yellow dots. They swarmed particularly around the continent of Europe and the southern part of the Americas. Every week another flag was added until it was difficult to find room for the new arrivals. He ordered a larger globe from the Royal Society in London, one mounted in a magnificent bronze bracket which he planned to illumine with electric markers. More than any mere event in the physical world this agglomeration of yellow signs sprinkled around a revolving globe on which nations were printed with the bright and unreal colours of postage stamps was the materialization of his childhood wishes.

Then, of course, there was the Barbarossa Suite . . .

A relentless ornamentation contained at its centre, shadowed under pendulous flounces of aubergine Formosa silk, a buhl bed filled with a ton of duck feathers.

Here the obese emperor of shells reclined in the afternoons dictating letters to minor potentates, dukes, mercenaries and shipping companies with a box of candied figs not far from his left hand, on which the knuckles had disappeared. The telephone rang constantly. Servants rushed in and out of the room with pots of flowers, letters, bottles of iced water and mounds of fruit. The secretary camped by the bed, typewriter on his knees, and made suggestions in a voice so quiet that the Dane was always shouting, 'What? Speak up! The Minister of Finance? Send a yacht to his daughter!' Manicurists fluttered around his exposed toes, which were covered with swabs of cotton-wool, and runners from the Berlin stock market constantly interrupted business in high-pitched adolescent voices warped with fear.

The padishah of Suger-Sarfati sat and lay in state.

But towards the autumn of 1902 the secretary was obliged to record a falling off of profits in the new Modesta tungsten-tipped shell which the master himself had helped to design, despite its having been successfully sold to at least five sovereign states.

The respective Ministries had their quotas and stockpiles were at a satisfactory level. The depots were full. The shells were not being used, and at one hundred and seventy dollars a piece . . .

It was a cold morning in October, breakfast was laid out over Hauser's quilt and he was stuffing four quail's eggs into his mouth with eight pieces of toast covered with caviar butter. His jaw stopped masticating.

'Stagnant revenues from the Modesta?' he spat through the half-crushed eggs. 'With my own new detonators and twenty-four-carat cases? Not being used?'

'As I said, sir.'

'*Sapperment!*'

He expelled the eggs and sat up.

'Go to the bathroom, Frisch. Get me the packet of soap that Henckel opened this morning. The potassium soap by the bath.'

The secretary came back with a soap box in one hand and a wet table in the other. The master wanted the box.

'Look at the cover. An angel of death!'

The soap box showed an adolescent reclining in a bubble bath under a legend in Gothic script: 'NYMPHUS TOILET SOAP (With Potassium Ash)'.

The master of Suger-Sarfati had seen enough.

'Who produces the soap?'

'The Lino Oil Company, sir.'

'How do they find their models?'

'The Venus Liebstrahl Agency, sir.'

'Proprietor?'

'Herr Paolo Sainctavit, sir.'

'Modelling fee?'

'Forty marks, sir.'

'Corruptibility?'

'Ten out of ten, sir.'

'Fine. Get the nymphus.'

The secretary rushed downstairs and so into the street, hailed a taxi and within half an hour was at the Venus Liebstrahl Agency on Kreutzdamstrasse.

Herr Sainctavit was on holiday, could the assistant manager help him?

'I take it your models work incognito?'

'Of course, sir.'

The secretary held out a roll of two thousand marks.

'But, of course, there are circumstances in which . . . this way, sir!'

Within another half an hour Frisch was at the door of a small apartment near the Charlottenburg Palace. When the girl on the soap box answered the door he smiled and bowed.

'Miss Dorziat? Here is three thousand marks. I would say it was your lucky day.'

They took the same taxi back to the Renoma.

'Take your hair down,' the secretary advised. 'Herr Hauser likes a full head of hair.'

By the time they entered the Barbarossa Suite the master was fully dressed in a serge suit and opening his correspondence with a silver paper knife. A young man was shrieking into his ear: 'Transoccidental Spices, sir, seventy-eight per cent since April!'

The table was covered with large bowls of figs and bananas and in the middle of them stood a bonsai tree with a label attached to one of its branches: greetings from the man in Krung Thep.

Hauser rose and held out his fat hand. His eyes flared up. A nice specimen. Far too good for a soap box.

'So here she is,' he murmured. Then, turning to the exhausted secretary, 'You were a little late in delivering the goods. Really, Fisch, I thought you were cold-blooded.'

And the entire room exploded in rachitic laughter.

18

'My secretary', Hauser began, trying to get a good look at her buttocks, 'has given me the Venus accounts for the last three months. I see that . . . yes . . . since arriving from France you have worked on three assignments. A garden utensil advertisement, a cough mixture label – Streptotherapic Balsam with Mexican Honey? – and the, yes, soap box. In total your earnings were below seven hundred marks. A crime, Miss Dorziat, a financial slander! Your charm shines from every object. In fact I think I'll go and order some hoes right away, and I don't even have a garden!'

The room burst into laughter again.

'However, being serious. We could not tolerate seeing your talents undervalued. Furthermore, we would not allow it. Now, what are your measurements?'

'Sir, sir, the tape measure!'

Frisch sprang forward.

'Oh, you again? Oh well, I suppose I'll let you do it. I have to make concessions once in a while.'

Hysterical laughter.

'Thirty-five – twenty-eight – thirty-two,' the secretary reported.

'Got that? Now go and get a Loie Fuller dress and something by Paquin. And get her a Doucet tea-gown as well.'

Frisch vanished.

The master rubbed his hands and split open a fig with his fist. A youth appeared in the door and shouted: 'Vickers up four per cent! Eight per cent since Wednesday!' Hauser waved his hands dismissively.

'Sit down, our soap-box beauty. Breakfast is prepared. We'll wait for the dresses and then we'll see what they look like.'

As they drank the cinnamon-flavoured coffee served in strange oblong boats bearing the Renoma insignia, Hauser chattered comfortably while shouting orders left and right over her head, the rings flashing on his fingers and the flower in his early morning lapel wilting in its hole.

'Cinnamon is an aphrodisiac, of course . . . when I was your age . . . headaches and nervous disorders . . . the tumultuous state of the world . . . no one but myself . . . Polignac? Let him wait! . . . Now, where was I?'

As Hauser examined her with one eye, putting his knee into contact with her thigh, he was not filled with desire. True, the mouth had worked its foreseeable effect upon him at first, but as soon as he had felt its pull he had distanced himself from it and persevered in looking at it from the outside, at a calculated remove. It would be tempting to tweak her thigh, yes, he would happily and gaily tweak the thigh, but what would be the point if he was only going to end up enmeshed in the mouth? The mouth of a woman is a dangerous thing. Especially when it looks as if it's going to leave its face. He had seen the alternative uses her mouth could be put to. If it could be harnessed and controlled, disciplined and bribed . . .

'The one thing I learned when I was directing the nickel mines in Noumea', he whispered close to her ear, 'is that if a secretary is late, you cut off one of his balls with a razor.'

She laughed; the mouth wagged like the female spiv he knew it was.

And he thought: she's not shocked, she's laughing at the thought of Frisch in agony. How common it is when it laughs.

Frisch returned forty-five minutes later with the dresses. She changed in Hauser's bedroom, surrounded by tapestries and alabaster Rapes of Daphne. The wad of marks was still fixed in her underwear. Since leaving Paris she had been haunted by the fear of the French police tracing her across the border with her stolen articles and her record of participation in a mutilation. But the fat man with the rings was her safety. Men in buttoned uniforms waited in the anterooms. A grovelling subservience filled the eleven vast rooms of the Barbarossa. The world of Hauser was a labyrinth in which entire nations could lose themselves.

When she came out, the master was browbeating a little man in a grey goatee.

'That's right, de los Caballeros, I invited him to dinner, I won't take no for an answer, Bolivia will regret the insult, sir, I assure you . . .'

'But', the little goatee-man was protesting in a thick Spanish accent, 'at such short notice, he will have to put off Frau Berthe Krupp von Bohlen who is, you will appreciate, by far the richest person in Germany, I cannot . . .'

'Mr de los Caballeros is in no position to refuse an invitation to dinner, especially when his government . . . ah, excuse me . . .'

He walked over to Lili and took her hand.

'Mr Tolmezzo,' he said, 'this is our latest addition to our army of contented employees. May I introduce Miss Dorziat from . . . Paris.'

'Ah, Parees!'

The little man kissed her hand.

'Mr Tolmezzo, Bolivian embassy . . .'

'An exquisite *créature*, Herr Hauser.'

'You can tell Mr de los Caballeros that she will be there as well.'

'Is that so?'

The Bolivian looked up at her breasts.

'Besides, there is a problem with the twenty-four-carat casings. I can't permit any misunderstandings to come between us.'

'Well, it's true Frau Berthe Krupp von Bohlen is not as . . . alluring . . . as your new employee, Herr Hauser, a fact which I will, with all . . .'

'Yes, yes. I want him here now, tonight. Who knows, Mr Tolmezzo, you might find it's to your advantage, what with Chile grumbling . . .'

'Ah yes, Chile.'

With a long face, the Bolivian exited after covering Lili's hand with his mouth and Hauser lit a cigar while continuing to crush puny fruits with his fist.

'You look beautiful. What do I smell? *Kokottenduft!* The smell of a cocotte. The attachés will not miss a thing. Remember that they are very proud. Frisch!'

The secretary appeared immediately, as if summoned by a conjurer, with a telegram form thoughtfully ready.

'Telegram to Chilean embassy. Señor Luis del Pilar Angelo Patrocinio Simone de Muguiro y Beruete, military attaché. Greetings Hauser stop. Request presence Renoma dine stop. Insist stop.

Favourite duck women charm stop. Eight if convenient stop. Must insist if convenient stop. Urgent matter confidential man to man hostilities imminent Château Margaux promised stop. Yours Hauser stop.'

Beaming and filled with vital health, the mikado of Suger-Sarfati dismissed his secretary and admitted a Romanian barber who rushed across the room with a tiny pair of scissors. He sat.

'They're all the same,' he sighed, patting Lili's knee.

The barber, sweating with terror, brought his minuscule scissors to bear on the waxed tips of the master's moustaches while the master swatted him like an irritating fly.

'Monsieur wants the moustaches linear or curved today?'

'I want them . . . unforgiving!'

As the barber snipped, the master watched his progress in a small hand mirror. And, as happened every morning, the Romanian cut off the wrong hair on the left side. Hauser grunted, lifted his hand and brought it down with vicious force into the barber's bald spot. The red image of a hand appeared on the spot. The master turned smiling to Lili.

'You must never forget, *Süßchen*, that the most profound, the most intense emotion that a man can feel is . . . humiliation!'

19

In 1884, on the other side of the world, a short war erupted on the South American continent between the states of Bolivia and Chile. The object of the dispute was the small corridor of land stretching from the vast Cerro Sairecabúr to the Pacific more or less along the Tropic of Capricorn and comprising the region known as Antofagasta, with its three principal coastal towns of Antofagasta, Mejillones and Cobija.

In the event, the Chileans won the day and Bolivia was forced to cede not only the Antofagasta corridor but the whole littoral and Andean region between Africa and Calama as well – that is, the northern tip of what is Chile today between the seventeenth and twenty-third parallels. The effect of this was to inflict a profound and unbearable humiliation upon the Bolivians, who naturally mourned the loss of that great Federation of Bolivia and Peru that had once comprised everything between the port of Tumbez and the Chaco. All peoples mourn the loss of territory with unconscious bitterness. Humiliation sharpens and deepens the national collective grief. A culture of humiliation emerges, an ethos of nostalgia and revenge.

With his fine instinct for the nuances of humiliation, Hauser had formulated a masterful plan in the light of the loss of Antofagasta, one which used the weapons which had built his incomparable career.

'As I was saying,' he went on, throwing off the barber with a flurry of slaps to the cheeks, 'we commonly mistake the nature of our true passions, we misunderstand the basis of our own natures. We are told all the time that we are dominated by timeless passions, a register of emotions all carefully notated in the language of the arts. But, as I said, the most powerful feeling that a human being can feel is the feeling of humiliation. Humiliation is the most intense experience we ever have. Nothing approaches it for its shattering effect. A humiliated man is a natural predator, a dangerous animal. And he is dangerous not just in moments of anger, but at all times – his itch for compensation, for revenge, is permanent. His entire being is disturbed in a way that no one else's is. Humiliation is a form of spiritual destruction so complete that there can be no recovery. And in no sphere is it so potent as in the sphere of culture itself. The nation or individual that suffers from an inferiority complex on the level of culture is naturally disposed towards genocide.'

That night she sat behind a spray of ink-stained carnations at a table so large that the face sitting diametrically opposite at the further edge of the ellipse from her was no more than a smear of mobile pink and black dots obscured and refracted by globes of lead crystal and silver lids. But the face just to its right, for some reason, was more clearly visible and, as if recognizing a mutually inexplicable visibility, it leered and gestured in her direction. It was large and handsome, with thick black lines painted on it: a firm moustache and a slick arc of macassared hair.

It was Beruete, fresh from lecherous promenades on the Unter den Linden.

His own carnation curiously complemented a diagonal white scar across his left temple, the kind of picturesque and unspoiling scar that duellists acquire.

The red Paquin dress and Japanese fan had caught his eye: a fat black eye that swam behind an aristocratic lens.

On her right sat, rigid and uncomfortable among Hauser's guests, de los Caballeros, a shrivelled middle-aged man with a single tuft of grey hair glued to the back of his skull and a slightly deformed nose shot through with the blush of exploded varicose veins. Hardly touching his *Canetons Duclair*, he too was casting nervous and admiring looks over the top of his glass at the fine red line of a *décolletage* that glistened with rows of tiny stones.

After dinner the guests adjourned upstairs to the Barbarossa Suite and Hauser ordered crates of Krug to be opened by waiters dressed as khedives in maraschino breeches. Baccarat tables were set up. Smoke began to fill the rooms. Lili was the only woman among the black jackets.

As midnight passed it was clear that Beruete and de los Caballeros were both concentrating upon her face. They appeared to have lost interest in everything else around them. And in addition they were both aware that they were fixated by her mouth. Beruete, in his childish way, scribbled *billets-doux* on to the backs of matchboxes and sent them by devious routes across the wide spaces of the suite. They were written in Kama Sutra mode: 'The lokri of summer evenings', 'The pale pathma of the moment', and so on. The more reserved de los Caballeros limited himself to moving the edges of his facial hair when her eye came across him. He did not lose a single opportunity. And as the evening wore on the movements of hair were accompanied by the scortatory tip of his tongue, which peeped out like a secret organ and gave the lie to his ordered and shrivelled face.

And since the two attachés were poignantly aware of each other, they kept a close watch on each other's movements, so that de los Caballeros followed with an eagle eye the trajectories of Beruete's matchboxes and the latter watched with mounting apprehension and disgust the sly performance of de los Caballeros's moustaches.

In between them, at the focal point of their national enmity, was that mouth copied from a Levy Durmer painting, black, wide and rapinous.

As each of them left the suite they discreetly asked the secretary if it might be possible to acquire the address of the woman in red. Frisch wrote it for both on the back of the master's calling cards. The Americans blushed and bowed gratefully. Throughout the evening their host had said nothing about business, but clearly he had provided compensations for his political withdrawal. They were uneasy in the Barbarossa Suite. Hauser watched them with a wet smile. Beruete remembered him in a whorehouse in Asunción during the Chacos war, the same smile, the same clicking fingers.

But in his haste to memorize Lili's address, he forgot all about it.

De los Caballeros hung back in the vestibule until Beruete had taken his cab, then stepped out into the street himself feeling thirty years younger.

Within a week they had both called at the apartment in Charlottenburg, both of them bearing clichéd bouquets of red Christmas roses.

The supplicants soon learnt each other's routines. When Beruete was there, de los Caballeros hung back. When Beruete knew that Caballeros was upstairs, he prudently stayed in the background. But it was eventually inevitable that they would meet by accident on the stairs or that their duel would be resolved against their wills in some way or another.

Beruete for one had decided to attack aggressively.

He went up to Lili's rooms one day and took out a handkerchief.

'It's not enough', he said theatrically, 'that we exchange our little pleasantries, however pleasant they may be, or that we give and take small but dangerous kisses . . . Oh no, I want something more. I want a living memento of your mouth. I want an imprint of your lips to look at twenty-four hours out of twenty-four . . .'

Making sure her mouth was heavily coloured, he had her put it against the handkerchief, which was then stained with a perfect reproduction of a pair of lips.

Carefully folding the handkerchief with the image of her mouth, he placed it in his pocket and when later he was on the boulevard alone, still moist and perfumed from being close to her for over an hour next to an open fire, he took it out and held it up to the sunlight. The print had captured her mouth. It was better than a nude photograph.

He took it with him to the Café Rex, where he sat inside and ordered a rum punch. Hardly had he sat down, however, than he caught sight out of the corner of his eye of his rival sitting on the other side of the café and in the act of taking out a rubber mouth spray and directing it towards his mouth. Evidently preparing to make a call on the woman he himself had just left dressed in nothing but a tea-gown and with heavily coloured lips! Barely controlling his rage, he rose and walked towards the Bolivian.

He stopped only three feet from de los Caballeros's table and the Bolivian, seeing him only at the last minute, blushed to the roots of his hair, passed a pale hand in front of his mouth and hurriedly put away the spray. They confronted each other in silent monomachia.

A minute passed. The waiters rushed past them ignoring the silent confrontation. Then Beruete revealed his secret weapon. With slow and deliberate movements he took out his handkerchief, moved his nose as if to sneeze and held the handkerchief to his face. And as he did so the corner of the handkerchief that bore the mark of Lili's mouth fell outwards and displayed itself to the Bolivian, who observed it with growing consternation.

He immediately recognized the shape. There was no other mouth like it. It was the very mouth towards which he was continually launching himself!

Perspiring rapidly, he squirmed in his chair.

Beruete sneezed and sneezed and the lips continued to dangle in front of de los Caballeros's face, taunting and reviling him.

The Bolivian felt rising within him the irresistible force of humiliation. The lips had been stolen from him, turned against him, so proudly emblazoned upon his enemy's handkerchief.

Rising himself, and understanding now the connection between the mouth imprinted on to Beruete's handkerchief and the lost province of Antofagasta, he burst spontaneously into the national anthem and ended it with a military salute, shouting: 'Long live free Antofagasta!'

The Chilean responded by saluting in kind.

'God bless Antofagasta!'

De los Caballeros, unable to further restrain his unleashed nationalism, leapt forward with the blessed name of that splendid and scenic province on his lips and there was a diplomatic incident.

De los Caballeros left the Rex with a smear of lipstick on his face and Beruete, laughing loudly, was escorted from the establishment with a loop of saliva covering his cheek from nose to ear. Within hours, telegrams had been exchanged across the Atlantic and Tolmezzo had again presented himself at the Barbarossa Suite.

'An unimaginable insult,' he spluttered, walking up and down. 'The army has been mobilized . . . there have been formal threats . . . movement on the other side . . . the border on alert. Needless to say, Herr Hauser, we count on you to fulfil your obligations on the supply front, who knows how quickly the stockpiles will deplete themselves? In fact, my orders are to request fifty thousand Modestas for immediate delivery in Panama. We trust your agents . . .'

Four days later detachments of the Bolivian militia proceeded from the south-western towns of Uyuni and Quetena and entered the wild and mountainous border zone dominated by the heights of the Cordillera Domeyko. They were armed with two German cannons bought from the German army after the siege of Paris, including an eighteen pounder which, being set up fifty yards from the border, was set to an elevation of twenty-seven degrees. At the same time, a hundred Chilean soldiers despatched from the small outpost of San Pedro de Atacama arrived at the border on the same day and hastily excavated conical dugouts and set up a fourteen pounder dragged up the mountain sides by donkeys.

In shallow covered ditches, the Suger-Sarfati Modesta tungsten-tipped shells lay ready for the sign of a flare.

Responsibility for the righting of humiliation lay with them.

On a cloudy night towards the end of April, after the three cannons had been mobilized and prepared for over two weeks, the Bolivian commander thought he saw a flare drop to the east and ordered the eighteen pounder to open fire across the border. As the first self-detonating shells burst upon open ground a few miles north of the great marsh of Atacama, throwing the reflections of bright pink flames against the low layer of cloud, the Chileans responded with their fourteen pounder, sending a flurry of shells over the heads of the Bolivians and into the side of Sairecabúr. For two hours hundreds of shells rained back and forth across the border igniting trees, grassland, nests, burrows, fences, huts, flowers, alpine fauna and insects. Isolated bursts of flame lit up the night. At dawn, finding their ammunition had been used up, the two batteries turned on their heels, yawned and headed back to Quetena and San Pedro.

Several thousand shells were subsequently ordered from the Berlin firm to replete the diminished stockpiles.

Hauser's secretary, waking him with a fresh orange juice, read out the quarterly profits from the Modesta shell and suggested the possibility of a war between Montenegro and Serbia.

Lili filled her portmanteau with mark notes and de los Caballeros and Luis del Pilar Angelo Patrocinio Simone de Muguiro y Beruete returned to the Café Rex, where one ordered a rum punch and the other *crème de menthe* with iced water.

The Modesta was happily produced for five years to come, at an annual rate of increase of 8 per cent and at a pre-tax profit margin of 50 per cent per shell, increasing to 60 per cent with the introduction of equally conductive 18-carat casings – a remarkable achievement for a shell capable of piercing 5 inches of sheet metal at a distance of 40 metres and one which the industrial museums of the future will celebrate in display cases of unimaginable opulence and generosity. And under the murky black and white picture of its illustrious creator in a Homburg hat and a striped tie will read the appropriately elegant eulogy: 'Gustave Hauser, engineer and philanthropist, designer of the Modesta shell and the Lynx fire engine. Representative *Homo faber* of the middle machine age.'

20

Months, then years, passed. Lili stayed in Charlottenburg. The Hauser empire grew further into a massive organism equipped with tentacles, teeth and stomach. Minor wars provided it with nourishment. Nickel supplies from Noumea kept it healthy. Hauser escorted Lili to diplomatic parties in Berlin, where the fat man buffooned around with the ease of a gorilla and boasted to scandalized countesses about the whores he had inseminated in Quito. He corresponded with Turkish military experts and provincial governors who sent him boxes of ambergris and Egyptian antiquities. In return he assisted in the massacre of Armenians and occasional pockets of oriental Greeks. On voyages to Budapest and Istanbul (where he crossed paths in Tatavla with the cunning Zaharoff) the head of the Suger-Sarfati octopus, which now appears in the London Register of Companies as the Hauser Munitions Co., found himself rocked by gentle luxuries. His stomach fattened even further. His fingers bulged under Zuloaga rings and a surprise gift from a gun-runner in Sidon set with a painted enamel plaque by Charles Lepec. His breath smelt of kif.

But he was still unable to touch his concubine.

When he came near her, he was frozen. He could not possess her. At the opera he was stung with admiration: that skin, which shone with the procreative whiteness of albumen! Her throat was traced with veins bearing the evidence of blue and pink phosphates.

Unprepared for a human palette of such cunning he sat obediently at her feet. He could smell the oily moist patches behind her ears: marzipan and wet grass. The smell of his childhood, evenings on the North Sea islands. When he kissed her (the only physical contact he ventured to permit) the marzipan smell reached far down into his lungs and made him choke. A light desire to vomit and gasp for air. He might go as far as the armpits, with their layer of soft hair, but never further. His limited adoration inflicted upon him precisely that which he most feared and liked to inflict on others. He was about to discover the lurid world of humiliation.

One night, two years after the conclusion of the Antofagasta episode, the master was sitting alone in the Renoma dining-room with a cold meat *frokost* when he noticed a thick-set man also sitting alone and eating a joint of Culosses ham which the cooks had thoughtfully surrounded with paper flowers. The waiters spoke to him obsequiously. He wore a brown hunting suit with knee-high strapped leather boots. Hauser was immediately offended. The diner was dressed in the wrong way. But it was more the sawing motion of the knife against the joint of Culosses ham that offended him. Since the table was just next to his, he leant over with as much persiflage as he could muster and said, 'Are you enjoying your ham?'

The diner looked up with a smile: small red eyes, firm teeth. His grey hair was cropped over a military-style cranium. He smiled back just as sarcastically. Hauser had to retreat. He blushed violently. He wanted to wipe the smile off the diner's face and stop the sawing motion of the knife. It looked as if . . . as if this intruder had been humiliating him. Yes, he was sure of it.

Abandoning his meal and retreating in disorder he uttered an insolent and childish warning.

'And if I see you here again . . . if I see you . . . it's an *affaire d'honneur* . . . an *affaire d' . . .*'

The diner half rose and bowed.

The guests tittered.

Hauser went up to his rooms and restrained an urge to boast to Lili, who was in the bath. But his hands were shaking.

He knelt by the bath and wiped away the bubbles from her face.

'The funniest thing happened to me,' he said. 'Do you know the man who comes in with a pair of hunting boots?'

'I've never seen him.'

'Haven't you? Well . . .'

He couldn't think what to say. What had the man in the hunting boots done to him? The way he had looked at him . . . the knowing gaze of the cuckolder.

'Are you sure? You didn't see him at the opera or somewhere? He may have followed you here. He seems to want to . . .'

'You're dreaming things. Don't look at him.'

'I'm dreaming? Me?'

He clenched his fists.

'I never dream. I've never dreamed. Dreaming is everything I am not. I see things icily. I perceive them clearly. Dreaming would be an interference. No, I see him lucidly, as I always see every face, and what I see is a look of knowingness. And that costume! Where does he think he is – the Black Forest?'

His face had become puffy and flushed, the face of the cuckolded.

'You can't be jealous,' she whispered. 'You never did anything in the first place.'

'I've never been jealous . . . I've never been humiliated like that, either. I suppose that's his strategy. He thinks he can humiliate me, make me suffer what I cannot suffer.'

'Anyone can suffer anything.'

'Can they? My sufferings are extremely limited, as I have arranged. When I suffer it is so unexpected I am almost charmed by the experience. I might have been charmed by Mr Bloodsport in his strapped boots, except that I'm not charmed at all, I'm the very opposite of charmed, I am anything but charmed. The question is, am I suffering?'

And a venomous but puzzled expression crossed his face for a second.

He was suspicious. The girl in the bath was being cool. She did not sympathize with his suffering. How could it be proved that the Black Forest hunter was not playing with her bubbles as well?

The next evening he took the same table and found that, as before, the hunter was seated next to him dressed in the same serge suit and knee-length strapped boots and with the same joint of Culosses ham surrounded by paper flowers before him. And the same serrated knife was making the same motion against the joint, irrespective of his clear warning. Repeating his insult of the night before, he rose this time, walked over to the table and asked, with savage innuendo, if he was enjoying his ham.

'A little too dry,' the diner said.

It was too much. They were laughing at him, the waiters, the guests, the 'general' (for what else could he be but a general?). A cuckold is touching but absurd. His tie was loose. His hair was standing up. He was ruffled and they had seen. He was losing something: possibly his dignity, though he was not sure. And how could his dignity be restored if not by the act of slapping the 'general's' face? He spent a restless night fantasizing about the face he was going to hit.

But before tackling the 'general' he wanted to practise his slap on the Romanian hairdresser . . .

The next morning, as the coiffeur was clipping his neck, he abruptly threw off the warm towels and pointed angrily to his hairline.

'Look at that, you fool! One side is higher than the other!'

And flexing his biceps, he delivered a vicious blow to the hairdresser's cheek.

'Now how do you feel?' he boomed aggressively, raising his hand again.

'Thoroughly and most justly humiliated, sir, if you'll beg my pardon for saying so!'

'Exactly. And rightly.'

'Thank you, sir.'

'Not at all. You were only speaking the truth.'

Confident of his powers, he returned to the dining-room the following night. But as soon as he was seated he felt the sour paralysis of the coward. The man had massive fists. So she liked that kind, did she? He remembered the effect of her mouth on the South Americans. Who knew better than he himself how difficult it was to resist that mouth? Of course, the 'general' had given in. Something dashing about *les militaires*. Their canine necks, their thighs. His hands began shaking again as he approached the table loaded with Culosses ham and assorted pickles with wooden toothpicks stuck in them. The 'general' had powerful jaws. He could probably shoot. But then, wasn't he in the right, defending his dignity?

He went up to the ham man.

'Are you enjoying', he shouted hysterically, 'your ham?'

He was going to hit him, but couldn't.

'A bit dry,' the man said, and smiled. He carried on sawing.

As Hauser retreated the dining-room burst into loud laughter. A man who can't hit his cuckolder! He backed out, sweating. The world was becoming unreal and inhospitable. Feeling weak, he asked the *sommelier* to accompany him to his suite.

In his study, illumined by the clusters of yellow electric lights, he spent a feverish night smoking cigars. He had tried to make enquiries with the staff about the guest with the Culosses ham but they avoided his questions. He had no idea who the diner was. He had no idea why he ate Culosses ham. He had no idea why he sported a sarcastic smile. But, worst of all, he had no idea why he kept coming back. And what if he came back the following night – if Hauser's innuendoes had not been enough to consign him to oblivion? The man's teeth, his cheeks, stupidly red and healthy, the strapping muscles folded over his neck and the sawing motion of the knife . . . everything in him rebelled against Hauser's power. He could be defeated (because he never lost his temper) but at the same time he could not be defeated.

He smelt of the earth and wet parade grounds, dead rabbits and waxed saddles. The army and the land.

He was everything that the soft and pulpy merchant, offspring of a Danish government clerk and a school teacher, was not or could ever be. His mouth was part of the aristocracy.

And whenever Hauser heard the word 'aristocracy', the nerves connected to his spinal column radiated a chilling and resentful alarm.

However much you worked, however much you hoarded, they could still destroy you with those smiles of theirs, the restrained, comfortable smile of the patrician beaming down from the top of the social pyramid with the malevolent equanimity of a man observing an ant through a magnifying glass.

At eight o'clock the following evening, the fourth of his ordeal, Hauser walked into the dining-room with his hands in his pockets. The room was crowded. Mixed parties laughed around the tables under a penumbra of smoke. And he saw straight away that the table next to his was occupied by a journalist whom he knew. In the excitement of his relief he waved to the journalist and walked quickly out. He went straight back to his bedroom.

Lili lay asleep in the bed. A blue sheet covered half her body diagonally. He cracked his joints and poured himself a glass of champagne. Then he went up to the bed. Her mouth was open, brown and tasting of smoke. It quivered under the pressure of a shallow snore. It bulged in the darkness, thick and moist at the edges. And for the first time, it repelled him.

A sinister correspondence began to form. Her mouth and his

mouth . . . his own mouth and hers . . . a duplication such as could not happen outside the laws of nightmares.

Dropping his glass to the floor, he left the bedroom with a suffocating knot in his throat. He went downstairs. Entering the dining room again he was astounded to see that it was empty except for table 46, the one next to his own, upon which sat a joint of Culosses ham and behind it, as before, the diner with the cropped grey hair and strapped tan boots. The man rose slightly from his chair and performed a spectral bow.

The Dane did not know how to react. There seemed only one solution. He advanced as he always did, contemptuous now through familiarity, and said, 'Are you, sir, enjoying your ham?'

'A little too dry,' the 'general' answered sarcastically.

'In that case,' Hauser replied, 'I challenge you to a duel!'

The man bowed again.

'Accepted, most humbly.'

'May I have your card?' the Dane said.

'Certainly.'

The card read: Lojo, Tollsten Mining Corp.

Hauser, hiding his surprise, stood on tiptoe.

'At dawn. My seconds will call.'

'It will be my pleasure.'

'The pleasure, on the contrary, will be mine.'

They bowed. Lojo sat down and resumed the sawing motion of the knife against the Culosses ham without the slightest tremor. His face was calm. There is no point in hitting him now, Hauser thought, and it would breach the laws of honour. Every gesture of this Lojo made him feel sick. Before vomiting and losing consciousness he had to turn on his heel and walk away. And as he walked the words went through his brain . . . Lojo . . . Tollsten Mining Corp . . . metals . . . weapons . . . without cohering in the usual way. He didn't know him. Never heard of the Tollsten Mining Corp. The card was edged with gold. A snotty card for an industrialist. At ten paces he turned. The man was chewing his ham, oblivious. It was a disgusting display of nonchalance. And besides, more disgusting and relevant still, he himself had never fired a weapon in his life. The irony of this was not incapable of raising a smile on the mouth of the armaments emperor.

21

Fate has a way, from time to time, of inebriating her victims before the inevitable execution by suddenly granting their most shameful requests – the incessant requests made over and over again in the hollows and troughs of the brain. Posing in a handsome leather coat in front of the reception room mirror, Hauser felt in the weight of the regulation German army pistol in his hand – pressing against his inexperienced fingers – the pleasure of an obsession refound.

In the moments before dawn, as he waited for Frisch, his second, to arrive, he felt every object around him dancing to a disorganized and barbaric music. He had ceased being Hauser and was just another object tangoing around the room out of step. But as he felt himself sliding through chaos he caught his breath firmly enough to be able to hear the first streaks of rain on the street outside, the grunting of the horses – his cab – and the soft thud of the pistols being laid in their box. He touched his fine moustache, admired his face and looked through the mirror to the future, the next hour, and saw the corpse of Lojo laid out in the mud. He went to the guest bed and woke up Lili.

He kissed her sleepy eyes and dragged her to her feet.

He couldn't go without her.

A long drive through the suburbs. In the flat woodlands beyond the city sprawl the rain grew heavier. Hauser's face paled. The cab entered a wood three miles from Potsdam, the wheels churning in fresh mud. When it stopped they were in a clearing near a small river and a derelict wooden hut. The employee of the Tollsten Mining Corp had already arrived, was stripped down to a white shirt and was flanked by two funereal assistants in charcoal frock coats. Water fell heavily from the leaves above and around them, spattering their shoulders.

The same smile formed itself on Lojo's mouth. Receiving his weapon, he did not bother to inspect it. Instead he walked calmly to his place and waited.

The secretary turned to Hauser. 'He looks very calm, sir. We could end it with a mutual apology.'

The master in turn turned to look at Lili and his rival. The triangle of mouths was finally naked here, in the wood, under the falling rain. Their heads looked shrunken in the dawn light, with lurid, vulgar lips stuck to them. He shook his head. The triangle had to be broken. One of the mouths would have to go.

Taking up his position, and without removing his leather over-coat, he turned the chamber of the pistol with his thumb.

Taking aim slowly, and lining the sights up with the mouth he hated so much, he fired first. He missed – the bullet flew into the branches above Lojo's head and knocked off a small twig. His fore-finger wobbled.

Lojo aimed desultorily, fired, and blew a hole in the mud between Hauser's feet. Standing slackly, he was already grinning at the misses.

But they had agreed to two shots each. They recommenced. This time the Dane paused. Lili was shivering in the cab, but watching with open eyes. He wiped his mouth. The realm of desire enclosed all three of them, and how could he be sure that she was not sending winks at Lojo behind his back, or worse? He took aim with greater care and as he fired she uttered a hoarse croak that might have been, if he had heard it clearer, a cry of disappointment.

But his aim was a few millimetres too far to the left and the bullet did not touch the Spaniard. It smacked once more into the trees and zinged through the leaves on its way to nowhere. There was silence. Lojo swayed and licked his lips. The nightmarish smile was back. He called over: 'Butterfingers!' The Dane froze to the spot. Lojo swung his weapon up to shoulder level, brought the hammer back with infinite patience, though without taking careful aim, and fired.

Hauser saw and heard nothing.

The bullet sliced through his jawbone and slid into the cerebellum. Blood and brains splashed in all directions. A tiny splinter of bone hit Frisch in the face as the Dane, reeling backwards with astonishment, fell to the earth. It stuck persistently to his lip for a few moments. The secretary flinched and removed it with his hand, but without screaming.

More surprised than anything else, Hauser lay quietly in the mud and rain fell softly on to his face. He was perfectly awake, though technically dead. He could see Lojo walking away into the trees, melting into thin air. Lili's single kiss touched his cheek. There was quiet at last. And rain fell gently from a million leaves, falling on to the face of the corpse. His eyes were open. He watched everything. He watched the trees suffering under the onslaught of water while the dripping went on and on, all day until night, the branches sagging, the twigs vibrating, out of control, while the leaves . . . the leaves turned and twisted of their own accord.

And the worst of it was that the trees were real.

As she walked away from the tragic scene Lili could not help herself breaking into an uncontrollable fit of hiccoughs.

At the post mortem in a Berlin morgue, the pathologists removed the bullet, upon which they saw the word 'Antofagasta' scratched with a needle. Lojo, silent and efficacious undercover agent of the Bolivian secret services, had inscribed it carefully in capitals.

The Barbarossa Suite was evacuated to a sound of irritated obituaries.

Lili wore black to the train station, converted the government bonds Hauser had bought her for two birthdays running, sold the Paquin dresses and bought a ticket for Switzerland.

She flew past factories and stagnant pools.

Rain fell against the windows.

She was as anonymous as the ritual that takes place between millions of mouths in the course of a minute and which we must now turn to in the course of our improbable description of the mouth: the kiss.

V

22

Anatomy of the kiss   I

There was once a doctor in Bruges named Felix Paléologue, a distant cousin of the more famous M. Paléologue of the Belle Époque, who specialized in the apocrine glands and the oral fantasies of little children. The doctor was nervous, thin and hysterical. From time to time, he took his six children to the slum streets, lined them up in front of *lumpenproletariats* and shouted: 'Unfortunates! Victims! Examples of decay! Observe! Pity! Weep! Sob! Guilt! Introspection! Social awareness! Responsibility! Let us pray!' At other times, in moments of rare perception, he wrote sentences in medical papers such as 'The divine osculum is a black hole', or, 'We have to admit that the kiss is a clinical lacuna.' All of this brought a mixture of fear and loathing-respect on to the head of Dr Paléologue.

Never once did he limit his observations to the transmission of bacilli.

His work on the apocrine glands contained – like dark cobalt seams – unexpected streaks of lyricism.

On Sunday mornings he cut the family roast beef with the remark: 'May our mouths be grateful for the Lord's bounty which we are about to kiss.' And when he was exploring the mouths of children with his own precision instruments, he felt a queer repulsion which was related to the holy mystery of the kiss. It was true that, like the majority of the male species, his own mouth made him deeply uncomfortable.

'If only', he said to his children, 'we keep a tight rein on our mouths, we will avoid the terrible *regressum ad proletariam!*'

And looking at their rosy infant lips he wondered if it was necessary for children to kiss at all. The kiss was the first step, the first estrangement . . .

In 1907, at the height of his fame and glory, the doctor was appointed Professor of Psychiatry at a university college in London. As soon as he arrived in his new city his employers presented him with a similar problem: a series of cases of male mouths 'on the rampage'. Paléologue compiled a thick file of case histories. The alarmed authorities requested his advice: middle-aged men suffering psychotic disorders with their mouths . . . in the context of the kiss? The intrigued doctor took charge of the affected patients. And within days he had assembled the first case histories of 'oral schizophrenia':

Case History One – the Wandering Lips

The patient, an Irish labourer in his late forties living in a male dormitory, had felt a 'tick' one night in the region of his mouth as he lay in bed. He then felt his mouth detach itself from his face, climb down his neck on to his chest, make its way to his navel and then swing itself gracefully on to the floor. Having reached the floor, it displayed the agility of a large spider. It leapt around the room playfully looking for something 'to kiss'. He knew that it was searching for prey, an object upon which to unleash a moist kiss, because he still – despite his physical separation from it – felt 'attached' to it . . . as it were, by the umbilicus of the unconscious, as if he still inhabited his own mouth while watching it go its own way in the world in search of a victim.

Finding nothing to kiss in the wretched dormitory, the mouth made frantic efforts to leave the room. Finding the door locked, it mewed pitifully like a stray cat. It had to kiss or it would die. Feeling pity for it, the patient got up from his bed, crossed the room and opened the door. The mouth sighed, purred and shot out of the room.

From then on, he had no personal physical contact with his mouth. It fled the dormitory, scuttled into the street and jumped on to a no. 23 bus in the direction of High Holborn. Yet however distant he was from it, and however unable he was to keep track of its whereabouts, wherever it went he felt himself with it, as if proprioceptively bound to it. The mouth was a projection of his own soul detached from his body but bearing with it his sense of the world.

For days the mouth cavorted around the city, relishing to the full its new-found freedom. For whereas before it had been bound by its adherence to a face to observe the laws of decorum, social discipline and restraint, on its own it could fulfil all the suppressed desires that mouths feel. It was free to stick to anything it liked. It was free to insult, lick, pout, snarl, yawn, burp, sneer, despise, solicit, reject, bite and . . . kiss. For the first time it could enter restaurants on its own, order what it wanted, eat as much as it wanted, criticize, bully and humiliate, leap on the tables, dance around the kitchens, fly on to the faces of women it had never been allowed to approach before and sing Irish songs while reclining in bowls of leek soup.

The mouth had not yet come back. It was loose in the streets, free, unattached and disobedient. The patient felt deep nostalgia for it, though noted that this tenderness was not reciprocated by the mouth, which clearly relished its freedom. And yet at the same time the patient recorded moments of bliss, tranquillity and joyful excitement. He felt himself 'kissing' hundreds of attractive women. He felt the delicate and astonishing textures of food he had never eaten in his life. He produced vivid descriptions of pineapples, mango sorbets and chocolate éclairs. He smoked cigars, wormed his way into luxury brothels and discovered the secret world of crushed ice.

His mouth, in other worlds, like a talented and socially mobile offspring, had ascended the class system and left him far behind. Yet how could he resent its spectacular ascendancy when he too could share in its decadent life style? There were times, he admitted freely, when he wished it would not come back at all.

Case History Two – the Ape Man

The patient, a charming and cultivated retired tax inspector, lived in a bought property in Welwyn Garden City. He occasionally worked as a consultant for a firm of building developers in the West End. A stable family man, he frequently took his three grandchildren to the Natural History Museum to look at the suspended casts of whales and cases of arthropods. During one of these visits, he happened to look into a glass cubicle containing a stuffed lemur wrapped around a pole and saw a reflection, not of a charming and cultivated retired tax inspector, but a large, brightly coloured orang-utan.

Reaching up to his face, he felt not his usual slightly hard and puritan mouth, but a voluptuous, conical muzzle made of soft and inviting pink skin.

But more alarming still for a man who was used to regarding the act of kissing with hygienic and moral disdain, for the first time in his life he felt like kissing everything in sight, swamping everything with his new sensual super-mouth which was already – he could see it in the reflection – turning up its lips and pouting in the way that primates do.

He promptly kissed his grandchildren who, frightened by this unusual occurrence, ran away crying. He therefore progressed to the museum attendants, whom he covered with slobbering ape-like kisses, and then to casual passers by.

Chaos ensued. The museum authorities descended, tied his arms behind his back and carted him off to a back room.

'But all I did was kiss them,' he protested innocently, forgetting how out of character he was sounding.

'So you think kissing is an act of affection, do you?' they snarled.

The patient was resentful at this point. He was certain that the disgust of both his grandchildren and the strangers he had so warmly kissed was due not to the fact of being kissed as such, but to their being kissed by an ape. He was convinced his transformation had been real and not imaginary.

'Are they frightened of the ugliness of apes?' Dr Paléologue asked.

'Not at all,' the patient replied. 'But they cannot bear a kiss from an orang-utan. If I had torn their heads off they would have been less disturbed . . . they would have treated me better!'

In detention the patient continued to kiss everything in sight – walls, doors, sheets, bananas, cups, lampshades. His simian mouth had run away with him, not in the more 'literal' and paranoiac manner of Case History One, but in a gentler and more perplexing way, while still attached to his face.

Case History Three – the Hermaphroditic Mouth

This patient – a strong and muscular specimen – was a land surveyor residing in Dulwich Village. His masculinity was unquestioned as far as the development of his physique was concerned, and his mind followed the example of his body, being virile, resilient, independent and scornful.

Over the years, however, a contrary tendency had developed in his mouth . . . so much so that at the age of thirty-eight – at the height of his specifically masculine powers and self-confidence – he was forced to concede to himself that although the rest of him was male, his mouth – by some inadmissible perversity – was female.

'I have a woman's mouth,' he confessed nervously. 'Whatever I do, being a man, I feel my mouth pulling the other way. I hate to admit it, but my mouth is a fairy, a poof and a pansy, it's definitely dying to wear rouge. I won't let it, though! Not in a thousand years!'

For most of the time, however, the sexual opposition of the patient to his mouth could be concealed, even if with some difficulty. But there was one activity that threatened to tear him apart. When he wanted to kiss a woman, his mouth (propelled by perfectly understandable anti-homosexual tendencies) recoiled.

He could not force it to touch the mouths of other women.

On the other hand, it was strongly drawn to the mouths of men.

In danger of being misunderstood, his solution was to retire into self-imposed solitude.

Two years passed. He then re-entered society in order to find a wife. But at his first party in mixed company, finding a former woman friend, he planted a spontaneous kiss on one of her cheeks. The woman suffered the illusion that she had been the victim of a sapphic assault. She stared in amazement at the patient's face. There was nothing to do but slap it. And two days later, with a bruise on one eye (the gentlemen had shouted that they wouldn't have queens kissing their women) the patient surrendered himself to a clinic.

His pouting mouth was painted red . . .

Despite the alarm visible in the patient's eyes, it clearly moved of its own accord and, in a spirit of hermaphroditic libertinage, kissed whoever and whatever it wanted . . .

Dr Paléologue was speaking in front of an assembly of other doctors. He was pulling at his waistcoat pockets with two bleached fingers. From time to time, he looked around at the bald heads and monocles, licked his lips and smiled in a superior way.

A flavid smear from his pipe discoloured his left hand.

'Of all the works of art', he said, 'resulting from six thousand years of production, there is only one that is deliberately called "The Kiss". It seems that the kiss, gentlemen, has a secret history and pathology which has not yet been exposed to the professional eye, so that its true content, its true *infectiousness*, has not been understood. The kiss is an epistemological vacuum.'

His thick Belgian accent did not relent. And, as he talked, his voice became more vicious and committed to its content.

'Mouth-to-mouth contact has reached the inner sanctum of poetic subject matters, but only in the form of black verbosity and fumbling descriptions of man's most exquisite ritual. However, it is time to wrench it away from there – and also from the realm of beds and fairgrounds. For the first time it is a matter of professional imperative to inoculate ourselves against the kiss, recognizing it for what it is, a disease of the lips, a childish and febrile trauma, a passing phase and inflamed condition of the buccal cavity, an infection, a wound, a disorder, an apocrinal anachronism!

'Let us consider the following alarming possibility, gentle-men: we are descended from apes, but at some point in the early evolution of our ancestors, say between Dryopithecus and Eagytopithecus, the Divine Finger intervened by touching the forehead of one of the hairy brutes. From then, ape was destined to become Son of Man; except that, by an unintentional error, the body was far from perfect . . . islands of pithecoid elements survived like ice floes in a warm sea . . . parts of the anatomy spring to mind, gentlemen, but who has yet considered the possibility that the mouth is one of them, a vestigial feature of the ape left untouched by the remoulding hand of the Deity? Can the resulting uneven patchwork of *homo* as we know him contain the regressive aspects of the mouth without betraying the fact from time to time? And since, as we know, regression is a universal and mysterious force in nature, is it so unthinkable that the pre-hominid past should surface to haunt us in the form of brutal, instinctual and unspiritual mouths?

'It is for this reason, respected colleagues, that I have proposed to effect a cure with the second of our case histories, the so-called Ape Man, since it is he who manifests the problem in its purest and most essential form. If the mouth of a man who clearly identifies himself with the orang-utan can be brought back to the nest of civilization, then there is hope of similar cures for other oral organs. I will attempt nothing less than the redemption, reformation and rehabilitation of the Ape Man's mouth, a problem as complex as the moral and psychological rebuilding of the famous "animal boy" discovered in the wild forests of eighteenth-century France. And on the success of this cure will depend the future of all humanity's mouths, and therefore the future of civilization as a whole: it is unnecessary, gentlemen, for me to remind you that the Ape Man is not an isolated phenomenon, but the most visible realization of a widespread menace . . . the menace of resurgent apedom!'

The doctor's speech was greeted with warm applause. A laboratory consulting room equipped with psychoanalytic couch and library were put at his disposal and the Ape Man, the cultivated tax inspector who had not yet been set free, was brought to live permanently in the hospital wing where Paléologue's working area had been set up.

The doctor from Bruges was familiar with the latest techniques from Vienna and Berlin. His consulting room was screened on one side by a large mirror, through which an audience of students and guest specialists could watch the proceedings without disturbing the doctor–patient equilibrium. The sessions with the Ape Man were watched by three anthropologists, a wide variety of clinical psychiatrists and two physiologists from Belfast. They awaited demonstration of the Paléologue technique with intense interest, a technique which he had already elevated with the term 'selective induction'.

The doctor stood in the middle of the room alone. He talked with quiet emphasis in the direction of the tinted mirror.

'Through the technique of selective induction, gentlemen, we will attempt, by means of a direct appeal to the unconscious impetus of word association, to "drag" the mouth from the realm of apedom to the realm of humanity. This will be done in the first place by confronting it with images of what it knows best: food.'

The patient was walked in and sat on the divan. He was a charming and alert old gentleman, the tax inspector who so loved his grandchildren and who had so keen a knowledge of all things cetacean. He sat awkwardly on the divan, adjusted his small steel-rimmed glasses and smiled nervously.

The great Paléologue circled him thoughtfully; then pushed a hand through his mane of grey hair and lit a cigar. He sat in a leather armchair opposite the divan.

'Are you hungry?' he said.

The patient shrugged.

'Thirsty?'

Another shrug.

'Lunch,' the doctor said. 'Lunch.'

The patient pointed to his mouth.

'Banana,' he said.

Paléologue took a puff.

'Château La Mission-Haut-Brion,' he said.

'Banana.'

'A Graves red, rich and mellow.'

'Banana.'

'A gravelly soil fourteen metres in depth, twenty-five per cent Merlot grapes.'

'Banana,' the tax inspector insisted with melancholy, 'banana.'

'A spicy and harmonious repertoire, chewy, complex with a fully blown tobacco nose.'

'Banana, banana, banana.'

There was a long pause while the doctor picked his teeth.

'Not the thing in itself but the secondary pleasure,' he said, as if to himself. And then, louder, 'Wine, truly fine wine. The palette. The palette, and nothing else.'

The patient reached into his mouth with a finger and touched the roof of his mouth.

'Banana,' he said.

'A wine has a history,' Paléologue said, 'a year of manufacture. Think of a banana. What year can a banana be?'

'Green and yellow,' the patient said.

'Exactly. A banana . . .'

And pausing, he reached down to a bowl on the table and picked up a banana.

'. . . a banana is naive.'

The patient grunted and scratched his armpits.

Seeing the banana, he became agitated, flexed his legs, jumped up and down and flung his arms about.

Smiling pleasantly, Paléologue handed over the banana, which the patient gobbled up in a second.

When the patient had finished, the doctor recommenced. He tried Lapsang Suchong, curries and marmalades. He evoked smoked hams, peperoni and pungent cheese bacteria. He evoked the pleasures of discourse, the intricacies of conversation and contact with laundered napkins. But every time the patient sat there dumbly and said, 'Banana'. He ate banana after banana. His mouth was unable to negotiate anything but bananas. It was fused with the banana . . .

During a half-way 'intermission' of the session, Paléologue went behind the glass divide to join his colleagues.

'The patient is clearly resistant to gastronomic "improvement", which is often the case with severe personality disorders. We will have to try the "frontal sentiment shock".'

The specialists raised their eyebrows.

'Instead of inducing a breakdown of the complex by means of food-related associations, we use the images of sentimental prominence instead.'

The session recommenced with the doctor seated as before, now twirling a pencil in one hand and staring absent-mindedly out of the window. As soon as the patient was seated opposite him he said, coldly and indifferently: 'Your mother's face. Your poor old mother's face.'

The patient knitted his brows.

'Your poor old mother. Your poor old mother's eyes,' Paléologue insisted.

The patient crumpled slightly.

His eyes grew glazed and disconnected, as if he had ceased looking at the outside world.

The doctor did not relent.

'Poor dear old mother, alone in her rocking chair.'

'Ba . . . na . . .'

'No, mother, mother, mother in her chair with her knitting! All alone in the basement!'

'. . . na . . .'

'Her kind old dear face, her soft and withered hands . . .'

The patient's resistance was indeed crumbling. He put a hand over his eyes. Yes, he was sobbing gently to himself, his eyes were moist, he was shaking. The experiment was proving a hearty success.

109

'Her rocking chair . . . the knitting . . . her hot toddy . . . oh, her hot toddy!'

The patient buried his face in his hands.

He was speechless.

'Mother wants her hot toddy . . .'

'Mo . . . ba . . .'

'The shawl, the black shawl!'

'. . . ther . . .'

'Her kindly snores, her bedtime kisses!'

The patient was struggling with his mouth. Torn between the words 'banana' and 'mother', it had become the battleground of his psyche.

But before it could utter the full word 'mother' the doctor had leapt once more on to the offensive. Grabbing a small tartlet of sophisticated construction which he had had placed on the table beforehand, he guided it towards the dithering, incoherent mouth. It was made of strawberries and puff pastry, very fancy. The most artificial of dishes. The patient stared at it in horror. It was not a banana. He uttered a strangled cry. 'Mother, mother with her teacakes and scones!'

Stained with tears, the mouth opened and as soon as it did the doctor threw the exquisite tart into it as if it were a stick of dynamite.

The patient went red in the face and swallowed it whole.

'There!' the doctor bellowed triumphantly. '*Primus:* an ape does not eat French strawberry tarts. *Secundus:* an ape does not weep at the mention of his mother. *Ergo*, you are not an ape, but a higher species altogether. You cannot deny what you yourself have already done. Your action has betrayed you. You can no longer eat bananas because you have eaten a strawberry tart, the antithesis of a banana, and you cannot scratch your armpits while weeping over the memory of your poor dead mother. We are making progress, my friend.'

The patient was then removed by two assistants in white coats in a state of total confusion and terror. He shook violently and salivated over the carpet. But the victorious doctor, flushed with his brilliant success, beckoned in his colleagues and warmly accepted their heartfelt applause and congratulations.

'The subject is being unravelled,' he declared proudly and lit himself another cigar. 'As you see, gentlemen, with every day that goes by the so-called mysteries of the human psyche recede an inch, and sometimes a foot! Before long there is no question that we will be in total control of the mouth and everything that it desires. I have no doubt, in fact, as this individual shows, that as the mouth comes inexorably under the control of science, all traces of apedom will gradually but inevitably disappear.'

The fame of the doctor's method and his success in reversing the tendency of the Ape Man's mouth to be drawn only to the food of apes soon spread throughout the metropolis. He was invited to attend galas and parties. He exchanged scientific witticisms with Fellows of the Royal Society and famous missionaries. At the Empire he was the cynosure of the promenades.

The reputation of Dr Paléologue might have continued ascending without interruption and his cure of the Ape Man entered in the annals of medicine's triumphs . . . but one day an assistant rushed into his office with the disquieting news that the patient had escaped from the hospital, disappeared into the city and was at large, no one knew where.

The doctor, although convinced of the power of his cure, was alarmed. He contacted the police.

'It is imperative', he said, 'to recapture the patient as soon as possible before the symptoms of the disorder which I have begun to permanently rectify re-emerge in the chaos of the outside world.'

Three days passed with no word of the runaway tax inspector.

It was possible, after all, that he was now normal and could melt into the general public without anyone noticing. And the doctor himself insisted against publicity. His new-found celebrity was too precious to lose.

Then, on the fourth day from the escape, the first report of a kissing attack surfaced in the East End.

A severely shaken cleaner on Ellen Street claimed to have been kissed on the cheek by a huge, talking orang-utan.

The police smiled indulgently.

'You did say it was a man and not an orang-utan?' they asked the doctor sarcastically.

'Can't you tell the difference between reality and a psychotic delusion, you imbeciles?' Paléologue retorted. 'A mental image has been imposed upon external objects.'

'But it was the woman who reported an ape.'

'Ah, the woman . . .'

Paléologue was perplexed.

'So the woman said "ape", did she?'

'She said it was orange, too.'

'And what was it doing, this "ape"?'

'It seems it was eating a banana and . . . kissing the ladies, sir.'

The doctor felt his heart go cold.

The patient was regressing, and if his rapid deterioration were discovered . . .

He then told a deliberate lie to ensure that the police would redouble their efforts: 'You have to understand that he's dangerous. He's suffering from "ape fantasies" . . . schizoid ape tendencies . . . he has to be recovered by the hospital immediately. Any delay and I can't answer for the consequences.'

The police mounted a full-scale operation.

The number of officers on the case was doubled.

Yet only two days later another attack occurred in Whitechapel, this time on Gowers Walk, a stone's throw from Ellen Street. A prostitute walking on her own was dragged late at night into a small alley and passionately kissed on the cheek by a loud-mouthed and sentimental ape covered in orange hair, the same orang-utan who had already struck.

She had struggled free, with ape saliva on her cheek.

A panic suddenly developed in the Whitechapel area. An ape was loose, a skilful kisser of female cheeks who was evidently tortured by his desire for more secret kisses.

Armed with more clues, including some strange long reddish hairs on the victim's clothing, the police began to spread their nets wide.

They issued descriptions on wall posters and inspected all the orang-utans held in the London zoos.

But they were still empty-handed by the time the 'primate' struck a third time – this time in Spitalfields: a match-seller kissed in broad daylight by the soft and nightmarish lips of an 'intelligent-looking ape'.

The description multiplied. A complex picture of the assailant was emerging. For the fourth assault, if it came, they were fully and finally prepared, wherever it might occur . . .

But it was not until two weeks later that the ape re-appeared, this time in the middle of Mayfair itself, and this time his arms were wrapped enthusiastically around a housewife, smothering her with apish kisses, fondling her cheeks and covering her mouth with his own lips, which, she said, were rubbery, elastic and 'vibrant' to the touch.

The task force was on the spot within minutes.

Dr Paléologue was with them.

'Remember,' he advised them, 'he is not a real ape, but a man who thinks he is one. You can talk, reason and discourse with him. There is no need for irrational physical force. Above all, no damage to the patient, please!'

An orange shape, however, was seen slipping through the crowds in the direction of Hyde Park. The police gave chase, with the anxious professor in tow. It must be costume, he thought, an external creation to match his inner deformation. But in addition, the orange figure – they could see it quite clearly now – was running at a fantastic speed across the expanses of grass, weaving in and out of trees and occasionally running on its knuckles.

The park was sealed off at all gates.

Armed police patrolled the adjacent thoroughfares.

They had been told that a wild animal was loose in the park and that they should shoot it on sight if it scaled the walls.

Meanwhile the principal posse had quickly cornered the hirsute fugitive among some huge oak trees, which the 'ape' had unhesitatingly scaled and in the topmost leaves of which he was disporting himself with ear-splitting bellows and roars.

The police massed around the trunk of the tree and the doctor sprang forward armed with a megaphone.

'Now, now,' he said soothingly, 'you don't have to be afraid, we know who you are and what you've been doing. You can take off that absurd disguise now and come down peacefully. No one wants to hurt you. We can arrange for you to kiss things in the hospital, even women, yes, we can arrange for you to kiss women, too, if you like – nothing is impossible. You have a sickness, that's all – your sickness can be cured. Please think carefully!'

The 'ape' raised itself on its legs and struck its chest.

Its face was filled with sadness.

'Talk to him,' Paléologue urged the policemen. 'Treat him with respect.'

The sergeant with the rifle came forward.

'Forgive me, sir, but tawk wiv' a monkey, sir?'

'A schizophrenic,' the doctor corrected contemptuously.

The sergeant squinted at the tree top.

'Go on,' the officer said to him.

The sergeant blushed and took the megaphone.

''Ere you, get dahn from that tree. Gow on.'

The doctor rolled his eyes in despair.

But at this point, the fugitive in the tree, aware of his encirclement, began pouring a torrent of acorns on to the heads of his pursuers.

They rained down with deadly accuracy.

'All right, sergeant,' the officer said, losing his temper, 'knock him orf that bloody tree!'

The sergeant licked his lips with pleasure and took aim. In vain did Dr Paléologue explain the subtleties of the method of selective induction! He went in great detail into the resurgence of the atavistic mouth to no purpose. The sergeant took aim. The 'ape' whooped in his nest. And with a loud bang, receiving a bullet in the centre of his solar plexus, he crashed to earth in a flurry of leaves, acorns, twigs and flying drops of blood.

The doctor ran forward to where the corpse lay and knelt by its side. The police crowded round them. Frantically, the doctor pulled at the thick hair of what looked like a perfect specimen of a Sumatran orang-utan with his fingers looking for the seams of the uniform.

But there were none.

'It can't be!' he spluttered. 'It can't be!'

The commanding officer whispered to a constable to fetch a vet. The ape was dead. The doctor examined his eyes, then his fingers and his genitals. It was an ape, an ape, an ape!

His world was turned upside down.

And its mouth . . . so human, so humanly moist . . . so unlike the mouth of an ape!

Holding his head in his hands, the eminent Dr Felix Paléologue of Bruges ran from the scene nursing a spiritual wound the size of a gangrenous limb.

He was never seen in the company of an ape again and never again ventured from the safe confines of his home city.

His work on the mouths of children continued in obscurity

and twenty-nine years later, in 1946, he died, surrounded by his six children and his wife, mumbling incoherently about a tax inspector and a fancy dress costume made from the skin of a Sumatran ape.

In his will, it was discovered, to the amazement of his family, that he had left his mouth to science. He had died of a labial cancer, it was true, but the bequest was difficult to accept. At the faculty where his body was cut up for its autopsy the students laughed when asked to shear off his lips with a surgical scalpel.

What were they supposed to do with it?

Store it in a jar of alcohol?

Break it down into lesions, cancerous cells, glands, tumours and membranes?

There was no answer from the establishment; but the wish of the dead man had to be respected nevertheless.

In the end, the mouth – a hideous medical trophy looking from a distance like a shrivelled kitten's gut – was suspended in embalming fluid and donated to the faculty of medicine.

A strange destiny for the inventor of the method of selective induction . . . but one suitable to a persecutor of man's most redoubtable organ of pleasure.

And in this way concludes the strange and wonderful story of Dr Paléologue.

VI

23

In April of the year 1909, in the orderly city of Lausanne, a riot involving two hundred housewives erupted in a bookstore on the Avenue Benjamin Constant. Armed suppression of the housewives by mounted police followed, and the confiscation of the copies of *The Dictionary of Secret Fruits* by Mr Pepe Lullio (Editions Paulus Kruft) held by the shop. And as the truncheons were crashing into housewively faces and spines, a dirty, rat-like intellectual in a serge overcoat who happened to be sitting at a nearby café turned to a dwarf sitting next to him and said – in a patronizing drawl filled with redundant saliva and obvious misunderstanding of the phrase – 'Look at that. *Aurea mediocritas!*'

And licked the foamed back of his coffee spoon.

The housewives being vigorously beaten up within earshot could hardly have guessed that the rodent in the serge coat was none other than the author of that same book which they had defied the social order to get their hands on. Nor could they have ever guessed the depths of his contempt for the ordinary housewife. Lullio himself, a former Communist whose knuckledusters had once been encrusted with teeth, had turned gentleman and writer, taken up the pleasures of soda water and shoe shines and begun to quote Latin tags ignorantly as he sat in the sunshine at the café tables where he found displayed all around him that organism which he loathed more than anything between the biological extremes of scorpions and spirogyra: bourgeoisdom.

Seeing a woman with a bleeding nose being led away by two cops with a handkerchief tied around her face, he burst out laughing and slapped his knee. So they were bleeding through the nose for his very own masterpiece! 'Never forget something about the common housewife,' he sneered to the dwarf, who was not listening. '*Parthis mendacior*. Yes, more cunning than the Parthians.'

And he added bitterly, 'More cunning than the Parthians.'

The former dye-works apprentice from Altafulla, admirer of the terrorist Sipido and former puncher of cardboard Moorish faces in Catalonian fairs, was full of autodidactic one-liners. When he ran up against an intellectual, an entity even worse than the housewife, he put a toothpick into his mouth and simply said: '*Abnormis sapiens*', thereby suggesting, at one devastatingly erudite stroke, the sexual deviancy of the bookworm class.

When people asked what he thought about a government, the reply was always the same: raising his finger and licking it, he rolled his eyes like a priest uncovering a cache of pornographic manuals and said, 'Pantoffel-regiment!' as if nothing could follow this thunderous statement but silence.

At the age of thirteen he had read Karl Marx and clicked his fingers as if hit by a shaft of celestial light.

The young Lullio was schooled in a hard world.

At the age of eighteen, with a shock of anarchist hair the colour of *nero antico*, he debarked from a cargo ship at Antwerp to discover the miseries, the concealed splendours and stoicism of the proletariat.

Six years later fate found him punching the faces of Swiss chocolate workers into the intricate shapes of *hari-nuki* in Lausanne side streets while stealing their pay packets.

Life was all one big paradox, no?

By a law of secret parallels, his life came more and more to resemble that of another exile in the same city . . . not Lenin, but the greasy socialist woman-hater-and-lover Benito Mussolini.

Like Mussolini, he bore the mark of a swift-fisted father inflated with articulate bigotry. Like Mussolini, he thought it indispensable to slash the odd girlfriend with a razor to demonstrate his mastery of the medium of love. And like Mussolini, along with a noble, fortified and multi-lingual hatred of capitalism and that vast tentacular cancer bourgeoisdom, he hated above all the unstoppable propagation of the housewife.

As it happens, the phrase '*aurea mediocritas*' refers naturally to the Golden Mean, but it only took the sight of a housewife in all the glow of her inviolable and superior domesticity to make him blurt it out with all the venom he could muster.

Oh yes, he agreed that the worst of all was a housewife.

He couldn't abide a simple *Hausfrau*.

She provoked his mean side.

When the subject of the housewife came up, he immediately raised his hand sombrely and intoned: 'This is the heritage of Adam!'

Which is tantamount to saying, 'The housewife is our misery.'

Here was the enigma he had puzzled over for years. Why, when history is moving in all its vicious grandeur in exactly the opposite direction, that is in the direction of combine harvesters, smoke stacks and interstellar rockets manned by militant worker hoplites, why is it that there are more and more housewives, that their numbers are increasing, that they are proliferating everywhere with the dizzying reproductive agility of aphids?

Why is it that they have not been made illegal?

Exterminated with pesticides?

'Ah well,' he said to his admirers, 'woman is made of glass and our hordes of husband-johns cannot do without a piece of glass stuck in their throats. Without memsahib bibis, fellow workers, the international system could not work.'

Spouting proverbs and maxims, Lullio established a reputation for acumen and when the same Bonmart chocolate factory workers went on strike they elected him their principal agitator. He relished his cynical turns of coat. And still he molested women in trams, visited padded brothels and wrote articles for the Spanish anarchist press on the emancipation of women.

As for himself . . . he couldn't get round them. Pity me brothers, however hard I try I just can't shake them off. Take the *joro* he stumbled over after a fracas at the same café where he had pointed at the sprawling women: a year earlier it had been him in the street on the offensive, a stocking pulled over his head and armed with a cricket bat. A year ago to the day . . . he had descended there to make a sacrificial victim of one of the book-eating babus he often saw there leafing through slim volumes of expressionist poetry with damp patches on their lips and topaz cufflinks and he had gone masked like that, with the cricket bat, to make a sensational scene which would raise the hairs on the backs of their princely necks. And he had picked out a likely Swiss *gospodar* complete with monocle and monogrammed tie with a pile of books on the table before him – he was cutting

121

the pages open with a pair of nail scissors – and, approaching him like a rocket straight out of the crowd, brought the cricket bat crashing down on his hand, breaking the metacarpels, eliciting a terrible but gratifying feminine shriek out of the poetry lover . . . who then rolled on to the floor and recited some lines of he didn't know what! And as he was running off laughing to himself and congratulating himself on this cruel blow against the proliferation of books, toffs and housewives, he collided with a tart eating a bar of chocolate on a bench, or rather he was sent sprawling by that shoe of hers which tripped him up, sent his face naked of its protective stocking skidding into a pile of whitened dog stools and brought up a multi-coloured bruise on his left ear.

He had risen swiftly armed with his razor ready to slice her face open. But she did not move. She threw him a handkerchief.

'Wipe your ugly face,' she said quietly. 'You look stupid with shit on your nose.'

And, crossing his eyes, he saw that there was a bit of stool gleaming white on the end of his nose.

Humiliated by a dancing girl!

By a twitching soubrette!

He swore and used the handkerchief.

'I've just hit a poet with a cricket bat,' he blurted, needing to boast about something. 'Broke his left hand, I think.'

He put the razor away, she made it absurd. Her mouth was open, swallowing up his razor, his smallish pudgy bloody-nailed fist and his high-pitched voice. She squinted down at him.

'That's strange,' she said, uninterested. 'I could have sworn you were the poet.'

It was at that moment, he said, that the insolence of the bitch got on top of him and changed the course of his life.

He straightened his jacket, wiped a smear of blood from his ear and struck a matadorial pose with his head.

'Me?' he said, sneering and revealing his peasantish yellow teeth. 'Not in a thousand years, you tart.'

But the red oval of her mouth had already – before he knew what was happening – filled him with an emasculatory and degrading desire for words.

A trash author was born.

24

'Imagine a book', Lullio said one day, 'in which every permutation of human crime is set out under its own heading, in its own class, according to a classification like the ones for labelling minerals or spiders in museums. You'd have a section for crimes with instruments (metal, wood and leather sub-divisions). You'd have a chapter for crimes with the mouth. You'd have forty pages for transgressions with fingernails. It would be endless. There would be crimes against housewives, crimes against schoolboys, crimes against newts, crimes against anchovies, crimes against dwarves with birth marks. And there'd be thirty types of notched whip. Imagine the book as it would be when it was finished . . . a massive tome, complete with index, references . . . fat, slick, shiny . . . a pillar of bourgeoisdom from the outside . . . and then you'd sell to millions of housewives. They'd take it to bed with them under the guise of a title that deliberately misled them . . . *Fourteen Sauces to Keep Your Husband, Aphrodisiac Shrubs from Korea*. They'd steal with it sniggering into the bathroom and read it with a naughty cigar. They'd open it secretly, with one eye on the lock waiting for hubby's censoring hand on the door handle and with all their adrenaline going . . . and lo and behold as they start reading they realize they've made a mistake. It isn't what they thought. But at the same time, no, they can't stop, it's too interesting, too much what they knew all along but were afraid to ask. They begin sweating, they forget the bath water turning cold, they forget the time . . . they are immersed. And they are disgusted, yes, they are disgusted through and through, and the more they read the more disgusted they are, and yet they feel their bowels are being turned inside out and, how can they say it to themselves, it's a pleasant feeling. More than pleasant! In fact, they are transformed. They are weeping with pleasure. So this is what life can be! Bamboo shoots and cantharides! Steel studs and whips! Out of the blue, the housewife has been subverted. She has been catapulted into a neutral void. She has reeled and taken two maybe three steps backward. In direct contradiction of present trends, her abrupt end is suddenly, and for the first time, conceivable . . .'

He said this to Lili in a room at the Hotel Andaluse in a soot and brick suburb where a whiff of the mountains still swept at odd moments through the streets. He had persuaded her to come there. And as soon as he was able to touch the mouth that had turned him into a trash author, he was articulate.

He paid her in boxes of chocolates and marzipan eggs.

And as he watched her eat, the structure of his book passed through his mind in detailed and luminous scenes.

'There's a castle in Wallachia,' he said dreamily. 'It's owned by a former pistachio-nut importer from Bucharest. Now he's retired so that he can devote himself to his erotic fantasies . . . or rather, his erotic nightmares. He sends to the villages for human fodder. After a while, the peasants begin to nickname him Dirty Dak . . . or the Impaler, if you get my meaning. In the castle there are a hundred rooms. I have constructed the contents of each one exactly. Each one is a different size and shape, converted by the pistachio-nut importer to meet his requirements. The equipment found in each one is unique. It has been designed and built to meet one precise need, or rather to enact one precise scene. For example, in one room there is a thumbscrew and a velvet mask. The Master uses the thumbscrew on himself while a village girl, blindfolded, listens to his screams: he is aroused not by the pain of the screw but by the twitches of her face as she is provoked by his voice as it rises in frequency into the upper reaches of pain. The more she twitches, the more he is aroused. Great damage to the thumb is required before he obtains release. This is an abstract torture which the housewife will not understand, but it will successfully challenge her preconceptions about romantic love.

'In another room (as a matter of fact in the same wing, only four doors removed) we find a still more ingenious arrangement. Here a nasal peg which has been specially designed for the Master by his own blacksmith lies on a table with a razor and a shaving bowl. The hedonist brings in his *Backfische*, as unknowing and innocent as the last one, and lathered in her armpits. At the same time he dons the peg. It is well known in Wallachia, you see, that when the armpits of an adolescent girl are shaved they release a hormonal odour of exquisite delicacy. Our hedonist knows this perfectly well. Hasn't he shaved hundreds of them for just this reason? But in this case he denies himself the ultimate erotic nasal experience just when it is most easily available to him – and he's naturally chosen an armpit that's youthful, strong and pungent. The girl looks in wonder at the expression of agony on her employer's face. And as he sees her expression mirror his expression, a spiral of expressions is created that brings the Master to his release.

'Naturally for the adolescent it's incomprehensible, and so it will be for housewives . . . but at the same time, of course, they will have their doubts, they will be brought face to face with the unknown, the very thing they will least expect to encounter when they trip off to their four-poster beds to make plump blond children for Mr Husband Hair-pin Factory Boss with gritted teeth and a handkerchief soaked in scent. And when it is remembered that there are a hundred rooms, each one with a different utensil, the effect on the housewife cannot be underestimated. This book, *The Dictionary of Secret Fruit*, is a wishbone sent into the housewife's throat. It will make her choke and as she chokes she will throw up everything she has learnt, everything in her digestive system that makes her a housewife!'

These outbursts of articulacy came over him when he had been kissing her mouth. So she lay in bed all day painting it surrounded by a constellation of moles – he didn't object, but when he touched it it transmitted a bibliophile vulgarity to him, a vulgarity which stuck to him like a sulky discoloured comedo on the end of a schoolboy's nose.

Flinging reason and skin creams to the wind, however, he began his long and arduous assault on the housewife, and before six months were up he had a manuscript which, surprisingly, was not yet covered with tell-tale drops of blood.

He read it out loud to its attentive originator.

She rubbed her mouth and groaned.

'I can't understand that chapter on the nose peg and the razor at all,' she said. 'As if a pistachio-nut importer would want to smell an armpit. I can't see what nose pegs have to do with love.'

He stared at her in disbelief: even her . . . a housewife?

25

In June 1772, the thirty-two-year-old Donatien Alphonse François de Sade, fresh from his incarceration in the prison of Pierre-Encise for the flagellation and rape of Rose Keller, descended upon the city of Marseilles in the company of his lackey Latour and visited the brothel of a Mariette Borélly, where – in the course of repeated copulations with a variety of prostitutes – he passed round a box of chocolates tainted with the dry skins of aphrodisiacal beetles. In this way he poisoned his favourite partner of the bout, one Marianne, along with one Marguerite Coste, and so, found guilty *in absentia* of intent to kill and of sodomy, he was condemned to death by decapitation. The Marquis in the meantime had escaped to Italy with his sister-in-law Mademoiselle de Launy, where he charmed the Italian courts with his new 'wife' and their façade of domestic happiness. While his straw effigy was burned in public in the principal square of Aix, the young nobleman recorded his subtle and perceptive meditations on the statue of Hermaphroditus in the Uffizi. He had begun to turn his life into a novel: his own.

The Marquis had achieved what Lullio dreamed of doing.

And the habit of classification, enumeration, repetition and tedious uniformity of tone was carefully learnt by the book-hater.

By the winter of 1908 he had presented his text to a publisher in Zurich.

It was brought out three months later under the title he had designated himself.

It was important that the market for the *Dictionary* be carefully chosen, and so the author insisted that on the cover of the first edition a picture of a virile Romanian should appear, one hand filled with pistachio nuts and a cigarette lighter in the other. He is shown unravelling a half-dressed naif.

There is a caption: One Hundred Oriental Transgressions in Original Language. 'Literature is crap,' Lullio used to say in the beer halls, as he treated his companion to sausages and Bavarian beer, 'but the housewife is even worse.' In this respect, he shared the young Mussolini's ethic when the latter was writing his famous *Claudia Particella*.

When the book appeared the couple escaped to the Bodensee on the publisher's advance and Lullio read the newspapers every day for news of its progress.

But there was nothing.

The Swiss intelligentsia had snubbed him.

After a week, however, a letter arrived from Paulus Kruft, his publisher.

'It is true', it said, 'that our *geistige Welt* has thrown it in the trash can without so much as a perusal. However, I can assure you that the ordinary people in the street are buying it in their thousands. Perhaps even in their hundreds of thousands. It seems that it has already acquired a certain reputation . . . that women, in particular . . .'

As they moved around the high lakes from cottage to cottage, Lullio's impatience increased.

'It is impossible', he whined, 'that the middle classes are impervious to the insult which I have so carefully thrown in their faces. Or do they think that they can merely turn the other cheek? They may think that now, but wait until their servants get a hold of a copy. It's not just the housewife that is under threat, but the household as well!'

They moved from Bodensee to the Vierwaldstätter See, where Lili took out bundles of banknotes from her crocodile portmanteau to the Spaniard's astonishment. And his affection turned bitter at the thought of what she must have done to earn them.

Housewives . . . whores: two sides of the same grubby coin.

One was the chrysalis of the other.

His depression deepened as spring came and he missed his anarchist friends, not to mention his sausages and Bavarian beer.

He missed the way they spat into their beer and then at themselves.

Then, just as he was at the end of his patience, a letter arrived from Lausanne. It was from Kruft, and contained a bright blue and yellow cheque made out for a four-figure sum. A cut-out from a newspaper was included, giving details of a riot in a bookstore on the Avenue de Cour.

Lullio yawned and winked at his lover.

'There, you see,' he drawled. 'The housewife has taken the bait.'

They returned to the city immediately and the writer went round to inspect the broken windows of the Librairie Bissolati. A blood-stain on the pavement raised his spirits even further.

Within a week, however, the disturbances had multiplied. The city's married female population had unexpectedly lost its com-posure. The orders placed with the printers were doubled and Lullio received yet another blue and yellow cheque. With the proceeds, rich for the first time in his life, he bought a Krieger Electric automobile and sailed round the Place de la Gare in a pair of doe-skin gloves.

As summer approached, the husbands of the metropolitan housewives, aware of the violent behaviour of their wives combined with their unusual immersion in a certain large text, alerted their insurance companies.

The insurance companies let it be known that if intellectually 'adulterous' housewives haemorrhaged in the bath with a copy of *The Dictionary of Secret Fruits* in one hand, they would not pay the funeral expenses.

Not until May, however, did a husband pick up a text. It happened in the suburb of Bussigny. A husband, returning early from work, entered his calm suburban bathroom one evening to find his wife asleep in the bath. By her side was a copy of the book, earmarked in twenty different places. He crept up to the bath without waking her, picked up the text in curiosity and opened it at page 278. At the top of this page he came across the following sentence: 'Georgos Dak, even after a lifetime's experience in the deflowering of the axilla, had not wearied of the smell of armpits.' The husband dropped the book as if he had been burned, but then picked it up and continued. There followed a section on phallic fruit. The insertion of fruits into orifices took up fifteen pages. The insertions were facilitated with nitro-glycerine (which was then consumed by the participants as a pleasurable drug), soap, mustard and olive oil. The husband reeled. Figs, dates and green bananas were consumed after use, along with the nitro-glycerine, and arranged by a chef from Paris in gorgeous silver boats. Grapes did not survive the treatment and so were converted into a rough but palatable wine. He flipped to page 345. Nails, poodles and greased walnuts. Page 401: leather hoods and swords. He had to sit down. The pages that his wife had earmarked went on to the end of the book. The last was on page 513, six pages from the end. But he had never even heard of a 'Moroccan sandwich'.

Little had husbands suspected what housewives were reading in their mineral-water baths.

Wiping the sweat from his forehead, the husband sat down and, in a long letter to a leading newspaper, exposed the anti-domestic propaganda that the housewife was now imbibing.

And he concluded (restraining a moist eye): 'Never before would a devout and fertile husband have divined the muck and squalor in which the housewife wallows when she is left to her own devices. It is time that the family was reasserted, the battle lines drawn and discipline once more exercised over the wanton housewife. What can result from the absorption of this Hispano-oriental *saloperie* but an inexorable decline of the national productivity, our GNP, national security and treasured national resources? And as for our gastronomic values, it is impossible to think what slavery is waiting just around the corner . . .'

The husbands joined forces and wrote a five-point proposal to the newspapers.

They demanded tests based firmly on the *Psychopathia sexualis*.

They demanded expulsion of the criminal who had excited the housewife.

They reclaimed the right to use canes.

The buttocks of the housewife, they solemnly assured the nation, were in need of severe correction . . .

But one day Paulus Kruft appeared at the door of Lullio's apartment near the Grand Chêne. The old man, who seemed to be suffering from acute kyphosis, was carrying a box filled with women's action committee pamphlets tied up with coloured elastic bands, and laughing softly to himself and thrusting one finger deep into first one ear then the other. Beneath his shock of white hair, his eyes were dancing backwards and forwards with the speed of little blue rockets.

129

'I've just been to all four corners of the canton,' he announced gaily. 'I've been to eighteen Housewives' Defence Committee meetings all over the city. They're springing up everywhere. I was expecting to hear some bitter stories . . . but no, the housewives are conciliatory. They are even contented and happy with themselves. They are not, I repeat, in a state of agitation. An aura of bliss surrounds them. Look at this.'

He held up one of the pamphlets. In sober blue letters it proclaimed

GRATIFICATION
The New Hope of the Home

Underneath a collection of housewives' comments followed in petition form.

Kruft held them up to his nose and smirked.

One had written: 'Since reading this catalogue of deviant acts, my sense of equilibrium has strengthened, my contentedness, placidity and passive submission to housewifely chores have enlarged and I am happier with my utter subjection, slavery and suppression than ever before.'

Another had written: 'The *Dictionary* has filled me with an intense and unswayable desire to breed, sew, bake, menstruate and make strawberry tarts. Hardly a day goes by without my rushing to the flour and eggs, the mothballs and the disinfectant. I'm consumed with love for milk bottles. I'm burning with lust for husbandly spanks. I'm desperate for discipline to be applied to my disobedient maternal buttocks. I only wish my husband would pick up his whip and thrash me while I'm baking his favourite fish pie with fennel and lentils. I'm ready to be soiled with cooking fat and garden mud. Never before have I so longed for the stream of insults my miserable attempts at *bouches de reines* elicits in my utterly correct and irreproachable lord and master. I only hope that he can be his true violent self. It's the beginning of a new life . . .'

And yet another: 'At last I've discovered the meaning of real pleasure. With each page of the *Dictionary* that I read, I felt my craven acceptance of the status quo increase. And the more I accepted the status quo, the more I enjoyed my acceptance. My one overwhelming longing is to re-enter the matrix of the nuclear family, sit once more like a lap dog at my husband's feet and engage in some innocent, artless and politically neutral embroidery which I will then present to him as the symbol of my joyful and heartful acceptance of modern housewifedom. A blow has been struck for the cause of the rejuvenated housewife and just when we thought . . .'

Lullio could not believe his ears. He covered them with his hands, as if they had been burned with acid.

'So you see', the obviously cowardly Kruft whistled, 'there's no fear of a scandal. As a result of your timely and moral stimulation, the housewife has become more domestic than ever. All we have to do is inform the husbands that their suspicions are absurd and we can continue selling thousands of copies to all concerned. You sly saint! You knew it all along.'

'I can't believe they've read it,' the author gasped. 'It's government propaganda.'

'But not at all, not at all. I've seen them at the meetings. Their faces are rosy and shiny. Their bellies are dying to be pregnant. They're smiling and knitting. They're doing the shopping and darning the socks. It's . . .' Kruft put his hand on his heart, '. . . beautiful.'

'Darning? Sewing? Knitting? Strawberry tarts?'

'Yes, all of it's true! I've seen it!'

'They've gone mad.'

'Oh, gone mad have they? Ha ha. What a wit you are.'

Lullio squinted at the publisher.

'*Abnormis sapiens*,' he said bitterly.

'Ah, Pepe, you're so erudite when you're excited.'

'You haven't understood anything, Kruft. The housewife is playing games with us.'

He felt a sudden desire to don his knuckledusters and smash the old man's face in.

And he went on: 'It isn't normal. They didn't get the point. Or else . . . *Parthis mendacior!*'

'Excuse me?'

'More cunning than the Parthians.'

'Women?'

'Housewives.'

'Ah. I see.'

Kruft replaced the elastic bands around the pamphlets and stuffed them into his briefcase. The Spaniard was a Spaniard, that was all. All the housewife wanted was to be happy. What was wrong with that? If it took a book, a single book, a book encompassing all other books appealing to her . . . what of it?

'Don't be so alarmed,' he advised. 'If you like, go to a resort until the riots subside. I'll send on your royalties.'

'That isn't the point,' Lullio said, clenching his teeth. For a moment he saw a black anarchist flag in front of his eyes. 'I won't be outwitted by a gang of *Hausfraus*. It's they who should retreat, not me.'

'Retreat? Outwit? My boy, this is not a war!'

Lullio threw up his hands and burst out laughing.

'He says it isn't a war!'

He collapsed in a chair and heaved with artificial guffaws.

After a minute he grew tired and wiped his eyes.

'It all depends on how you define a war,' he said quietly. 'There are those who think wars have neat beginnings and ends and that in between there is peace. And there are those who think of war as perpetual and unresolvable. We are different breeds.'

The publisher looked completely confused.

'But surely . . .', he ventured cautiously, '. . . surely you aren't at war with . . .', he could hardly say the word.

'Exactly.'

'But that's absurd. How can you wage a war against a genus, an institution, a way of life?'

Lullio looked up with his cold little eyes.

'The housewife is not a way of life,' he said coolly. 'She is a way of painting one's mouth.'

26

Yes, the more he thought about it, the more he understood that it was the way the lips were painted that mattered. Like the eminent Dr Paléologue, like the vast majority of the male species, he was uneasy with his own mouth. What was it for if not occasional but traumatic contact with the other mouths, the feminine organs? But his unease with his own mouth extended to an even greater unease about the other mouths. They were the same but they were not. Certainly you felt these other mouths during the course of your life, it couldn't be altered, so that they had to be dealt with . . . yes, even bloodied and split from time to time just so they knew where they stood, but after all in the end you had to feel their creases and saliva, their paint and their lust. A case of attraction and repulsion. A case of uncertainty about their moistness, the shape that fitted so comfortably, the mixing of microbes. Ah, what would women be without those mouths of theirs? Nothing! Nothing at all! Walking lumps of barbaric impulses. Formless nothingness, night without light, hedgehogs, lamp-posts and worse!

But as soon as they 'acquired' a mouth, everything was changed.

It was then that the trouble began.

And then the mouths themselves split into tribes. The dominant form of the female oral equipment was the housewife form (that wet fuchsia colour pencilled too thinly, the tightened corners resplendent with chastity) and perhaps for that reason it was the lips of the housewife that he was least able to resign himself to. But deeper still, the desire to transform the mouths of house-wives stemmed from a desire to remove the mouths of women altogether. Or at least to render them impotent. Or incoherent. Or dilapidated . . .

Nor was there any question whose lips had started him thinking of the social order in this way.

Lullio, however, misanalysed.

'What insults me more than anything else', he complained to Lili, 'is the way they eat. I mean, do they have to do it in the way that they do? It's as if they're doing it deliberately, or else like little dogs . . . chewing, I mean, using their mouths as if they want to pick a fight. As if they own the world. Do they think they own the world because they eat in a certain way?' And he forced a laugh. 'Who are they kidding? If there was a revolution, do you know what the first law to be passed would be? The banning of lipstick. Ban lipstick and you ban the housewife. Unfortunately, of course, the powers that be will never ban lipstick. No, they know as well as I do that lipstick is the cornerstone of the entire putrid system!'

With the failure of the book to dent the omnipresence of domestic women, though, he knew that it was pointless to stay in the city. Kruft's suggestion seemed more attractive. What he needed to do was hunt for congregations of these irritating species elsewhere, in places where they were more vulnerable. Where does a wild cat go when it's hunting zebras? To the waterhole, of course. And the waterhole of the bourgeois Swiss housewife – in its grandest manifestation – was the nearby casino town of Montreux.

In the second week of 1910 they took the littoral train.

Lullio caught a cold as soon as they arrived but could not be stopped from converting his cheques into red and black chips and entering the casino at the Bristol Hotel.

The place was full of housewives in *bouchon-de-carafe* diamonds.

In the distance, above the hum of the roulette tables, the sound of tennis balls being hit in the evening air, the trickling whine of a string quartet and the click of dentures on silver forks alerted his nostrils.

The delicate membranes inside them immediately registered the sweet and putrescent smell of unfaithful wives.

27

His gambling was compulsive and amateurish. The turning wheel was civilized, but did not prevent his catastrophic losses. The housewives soon identified him as he came down each morning, with a newspaper folded under his arm and his face sliding to the left, with murmurs of 'The incompetent conquistador'.

And why did his face slide to the left?

Was it an expression of his political sympathies?

In the evening, irritated by the empty blueness of the lake and the incessant tock-tock of pink tennis balls, he played harder and more clumsily even than during the day.

'You're letting these venereal widows get to you,' Lili would say to him. 'Double your stakes.'

And he would say: 'You're right. I'm behaving like a provincial. I'll treble them.'

'Why not quadruple them?'

'I'll quintuple them.'

And when he did the housewives in boas said: 'The incompetent conquistador. He's not afraid of pitched battles.'

But he lost it all before their eyes.

The more he lost, the more compelled to overcome his provincialism he became. At the moment of loss he looked momentarily like a corpse. Stupefaction eventually overcame him and he slid away from the tables in a numb silence. But the next morning he would be there again, starting with the crap tables and progressing by midnight to the roulette wheel.

A group of painted widows collected around him.

At the crap tables, they sat around him, fat and glittering, and interrogated him about his health.

After a week they were joined by a tall Russian with a lisp and a tangle of rhubarb hair who introduced himself as a glass-button maker from Königsberg, Mr Tutaev.

He took one look at Lullio and said: 'Allow me, sir, your eyes are dilated. A sign of chronic losing. I say this in all respectability. It could be a case of piles or pink eye. Or then again there is the possibility of spastic paralysis. I once saw a peasant in the Urals, frothing at the mouth . . . turning cartwheels, and . . .'

The new arrival fidgeted constantly with an iron ring on one finger. He brought his own worn-in cards. One of the widows (equivalent in Lullio's eyes to a housewife) immediately observed: 'It's a pleasure to have an experienced gambler here for a change. My husband used to sentence them to twenty years minimum, but only because he, like our dear Mr Lullio, was a perpetual loser.'

'*Concedo*,' Lullio said.

'I'm sorry?'

The Spaniard touched his nose archly.

'*Non precipitando.*'

Silence.

The Russian looked at his watch and smiled.

'All manner of medical possibilities,' he murmured and laid out his cards.

Lullio turned to the traitor who had uttered the word 'loser'. He didn't want to lose his composure by slicing up her plump face with his razor – it was better to annihilate her with erudition. He searched desperately for another erudite comment but could remember nothing. They smiled at each other. Finally the Spaniard, clenching his fists under the table, inclined his head and said sarcastically:

'*Deus ex machina*, madame, and *hasta la mañana!*'

Tutaev turned out to be an expert player. A mere two days later he had collected fifty thousand francs from the Spaniard, who resolved with every franc he lost to avenge the pride of his wounded provincialism. And as he won the Russian bantered about Chagas's Disease, yaws and the terrible Guinea-worm, covering as he went the entire spectrum of his hypochondria.

Five days later he had taken half of Lullio's disposable income.

The Spaniard wired to Lausanne for more money and raised the stakes.

The Russian was calm and methodical. His obsession with decay expressed itself in long lectures on parasites, cures and medicinal waters. The widows giggled as he raked in the notes. And then, under his mat of rhubarb hair, ignoring Lullio's blushes, he began winking at Lili.

A glass-button maker!

From Königsberg!

And worse than that, he was the favourite of the 'housewives'. They sucked up to him at every opportunity.

'Mr Tutaev,' one of them said pleadingly, 'tell us about the Guinea-worm.'

The glass-button man was so cosmopolitan: he could hold forth on the Guinea-worm!

'The Guinea-worm', Tutaev began, 'is a helminth, which our biologists tell us is a diverse and ill-defined parasite. I refer to the "worm".' The widows nodded like students. 'The proper name for our villain is *Dranunculus medinensis*, and its habitat is West Africa. The larva enters the body with water. The female worm then sticks under the skin – more usually in the lower part of the legs – and emerges to lay its eggs when the host stands in water.' The widows reeled in disgust. 'But you are going to ask how it is cured? Don't worry, ladies, I won't disappoint you. The Africans pull it out by winding it slowly around a stick over the course of a week. When it comes out . . . but, ladies, decency forbids me to . . .'

After this description, one of them turned to Lullio.

'And what do you know about helminths?'

'Yes,' the Russian said with genuine curiosity. 'Tell us about the worms of Spain.'

'The worms of Spain?'

Lullio spluttered and looked at them in amazement.

'You can't be serious.'

'It's no use covering your ignorance, Mr Lullio,' the fattest one put in.

'My ignorance?'

'Come now, Mr Lullio. You must have a story about a worm. Not necessarily the Guinea-worm, but some kind of worm. Don't tell us you know nothing about worms at all?'

Tutaev stroked his chin. The Spaniard squirmed.

'Why . . . I . . .'

'There. He's stumped.'

'Why should I be stumped? What are worms to me?'

'That's not the point,' the fat one said, wagging her finger. 'Ignorance is ignorance, no matter what the subject.'

'I've never seen a worm!'

'Oh really?'

They sniggered to themselves, as if he had been caught lying.

'Come now, my friend,' the Russian chirped, conciliating. 'Don't keep us in suspense. Stop hiding your light under a bushel. Let's share our stories and learning, our eclectic sophistication and wide-ranging cosmopolitan general knowledge. Let us discuss with polite and polished phrases the mysteries of the Bilharzia, the Filaria and the Trichiniasis. Let us delve together in a spirit of amiable respect and international friendship into the enigmas of the *Necator americanus* and the Enterobius, the Ascaris and the *Ankylostomum duodenale*. I know you're being modest. Or else you're afraid of offending the gentler sex. In truth, you needn't be restricted by such exquisite preoccupations. We are all in the exploration of the worm together – we are submerged in the sweet detachment of science, we are receptive to the poetry of helminths. Ah, the whipworm and the pigworm! The tapeworm and the hookworm!'

Deeply impressed, the women applauded.

Such a fine speech in defence of the worm.

'But that still doesn't get our Mr Lullio off the hook,' the fat tormentor continued. 'He claims he's never even seen one, while Mr Tutaev knows how Africans wind them round sticks.'

'That's right,' another one whistled, 'he's looking more ignorant all the time.'

Lullio sneered and then panicked.

'Worms? Worms? What a load of crap!'

The table was silent. The 'housewives' fidgeted indignantly. Mr Tutaev dealt the next hand with a resigned expression. And in the depths of this expression, hidden by occasional muscular twitches, could be seen the unmistakable colour of pity.

It seemed this Spaniard was turning out to be something of a provincial.

Lullio looked at them in alarm. Were they suspecting that he was the son of a peasant, a former dye-works apprentice, a stoker-boy in a ship, a miserable autodidact and – furthermore – acquainted with the worm, not intellectually, spiritually and suavely like the Russian but merely pragmatically and empirically? Were they suspecting him of being what he was: a low provincial, a being thoroughly permeated with provincialism?

The 'housewives' were now looking at him with open hostility.

Their mouths were tight and oppressive.

'We don't have to talk about worms,' the Russian said quietly, avoiding the Spaniard's eyes, 'if it offends you . . . we can move on to other subjects. The world is full of subjects. There is never any end of subjects. Subjects for civilized, courteous and knowledgeable conversation between reciprocating and subtle minds abound in all directions. There are an almost infinite number. Have you ever considered inflammations?'

The ladies perked up.

'Inflammations! Oh tell us about inflammations! We're dying to hear about inflammations! Did you hear that? He's an expert on inflammations! What a man! What a gentleman! What a scholar and aesthete!'

And the fat tormentor said to Lullio: 'Mr Lullio could redeem himself on inflammations. With inflammations he could redress the balance and we would let bygones be bygones!'

'Inflammations . . .'

Before he knew what he was doing, he was co-operating in their game. Their housewifely snobbery was enveloping him and forcing him to prove himself to them, as a child would have to prove himself to a board of examiners.

He blushed and looked around wildly for inspiration.

'*In flagrante delicto,*' he muttered uncertainly.

The ladies burst out laughing.

'Surely,' Tutaev said smoothly, 'our estimable guest has no intention of hiding from the ears of our gracious feminine company his profound and nevertheless eclectic perusals on the variations of *rubor et tumor cum calore et dolore*? Surely he is not an adherent of the outmoded theory of laudable pus? Adhesion, suppuration and ulceration, my friend, the three rules of true inflammations, which we are always mindful of. Ah, the work of Virchow and Cohnheim! Oh, the microscopy of frogs and the detection of the inflammatory exudate! How can we ever encompass the complex paradoxes and the remote subtleties of granulation tissue and the septic finger? How can we ever hope to exhaust the myriad possibilities of inflamed organs, auto-immunity and counter-irritations? Inflammations everywhere! A world of inflammations! Histamines and osmosis – that is what human life is, a cycle of Hunter's adhesion, clots, abscesses and irritations!'

'Bravo . . .', the fat one. 'As Mr Tutaev says . . .'

The Russian raised a terrible finger.

'Life is one long thrombosis,' he sighed.

'He's right. One inflammation after another . . .'

'I had one in my bladder . . .'

'I had one in my ear . . .'

'But remember,' Tutaev added with a stern smile, 'inflammation is useful. Yes, inflammation is useful!'

'Why, Mr Tutaev . . .'

'You mean . . .'

'Yes, ladies, without it trivial disorders would result in death.'

One of the jewelled 'pastries' turned to the fat tormentor.

'How useful, pertinent, practical everything he says is. How else would we have known that inflammations are useful?'

'It's true. He's saved us from irrational fear of inflammations.'

'Thanks to him we've lost our terror of inflammations!'

'His practical, useful and pertinent observations . . .'

'Oh, how can we thank you enough, Mr Tutaev?'

'Finally . . . the inflammation tamed.'

An orgy of congratulation followed. The Russian laughed it off gallantly and played his hand. Lullio crumpled in his chair and prayed that they would not torment him with demands for his opinions on inflammations. Black ignorance swallowed him up. And how is the presence of provincialism revealed if not by means of the exhibition of crass and unadulterated ignorance? He might have told them about dyes and steamships but being 'housewives' they would not have cared less. What they cared about was their health, their intestines, their inflammations. His knowledge of the world was provincial because it could not be related to them.

And before his provincialism could be increased he rose and excused himself. Tutaev rose too and granted him a shallow bow. The women nodded perfunctorily. They were dying to question the Russian about diabetes and gallstones and the existence or non-existence of a mere provincial could not concern them.

As he walked out he felt himself swearing like his father.

And a rustic red stain appeared at the end of his nose.

When they reached the lift doors, Tutaev waved and called out gaily: 'Tomorrow we'll discuss tonsils, Mr Lullio. And next time don't be so shy. I can see you're a tonsil man!'

28

From then on, when Lullio caught sight of himself in mirrors, he was surprised to see how fluffy, crude and protuberant his ears had become. And his nose, too, had become squat and square. In short, his face was becoming more peasant-like. His reversion to provincialism had become physical.

If he dressed in his English plaids, the provincialism did not disappear. If he snubbed the lift boys, they snubbed him back. Whatever he did, his provincialism displayed itself for all to see and as his provincialism intensified his resentment against the mouth which was the catalyst of his rusticity increased as well. He knew that when they were together his clumsiness, bad language and verbal incompetence were greater.

His face took on the healthy shine, plump inertia and vacant pragmatism of a small-time pig farmer.

His clothes looked awkward. His shirts no longer fitted. When he put a hat on his head it automatically looked pretentious.

When he pronounced the names of wines a syllable always jarred. When he walked, his feet splayed outwards and waddled out of control like the feet of a mechanical duck.

He was provincial, immersed in provincialism.

'Do I look different?' he asked Lili in a panic, turning first one side of his face into the light as he watched it in the mirror and then the other. 'My face looks rounder . . . more bovine. Am I eating too much? Am I eating something I shouldn't be?'

'Your cheeks look the same. It's your shoes that look different.'

'My shoes?', as he looked down at his feet in alarm. 'What do you mean? How are they different?'

Lili tittered.

'They look . . . inflated.'

'Inflated?'

'Puffed up.'

'You mean like the feet of an oaf?'

'Perhaps . . . more rustic.'

'Rustic?'

He blushed and shook his shoes off angrily.

'It's not just the shoes,' she went on, however. 'Look: it's your feet as well!'

It was true . . . the feet were also enlarged, oafish and vulgar. They could never be disguised.

He walked up and down the room looking at them.

A familiar nausea welled in his temples. When he was a child a count's son had hit him in the face with a whip, leaving a scar that had stayed with him for a year. The inflation of his feet in the Bristol Hotel effected the same destruction of his outer self.

'I suppose they were looking at them under the table,' he said bitterly. 'Housewives have an eye for discrepancies like that. They think I should be out ploughing fields. They think that I lose because of my feet. If my feet were more metropolitan they wouldn't expect me to lose to the Russian every time. I see that there is no way out of my provincialism other than a direct assault on the housewives and their fellow conspirator.'

He paused, still looking mournfully at his feet.

'What is the game most antithetical to the spirit and ethos of the hearth, the litany of domestic duties and the system of the housewife?'

'Russian roulette.'

He raised his eyebrows.

'You're reading my mind, *Süßchen*.'

They fell silent; and the assemblage of scenic views, slices of lake, thickets of trees, reflective parasols and steamboats visible from the window made no difference to the tragedy of Lullio's dishonourable provincialism.

Only Russian roulette could restore the balance of superiority and inferiority that held sway in his relations with the world.

He sighed and crumpled backwards like an old man.

Then brought his lips into contact with her shins.

'It might leave them indifferent,' he said sadly and desperately. 'But at least I might cover them all with brains.'

He wrote a haughty note to Tutaev. It read:

Sir,

A gambling man like yourself surely won't turn down an offer to participate in a game which makes all others seem empty and childish. I've heard that your nation invented it and I assume that you cannot be unfamiliar with its excitements. I refer, of course, to your Slavic 'roulette'. Naturally the bullets will be live. Are you susceptible to the implications of refusing?

There followed a harangue including details of the arrangements for the game, which was to be played in Lullio's rooms. Similar notes were sent to the housewives.

He expected them all to refuse. It was their refusal that he wanted. Their refusal would establish his cosmopolitanism, superiority and worldliness. It would deflate his feet in their eyes.

But within minutes the nightmarish glass-button merchant was at the door shaking a flower in his face and chuckling like a schoolboy.

'You are a joker, Mr Lullio, but you have the gift of springing surprises worthy of an officer. Russian roulette, as they call it! Our national pastime! How could I ever refuse? I've never played, as you seem to think, though I've shaken the hand of Bagration the famous life-and-death player from Kiev and I have a hunch . . . a hunch, Mr Lullio . . . that you've got an eye on his reputation.'

'Never heard of him,' Lullio said coldly.

'Haven't you? Well that's not surprising. Got his brains blown out in Yalta. What a way to go, Mr Lullio, what a way to go.'

He pushed his way forward and kissed Lili's hand.

'Are you going to watch? Why not? Imagine the scene . . . the sweat . . .'

'We can meet tomorrow,' Lullio suggested, and stood stiffly. 'I have a weapon. You can look it over of course.'

'Look it over? Whatever for? I trust you both with my life!' And he winked while handing over the flower to Lili. 'I can't speak for our widows, of course, but on my recommendation, they'll accept the weapon.'

'You think they'll accept?'

Lullio's voice was anxious.

'There's no chance of them not accepting. I'll insist that they accept. You see, Mr Lullo, they're gamblers. They can't resist a game.'

'But the possibility . . .'

'Of maiming, death, disfigurement?'

The merchant roared with laughter.

'What do you take us for . . . housewives?'

'But – of course not!'

'I'm relieved, Mr Lullio. For a minute I thought you had underestimated us.'

'Then it's settled,' the Spaniard said weakly.

'It is settled, and not a moment too soon. To be frank with you, Mr Lullio, I was getting a little bored with the Bristol. And believe it or not, I had a dream about Bagration a few nights ago . . . yes, I dreamt he was playing Wagner and they were down to the last chamber. Unfortunately, I woke up before the end. Let's hope that this time I'll be luckier.'

'You're very calm about it.'

Lullio's voice was strained.

But Tutaev's response was to take out his handkerchief and rub the end of his nose, which was shiny.

'It gets shiny when I'm calm,' he said.

The replies of the women came later but arrived nevertheless. They were all pleased to accept. They accepted without hesitation. They accepted with no reservations. They accepted with . . . ferocity!

His assault had backfired.

Downing a large Scotch, he rubbed his eyes and then threw up in the bath.

'They didn't understand,' he moaned, 'it was just a question of form. All they had to do was play with form. But they took it literally – what should I have expected from a bunch of bourgeoise domestics? For them form is literal. For me, it's just a matter of honour. That's the difference between a housewife and a peasant. Because that's what they're turning me into . . . a humble, worn-down, vendetta-waging, sun-beaten, illiterate, grovelling peasant!'

And as he retched, he saw before him, in the depths of the fouled water in the bottom of the bath, the face of his father.

It was Jacquerie or nothing!

He cabled back to the city and learned from Kruft that both husbands and wives had settled down to the notorious *Dictionary* and were using it profitably to reinforce and enhance, modify and deepen the nucleus of family values, homely disciplines and child-bearing duties. The riots were over. The book was being promoted by local government!

Kruft's telegram drove nails into his new coffin.

'*Dictionary* respectable stop family reunited stop more babies on the way stop defender of public morality stop possibility medal town hall stop.'

He cleaned the pistol he kept with him and placed one bullet in the revolving chamber. He then placed it in the middle of the playing table.

He sat with it all night. At noon the following day there was a knock on the door. The five players were there, all dressed in summer linen. The Russian, flushed red from a ride across the lake and holding a box containing a lump of snow he had hacked from some scree or other during the morning, took off his boater and threw it accurately across the room so that it landed on Lullio's bed.

'Fauna,' he said glowingly, 'fauna!'

'He's told us about fauna,' one of the women said. 'Glockenspiels and the like.'

'There's no end', the Russian said, 'to the bewildering variety of fauna.'

'I have no interest in fauna,' Lullio said, and guided them to the table. 'At this moment fauna are far from my mind.'

'Well, let me tell you that that's a mistake, my dear Mr Lullio. A man must never let fauna wander too far from his mind.'

They all stared at the pistol.

'Nor pistols . . .' he added quietly.

They sat. Lili closed the blinds. It was a warm day outside: huge blue butterflies flopped against the windows and scattered into sunlight. The room was filled with the humming of bees. An early spring . . . precocious exfoliations . . . an influx of insect life. Lullio took off his tie. His skin was boiled and pink, large patches of discoloration had appeared in it, giving him the appearance of a pinta sufferer. The Russian gave a lesson on fauna, detailing the beauties of blossoms, the wonders of trefoils and phloem. The widows, the surrogate housewives, were also pink and moist. Their maternal busts swayed and rippled in their flounced *décollétages*, *décollétages* that were attempts not to be housewifely but which were nevertheless fully in keeping with the panorama of domestic values. For as Lullio saw at once, they were in revolt, but their revolt itself betrayed them.

They had agreed to play for units of ten thousand francs. Whoever played the lowest hand was obliged to use the pistol. Lullio could not believe that they had agreed to such illegality. Why had he not arranged for the manager to find out discreetly and come storming into the room with the porters to stop it? But then the ultimate peasant revolt would be to force one of them to pull the trigger in an unlucky moment. In which case the game would be stopped, a suicide would be declared and Lullio would go back to Lausanne with his ideology intact.

Any unpleasantness would be worth this end result.

Tutaev removed his jacket, rolled up his sleeves and dealt the first hand. He did it slowly, so slowly that it seemed an hour had passed when he had finished. They laid their hands and it was seen that Tutaev himself had lost.

But the Russian was cheerful.

He picked up the revolver and spun the chamber.

The housewives looked uncomfortable for a moment.

'I have worked out the mathematics of it,' he said calmly. 'It's an acceptable risk. My only regret would be my inability to finish the book I bought in town this morning. A model book. An informative work. Maybe you're read it, ladies? *The Dictionary of Secret Fruits.*'

They all nodded vigorously.

'We've been reading it all week, Mr Tutaev. We've been discussing Room 98 – you remember – the thongs and the glass jars.'

'I do indeed remember the thong and the glass jars, esteemed friends, and may I comment, analyse and dissect . . . ?'

Hardly believing his ears, Lullio blushed and pointed to the pistol.

'But, you've forgotten . . .' he stammered, glaring at the glass-button man. 'You can't talk your way out of it.'

'Talk? Out of it?'

Tutaev looked at the pistol, gave a start as if he had just remembered it and smiled.

'I hadn't forgotten for a moment.'

And he put the barrel against his head, closed his eyes and pulled the trigger.

An empty click.

'As I was saying,' he went on, laying the pistol back in the middle of the table and ignoring the fact that the author of the book was sitting at the same table as himself, 'I feel it necessary to comment, analyse and dissect . . . to judge, embellish and anatomize . . . yes, the style, the sequence of events, the elaborations, the critical addenda . . . all of this, ladies, amounts to nothing more or less than . . . provincialism!'

'We quite agree, Mr Tutaev!'

They dealt a second hand.

As the cards were distributed, Lullio felt darkness invading his skull from the corners of his eyes. He gripped the edge of his seat with clammy fingers. 'Of course, far be it from me', Tutaev was continuing, 'to summarize, abbreviate and condense . . . but let me summarize, abbreviate and condense . . . what have we here? A litany of possible transgressions? Most unusual! Most fascinating! We are reminded of the castle of Sillig, aren't we? One Hundred and Twenty Days of Sodom, ladies. We are reminded of the esoteric de Blangis. Well, we are all Sadians these days, are we not, ladies? Not exactly imbued up to the hilt there, is it, ladies? Thought he'd give us an electric shock, didn't he, ladies? He mistook us all for housewives, that's what he did! But the modern housewife is a new animal. She is capable of any pleasure imaginable. She is vicious and experimental. She is bored of routines. She is after what Blangis can give her – or Mr Dak in this case. And that reminds me – Wallachia? Dak? Peasant girls?' He burst out laughing. 'Really, Sade meets Bram Stoker . . . what would the divine marquis have said? Our author is pulling our legs, ladies, beware, beware! He's being a little monkey! Oh, Mrs Betel, I see you've lost. How unfortunate. Do you want a blindfold?'

By this time he had them in stitches. Mrs Betel wiped her eyes and rolled around on her chair.

'A blindfold? A blindfold? You're the death of me, you naughty man. What do I want a blindfold for?'

'Allow me, Fraulein.'

'Oh you sly boy. Fraulein, indeed.'

He picked up the pistol for her and proffered the ivory handle. 'You spin this bit here.'

'Oh what a lark, Mr Tutaev, so I spin it, do I?'

Lullio's mouth fell open.

The palpitating housewife spun the chamber with a puggish little thumb. She put the barrel to her head, squealed and pulled the trigger.

The hammer snapped shut harmlessly.

Replacing the pistol, she took out a hand mirror and touched up her lips and cheeks. She was still shaking with laughter.

Lullio dealt the third hand.

'As I was saying,' the button merchant steamrollered on, 'it had us laughing on all fours. No doubt like me you laughed in the bath. We laughed ourselves to sleep, did we not? We've never been so amused, so titillated, so leg-pulled. Just what the jaded palette of our urban middle classes needed. We feel twenty years younger. Greased walnuts?' They roared with laughter. 'Spiked poles?' More roars. 'Nitro-glycerine?' They heaved. 'Rubber gloves?' Tears and guffaws. 'Table forks and marmalade?' Gasps. 'A wicked sense of humour, ladies! No, an impish, a mercurial, a Juvenalian, a Puckish, an operating-table, apocalypto-medical sense of humour! What a roaring gadfly he is! What a little *sal Atticum*! How our ribs ache, ladies! How permeated we are with muscular discomfort as result of our contorting, excessive and spasmic bouts of laughter! Our humorist has made his point. We are helpless on our backs. Ah, Mrs Sachs, you're unlucky today . . . a four of clubs and a seven of hearts in an otherwise commendable hand. I'm afraid it's the pistol for you, Mrs Sachs.'

Mrs Sachs was the 'fat tormentor'. She was dressed in a white lace dress that refracted sunlight to exaggerate her fatness. Trickles of sweat flowed down her bull neck. She sighed and picked up a fan. Lullio watched her gleefully, but there was no sign of panic in her face. The Spaniard had fielded two powerful hands so far and his third had not disappointed either. He winked at Lili. Third time lucky.

'Laughter excites my hormones,' Mrs Sachs declared, fanning, and wiped her neck. 'It makes me fatter.'

'Yes, Mrs Sachs, you know your endocrine system.'

She picked up the pistol and spun the chamber with a flick of her hand.

The players looked away. The fat tormentor put the barrel into her mouth, rolled her eyes and pulled the trigger.

Nothing happened.

Lullio choked and coughed violently.

'I'll deal,' Lili said.

As she threw the cards, Mrs Sachs began giggling. Her cleavage moved left and right and the small wolfish eyes spotted the Spaniard's dirty fingernails. He could not return the stares. Increasingly, he could not look any of them in the face. The failure of hands was moving inexorably around the table. None of them showed any sign of disturbance. A glass bowl of peppermint chocolates was placed in the middle of the table and the plump fingers of the housewives darted into it like painted kingfishers. They wiped their soiled fingers (the heat had made the chocolates soft) on small blue napkins as if eating a sacral meal at a wake. When they smiled their teeth were brown. What menacing edifices of chocolate and flesh, sprinkled with powders and scented insect repellents! Never had he imagined this species could be so potent close to, so inviolable and dangerous! Now he knew what they were: anthropophages. Overweight and thoughtless anthropophages. How could he have accepted to play a homicidal game with these female cannibals in flounces? And he looked down quickly at his feet. They were elephantine.

The fourth hand was even slower.

Even now his hand was not bad: a queen and a jack. The Russian did not stop talking for a minute. Beetles, soaps, volcanoes, the marquis again. 'When the marquis announced to the crowd outside his cell in the Bastille that they were going to kill the prisoners, what did he use as his megaphone? The pipe that carried his urine. Imagine, ladies, the pipe that carried the Marquis de Sade's urine and the amplification of that terrifying, original voice mixed with turds and bathwater . . . exhausting . . .'

The hands were played and another widow bit the dust.

And as before the pistol was raised, pressed against the head and the trigger pulled with no result. The game was becoming exasperating. And hours had passed. Lullio looked down at his watch: it was already five o'clock. He was feeling faint. The light over the lake was dimming, dispersing the blue butterflies and flies with it, mellowing into dull gold pools in the streets and turning a mountainside bronze. Coffee was brought up. The bowl of chocolates was replaced with a tray of pastries, puddings *à l' anglais* and rum babas. The ladies stuffed themselves with grunts. Tutaev lectured them on Mongolian polo and Lili stretched out indifferently on the bed.

She had been watching the game carefully, but at some point the collapse of Lullio had depressed her and sent her to sleep. The room became quiet. Lullio rang for sandwiches and beer. The fith hand was dealt soberly but without haste and they shifted the cards lazily, desultorily.

When the sandwiches arrived Lullio ate them savagely. He began to drink heavily as well. He played his hand before the others and sat back tensely. Tutaev followed, and then Mrs Sachs. They had beaten him. The two remaining housewives held back.

'Well? What are you waiting for?' Lullio snapped.

'We're savouring things,' Mrs Betel spat back.

'Savouring what exactly, if I may ask?'

'The moment.'

'What moment?'

His voice rose shrilly in a mad *glissando*.

'This moment.'

'And what moment is this? Are you guessing something?'

'We're savouring, Mr Lullio. That's all.'

'I would say', said Tutaev, 'that the ladies have the right to savour.'

'But savour what?'

He was almost shouting.

Lili woke up and came over from the bed.

The two withholders were grinning inanely. They held their cards coquettishly to their cleavages. The light dwindled further.

'Lay them,' Lullio ordered. 'You're not allowed to savour.'

'But we already have savoured, Mr Lullio. We have savoured it to the full.'

'They're savouring,' he said sarcastically to Lili. 'Look at them.'

But just then Mrs Betel laid her hand.

He was beaten a third time.

He turned brutally on the other.

'Go on, you stupid bitch, lay it down!'

The Russian smirked. And as he smirked the last widow laid her hand: it, too, had beaten him. Unintentionally, inflated with gaseous fear, Lullio scowled and farted.

'Oh, he farts!' Tutaev cooed, shaking his head.

Expressions of purely housewifely disgust . . .

Mrs Sachs pouted and looked down her nose at him, as if to say, he farts because he's scared.

Lullio blushed, experienced a great wave of nauseous provincialism over which he had no control and crammed a finger into his mouth, which he bit.

'It was just a game, you fools,' he snivelled. 'You all took it the wrong way. Now you expect me to put that thing against my head as if it didn't matter one way or the other, as if the world is indifferent to what goes on in this room, plus or minus on the Pepe Lullio front? I know exactly what you're thinking. Bourgeois honour. I could always refuse!'

Tutaev sighed and touched his lips.

'Mr Lullio,' he said softly but firmly, 'you're rapidly losing our respect.'

'Am I? Don't threaten me, you bastards!'

He picked up the pistol and immediately put the barrel into his mouth.

The housewives stared at him coldly.

Minutes went by. He couldn't press the trigger.

He heard them whispering, though their mouths appeared not to move.

'It's because he's more provincial than he looks . . . it's his peasant blood . . . look at his feet! What incredible, bovine feet! How can a man transcend such barbaric feet?'

The room went black.

Pressing two fingers together with all his might against the resistance trigger he suddenly moved it back, heard the click of the hammer and then nothing.

He rolled floppily on to the floor like a slapped child and curled into a ball.

And from far away Tutaev's voice floated towards him, buoyed up by its own mechanically accurate observations.

'Never seen it before. The hammer's jammed.'

'What?' Mrs Sachs. 'I demand a replay!'

'The hammer?' Mrs Betel. 'He's a Spaniard. He's rigged it!'

'No, no, it jammed spontaneously . . .'

'Pick it up.'

Lullio swung on to his knees but Tutaev already had the pistol and was turning it round thoughtfully in his hand. He pushed out the chamber in the position it had been. The bullet was in place.

'You're dead,' he whispered.

Lullio rose and then fell back again on to his buttocks. He was dead. And realizing that he was dead, with the careless-ness of the dead, he began snorting with merriment, guffawing softly to himself, grunting with accelerating laughter and then expectorating short purple bursts of intoxicated giggles. Dead! Dead as a stone! A dead provincial! Ha ha ha! The peasant as cold turkey! Magnificent opera! Swelling chords in the orchestra! Look at our humble, pink-faced, callus-handed hick reeking of grave mud and quicklime! How hilarious, ladies and gentlemen! What a dazzling *jeu d'esprit*!

And laughing with tubercular force, obliterating everything with his mortuary mirth, confessing his desperate and incurable provincialism, he suddenly forgot to exist.

VII

29

It is known that certain forms of neurosyphilis, contracted in their youth by prostitutes and libertines, are able to lie dormant in the victims for an entire lifetime before suddenly resurfacing in old age. When the disease re-appears at this great age, however, the effect of the spirochaetes stimulating the cortex is the very opposite of painful. The victims are filled with a unique intoxication. They feel rejuvenated, demented, ecstatic. They demand not to be cured but to live out this last fling of refound youth before they die: even at the age of eighty or more they suddenly feel amorous and alive . . . the cycle of the great sexual scourge so conveniently supplied by a vengeful deity turns out to be morally impish. The reprobate is rewarded, the disease – instead of cursing life – unexpectedly gives it back.

The principle is not confined to syphilis, however. Various diseases of the mind – obsessive ideologies and methodological revolt – lie dormant after the initial period of immaturity, in which they are contracted like the syphilitic spirochaetes and then, half a century later perhaps, after a long period of morose relapse, explode in the brains of old men like long-disused fireworks.

Pepe Lullio left the land of his unravelling and went back to Altafulla, the sleepy village on the coast of Catalonia, where he bought a bakery and married. His ideological intensity subsided. Dissatisfied with breads, he moved to Madrid and worked in a variety of factories. Years later, in 1936, he was working in a bottle factory when a cluster of phalangist bombs tore through the roof, smashed into the machinery and sent a large fragment of glass into his face, slicing the upper lip diagonally, giving it the appearance when it healed of a hare-lip.

During the fighting for the city he remained indifferent.

It was as if he had forgotten his abuse at the hands of the gamblers of Montreux.

The bottle factory changed places several times. At one point it was stormed and captured by the anarchists. Greeting the 'liberated' workers, an anarchist leader looked at him as if in recognition and said to his comrades: 'Hey, look, it's Garcia Ferrer, working in a bottle factory! So that's where he's been all this time!'

They crowded round and slapped his back.

'So Comrade Ferrer, how does it feel to have the blood of fascists on your hands, and so modest with it? We can't believe our eyes. Here you are making bottles, showing absolute solidarity with the proletariat as we knew you would, and they don't even recognize you. That's what we call heroic self-effacement. If only all the comrades were as iron-willed as you . . . there wouldn't even be a war!'

They asked him how long he intended to remain dormant undercover – obviously he was afraid of the shifts of territory in the city. They asked him when he would be rejoining his brigade and killing some more phalangists as only he knew how to. They praised and adulated him, cited his long list of astonishing single-handed victories against impossible odds and his luminous single acts of defiance, bravery and outright recklessness. And after a while he said: 'You're right. I've grown lazy working here at the bottle plant. I need to kill some more fascists again. As a matter of fact, I was thinking of making some grenades right now and going single handed into the phalangist lines and blowing myself up!'

'Incredible courage and self-sacrifice, Comrade Garcia!'

'My anger was building up. My indomitable defiance and inner strength were returning – I was once more feeling the necessity of risking my life every five minutes in the name of the Cause – if only there were more hours to a day, Comrades, how much greater would the purging be!'

'You're back on the warpath, Comrade Garcia: and not a moment too soon!'

It was his hare-lip that had singled him out. Garcia Ferrer of the split lip was a legend in the Madrid suburbs.

But in himself, Lullio had also felt the agitation of his long dormant disease. He remembered the face of Tutaev and Lili Dorziat's mouth. Now it was his own mouth that moved him . . . and he took off his factory apron, asked for a red and black arm band and told them all he had had his lips split by a fascist bullet.

They exited from the factory together.

But just as they were passing the main gates a cacophony of mortars and whistling shells broke out all around them and the courtyard of the factory suddenly swarmed with a hundred black shirts armed to the teeth and firing in all directions.

The anarchists broke ranks and fled. Some escaped over the walls or over a waste ground behind the warehouses; others surrendered on the spot with outstretched arms, Lullio included. They were herded back into the factory while the phalangist officers made their choices of whom to execute and whom to send back behind the lines.

The prisoners were arranged in rows. The officers walked up and down smoking cigarettes and eyeing up each face. And when they got to Lullio they stopped dumbfounded.

'Well kiss my ass, it's Garcia Ferrer! We've bagged the turkey, brothers!'

Lullio began pleading.

'It's not me,' he shouted, pulling his 'hare-line' around like a piece of plasticine, '. . . I mean, I'm not who you think I am . . . look at the lip . . . does it match Split Lip Garcia's? Look closely. I'm Lullio the bottle worker, nothing more. A piece of glass hit me in the face. It's not a hare-lip, God forbid! I grew up normal! You don't want to make a mistake, do you?'

'I don't give a shit whether we make a mistake or not,' the officer said, tapping his heel with a whip. 'And as far as I'm concerned you're Garcia Ferrer.'

'We've wanted to break your balls for years, you piece of anarchist scum.'

'Ha ha, gentlemen, brothers . . . I'm a member of the working classes, it's all a mistake . . . shoot one of them instead, the scum as you rightly say, they came breaking in here . . . just like that . . . it was a piece of flying glass . . .'

But it was no use.

He was dragged out to the waste ground by the warehouses and stood up against a wall. It was a bright day, which made him think of another bright day. He saw Tutaev's face: 'You bastard,' he said out loud. 'It's all your fault.'

The rifles fired, he slumped on to his side and died in a sitting position while overhead two vultures circled in a turning current. The phalangists had another look at his lip. Definitely the mouth of an atheist, they said, prodding it with their boots. They wouldn't want their daughters, their wives or their sisters being kissed by something like that. It was unthinkable. They shuddered, then threw a bucket of quicklime over him, slung their rifles over their shoulders and walked away.

The vultures did not descend, after all.

The author of *The Dictionary of Secret Fruits*, long out of print, had been marked out as an enemy of nature.

30

From the Branzi health resort Lili slowly drifted to Romanshorn on the Bodensee, a St Gallen clinic for an operation on her larynx and finally Milan.

She worked at the Milky Way brothel, a converted hotel with studded velvet walls and a tin-roll piano that played metallic *Liebesliedschen* through the night.

She took her promenades by the Bastione Venezia and the via Torino and on the first Wednesday of every month was inspected for signs of *Tabes dorsalis*, a disorder which nevertheless failed to appear.

The city was plunged in a proleptic terror. Plumed officers read the newspapers in the Galleria cafés with glazed and unstable eyes. The trees along the boulevards glistened as if underwater and a heated air filled with spores and grains of sulphur irritated the throats of millions of termites pouring incessantly and blindly across streets, squares and parade grounds. A bacterial vitality around the edges of an untreated wound festering in the heat of summer . . . in the claustrophobic room of the Milky Way, with its stained-glass window and silver tap, she lay on a mahogany bed listening to aged Austrian functionaries whisper about their *Torschlusspanik* – the fear of closing doors. She mopped up the sweat from their shoulders with a heated flannel. They stuffed dates into her mouth and complimented what they mistakenly called in snobbish French '*une main savante*'.

'It's not that you're the sweetest one,' they said, coughing with their glass of house vermouth while she stuck her nails into their vertebrae, 'but your mouth needs feeding, it needs pampering, it needs close attention. You were a glass blower, weren't you?'

Fusty nudges and winks.

'A pipe tester?'

Bronchial laughter.

'Come with me to Marienbad, you won't regret it. The spa
. . . the clean lungs. The minerals help me get it up – you'd be
surprised. You'll see another man.'

But she never went to Marienbad, or witnessed the amazing
properties of spa water minerals.

She stayed among the stars of the Milky Way, took her *pineau*
at the Café Carminati and waited for the aleatory colours of red
and black, the colours of a new order waiting in the wings, to
spread with bubonic speed into the streets.

'When the war comes,' the Madame opined, 'we'll be full
of eighteen-year-old peasants from Sicily smelling of piss and
garlic. The socialists will take over, punch everyone in the face
and invent a tax for brothels. Well, you're nearly thirty aren't
you, *maboule*? It's time for you to think about settling down.
Take my advice: if they want to use your mouth make them
buy you property in advance. Get them to hand over the deeds
and the keys and then let your mouth loose. They'll see eye
to eye with you. There's nothing more oppressed, elusive and
useless than a woman's mouth. In many ways, *mon chou*, it's
all a woman has. They want it because they want to soil it
– they know it's a holy organ, if you get my meaning. They
need to soil the same organ that speaks like a human being.
Ah well, I have a feeling that you're going to be lucky very
soon. Your mouth speaks volumes. They'll want it sooner or
later. It's in the air – a spin of the roulette wheel! *Bon voy-
age!*'

That very afternoon, thirteen days before war broke out, a
procurer of black-market soaps and bicycle chains named Paolo
Sainctavit called in at the Milky Way looking for 'the angel
look'. He saw Lili sitting by the mechanical piano and snapped
his fingers.

'That's the one,' he said under his breath. 'She has the malarial
air . . . a mouth of the times.'

He took her upstairs, biting his lower lip.

Why Sainctavit rather than another?

Why her face among dozens?

Why the biting of the lower lip, sign of incipient uncertainty
and nerves?

He fumbled with a tie pin. His shoes slipped on the thick stair carpet. His bow tie stuck unpleasantly to his thyroid.

In the airless room, he opened his cuffs and made a mistimed lunge for her buttocks.

It took a while, however, for his eyes to adjust to the light.

31

Slowly at first, but with gathering speed, the elements of the scene came together. The window, now opened over the street, disclosed a grey rectangle of wall and let a stream of light touch a silver tube: the tap. Yellow carpet-tassels, cushions, a pair of chamois slippers, a tub of spermicide by the bed table and next to it a fan folded up and tied with a small ivory clasp . . . one by one they came into focus, stayed obediently in their places and formed a room.

Finally there was the girl rolling down her stockings on the bed, rolling them too carefully inch by inch until they formed black rings around her ankles.

She was flicking piles of cold ash from the edges of her dressing gown and pouring some unguent ric-à-rac on to the tops of her bare legs. The shins bore the traces of shaved hairs and her nails were chipped. He stumbled to the bed, put himself next to her and laid his hand where the oil had been spilt.

'My wife's in Rome,' he said apologetically. 'I'll come every day while she's away and afterwards you can leave here if you want. I'll buy you your own place. I live in the Brera. Would near there be convenient?'

She kept oiling her legs.

'Whip?' she said. 'Harness?'

'No, nothing. I said the Brera.'

'Bring the keys first.'

'Aha.'

He couldn't resist slapping the fleshy inside of her thigh.

That was how Madame trained them all. All the same.

'I'll bring the keys.'

'When you bring the keys you can do what you want.'

'I see.'

'I want three rooms.'

'Three rooms . . .'

He chuckled.

'She wants three rooms . . .'

And after a lengthy interval of thigh-kneading: 'The war's coming and you don't want to screw soldiers. You're transparent, Signora Lili. And what colour do you want the carpets?'

The room was hotter than the street. Her face was blotched, as if in pain. On a single shelf tacked to the wall stood a china African carrying a pink parasol and a pink man on his back. The mechanical piano tinkled downstairs. The former puppet salesman and proprietor of an escort agency which was still running at a low ebb thought carefully about his future as he unpacked the lemon sherbet he had brought with him. He dusted her nipples with it and licked it up with the soft clucks of a mounted hen.

Her feet were the right parallelogram shape, each toe correctly separated cleanly from its neighbour.

The ministry employees he served with his agency would find her a change from the run-of-the-mill tart.

They might even pay more for her . . . they might pay for doing what he was doing then, lining her mouth with the lemon dust and kissing it off. A sherbet angel, a Turkish invention.

'You know, my wife, she started as a "houri" at my agency. That's what I call them. You know I run an agency?'

'The whores of paradise . . .'

'You know your mythology. Well chosen, wasn't it? Of course, the men don't guess it. They think of it as a harem.'

'You must know half the government, Signor Sainctavit.'

'Half? Half?'

He looked genuinely offended.

'Give me the credit at least of footwork!'

When they were finished she rolled upright on to her buttocks and fished out a pumice stone from under the bed with which she began to rub the soles of her feet.

As it happened, the part-time pimp had a unfulfilled affection for nature. He looked at her sentimentally. The woodland sprite. The river nymph. A suspicion of moistness rose to his eyes.

Controlling his rising nostalgia for the beauties of nature, however, he rose and went to the wash-basin and the mirror with a

165

smoked border above it. His slightly bloated and flushed face appeared unpleasantly to disrupt his visions of woodlands. He stroked his sharp stubble and stuck out his tongue.

'They say the Germans have airships,' he said dreamily. 'Zeppelins. It's going to be an aerial war. The first aerial war. People will look skyward. And when they look skyward what will they think of? They'll think of angels. They'll think of incendiary bombs and angels.'

32

At the age of forty-nine Sainctavit had reached the 'middle of life's path' and found to his alarm and displeasure that the forest around this path was not green at all, as the poet had claimed, but pink, an effete, plastic pink the colour of feminine bathrooms and decadent modernistic kitchens. In his heart the spiv longed for rustic tones, healthy landscapes and the divine colour green. But he had reached the middle of life's path and had to accept that that was not the road he had taken. His path had been, and was, theatrical and illusory; not green but profoundly pink. Looking back it appeared as a concatenation of minor accidents and coincidences. How, for example, had he started out selling women to high-ranking officials? A bracing trade. A stimulating and democratic profession. But why Paolo Sainctavit? How it was possible that so grotesque an incident could have happened to a man who at that time was dealing in international markets in nothing less than mechanical puppets he had no idea. It happened like this. One day, at the beginning of his career – in 1903 or 1904 – he had been in Berlin on behalf of the Patinkin puppet works of Lucerne negotiating a contract with a children's theatre. The firm was rich and respectable. It was anxious to make an impression. Accordingly it booked him into the most expensive hotel it could find, a place called the Renoma. He had taken a fourth-floor room. Everything was fine – he had even sold a couple of Punch and Judys to a theatre in Leipzig – when one night he went down to eat in the Renoma dining-room and suffered an extraordinary mental breakdown. Half-way through his *moules à la crème fouettée* (and he had never told this to anyone, not even to his wife) he had lost consciousness, but only for a split second – perhaps something they put in their mussels! – and when he had

167

woken up he was no longer in the dining-room, or even in the Hotel Renoma. He was in the back of a shabby suburban theatre, in the dark, clowns bawling at each other on the stage, and next to him, her legs artfully wrapped around his, sat a desperate and tearful minor actress named Lotte Zucker.

Such an amazing circumstance might not in itself have mattered (he had suffered food poisoning, delirium tremens, had walked around in a toxic trance, had lost his memory as a result and then gone to the theatre after taking a tram into the suburbs, but what could be more normal?), but the actress was in tears, stuffing a handkerchief into her face and sobbing on his shoulder. As a gentleman, even if only a fake one, what could he do but help her? They had just thrown her out of work. And he realized that he, too, since he could not possibly tell the truth to his company as to why he had failed to turn up at the critical rendezvous with the Kinderpalas's directors at half-past eight that evening, was effectively out of a job. The two of them were unemployed and stuck with one another. He nearly lost consciousness twice through grief.

But everything seemed to have been arranged in advance. He went to a friend in the business world with the minor, though extremely beautiful, Lotte Zucker. A meeting was arranged that night with a German banker. Lotte Zucker seduced him immediately and before they reached the bedroom he had given her a thousand marks in notes so new you could hardly bend them. Even divided by two, or three, that was more than his commission from the Patinkin puppet works for the deal with the Kinderpalas multiplied by four. It's curious, he thought in his thoughtless way, how things work out for the best in the best of all possible worlds. Sainctavit had landed on his feet and thanked the incompetent chefs at the Renoma for making him disappear from their dining-room.

The vertiginous world of the female then sucked him in. He set up his agency in Berlin. It processed every version of the female – the waitress, the street cleaner, the screen-test failure, the coffee girl, the tennis star, the power-station worker.

His network perpetuated itself.

In 1912 he moved back to his home country and began to subscribe to *Avanti!*.

The agency, now renamed Eroma, thrived. The artisan of

children's entertainments was at home, though the interrupted flow of his personal cash occasionally necessitated forays into the degrading soap and bicycle-chain markets.

After marrying one of his human merchandise, he settled near the Brera and collected plaster heads of Garibaldi. His head grew balder and balder, his infidelities accelerated his baldness and his baldness accelerated his infidelities, for its attraction was real to some. It was also true, however, that his baldness increased his familiarity with the cells of activists gathered around *Avanti!*, for they too found it irresistible, drawn no doubt by its similarity to the newspaper's violent editor and soon-to-be Ruler of the Italian Peoples. And so he gradually penetrated the enigma of how ageing men acquire greater and greater amounts of power, linked as this is to the hairlessness of their heads.

At the age of forty-nine, then, surrounded by the cheap pink forest of the middle of life, Paolo Sainctavit met Lili Dorziat, who knew nothing about paths, forests, baldness, middle age or the colour green.

He was seduced by her suggestion of greenness.

A glimpse of future greenness and radiant militancy, a world of tennis, harvesting machines and silent fertilizer airships nourishing fields of maize.

When war broke out, he entered her into the Eroma's books and farmed out his 'green' freshness to functionaries around the city.

She could be seen in taxis crossing and recrossing the metropolis with baskets of cinerarias.

Time and time again, his customer made a point of asking for 'the peasant'. Like her employer, they could not deny the tint of green in her skin. And as the colour grey, the colour of war and uniforms increased, so the nostalgia for the colour green – an oppressed and soothing colour uniquely attached to childhood – increased.

Once a week he climbed four flights of stairs to her apartment with a sprig of chervil in his teeth. Through the whole course of the war, his weekly appointment was never postponed. And when he looked at her face, he thought of the unbearable beauty of municipal parks. To him she was greener than a stick of celery, however pink she looked on the outside. His only regret was that he was obliged to share her. And as he passed the chervil to her mouth in the course of their kissing, he drew back, made her bare her teeth and smelt the greenness of her mouth. 'The next thing I'll know,' he said, kissing her chervilled gums, 'you'll be menstruating sap.'

To her disappointment, the Zeppelins did not appear. The front came nearer, then receded again. She continued to cross the city with baskets of cinerarias and Sainctavit continued climbing the four flights of stairs. Nothing happened; boredom increased. When the war ended he moved her to another flat and placed a Venetian table supported by four carved legs in the form of caryatidal Ethiopians in the centre of her front room.

Joss sticks burned in her bedroom at night.

Sainctavit became uneasy. He, too, was bored. He yearned for the smell of leather and jackboots.

And so a few months after the end of hostilities, the director of the Eroma agency found himself standing in a crowded hall on the Piazza San Sepolcro – it was 23 March 1919 – in the presence of the leftist congregation of Benito Mussolini. The first meeting of the Milan *fascio* was taking place and though his lazy mind was filled with memories of the chervilled gums the potency of the occasion did not fail to ignite in his heart a bilious, acidic and dyspeptic nationalism. He was converted on the spot. A new colour had come to join the colour green: black, the colour of patriotism.

Soft tears welled in his eyes.

Mother Nature . . . pasta and flags . . . chervil and gums!

His head spun and he felt faint. Mussolini was screaming at the top of his voice. Sainctavit couldn't help feeling that he too must have been familiar with teeth smeared with fresh herbs. And he too couldn't help mentioning haymaking and corn fields!

For the next three years he would put himself and his 'slice of nature' at the service of his brothers in black.

They rewarded him with increasing confidence.

Even the new order, after all, needed its secret erogenous zones.

33

In 1922, a few weeks after the March on Rome, Signora Sainctavit, who was on holiday in Bari, was stung by five wasps on the beach and was carried to hospital unconscious in a toxin-induced coma. Who could say whether her coma had been induced by the indignity of being attacked by mere insects? Whatever the reason for her lapse into unconsciousness, she did not recover from it and died the next morning at nine thirty precisely, the cause of death being given reluctantly as the wasp stings in the region of her buttocks. A sad end for a former Eroma girl, but one appropriate to her talent for burlesque parasitism.

The editors of the government press, reporting this death, incidentally extolled the virtues of marriage and reproduction and so the bereaved husband was able to marry Lili a week later in a ceremony at the church of San Satiro at which a clutch of Eroma employees wore vulgar orange dresses with carnation motifs and Lili wore a bolero embroidered with fleur-de-lys.

'Fra Filippo Lili,' Sainctavit said when he saw the official photographs, 'painter of angels by appointment. You've been created by a brush. The brothers will get a thrill cavorting with a seraph who also happens to be a wife. That's the way their tastes run . . .'

They moved into a house in the country and Sainctavit, like Lullio before him, tried to make Lili pregnant, without success. If she's not going to obey the needs of the Motherland, he thought, at least she can help with the economy. With this elevated thought in mind he set out to produce Italy's first hand-distributed pornography album, a tasteful, fanciful and cultured concoction of the best of the Eroma stable arranged in an artfully pro-fascist form and never transgressing the laws governing the determination of female virtues. The clients receiving this historically valuable document never doubted for a moment that inside every issue they would find not only the cream of the Eroma Agency but also the wife of Sainctavit himself, hopefully still dressed in the orange lace of her wedding day. Their hopes and fears were manipulated shamelessly, but all was forgiven for the former were inevitably gratified. And the more politically significant of the voyeurs began to ask themselves if it wouldn't be possible for the moral perceptions of the New Age to be made flexible for passing moments, in the way in which one cheats at cards, as a concession to the weakness of everything human . . . and in places that would be secret. Not that a wife could be leased out exactly, but Signor Fixit Sainctavit could be made to accept, perhaps, a rank in the militia, or in the newspapers, or in the radio and cinema business . . . and all for a taste of Lili's thigh, or – more precisely – Lili's green gums, which did not hesitate to reassert their charms.

Her first extra-marital affair, conducted on the shores of a small volcanic lake in the Abruzzo, was with Bartolomeo Tollini, ex-squad leader, paint salesman and later a colonel in the *bersaglieri*. He had gained prominence in the bureaucracy as a wheat inspector but then returned to the military environment, where he felt comfortable. In the summer of 1924 he drove her out of Rome, where Sainctavit had sent her, to the village of San Demetrio nei Vestini in the mountains and undressed her in the car by the lake. Next to Lili he became exceptionally unbrutal for days at a time. It was the first time she had been in an automobile and the first time a former black shirt had taken off his hat before slipping between her legs. His head was covered with hair and she ran her fingers through it with the uninterested pleasure of an Eroma employee. His thighs and buttocks might have aroused in her a passing interest had they not been corrupted by the vulgarity of parade grounds. When she returned to Milan she found that Sainctavit had been given a job in the editorial office of a fashion magazine, where with high authority he selected toothpaste advertisements and anti-radiation skin creams from America. He had been promoted in income terms. He shook her hand as she got off the train and the same day again tried to make her pregnant. In the back of his mind was the mounting tension of jealousy and he wanted to make her fat. But his semen was no more successful than before and within six months he had to lease her out again, this time to someone considerably more important.

Carlo Licata was the director of a Milan hosiery firm. He had helped to bribe Lusignoli, prefect of Milan, when the latter had received orders from Rome to arrest Mussolini the day before he had taken power. His dark brown, lilac and black stockings could be seen in a thousand bedrooms, easing the achievement of an ever-increasing population. Like Tollini he took Lili to a lake, although he had only to drive north to Garda. At the Grand Hotel Salò he presented her with a pair of his finest elasticated silk model in 'mulberry black'. Sainctavit's prophecies regarding the taste for angelic mistresses were proving themselves correct.

'Put them on,' Licata said, breathless under his double chin. 'Your legs are going to look more whorish than your stupid little husband ever imagined!'

From Licata she progressed to other patrons.

Within a week she was in the Alps with Teodoro Sforza, academic specializing in naval history and nautical clocks. An adviser to the navy, his respectability came into tantalizing conflict with her underwear. They tussled with unseemly haste in a chalet bedroom in the Val d'Aosta while Sforza lectured her on the recent evolution of torpedoes. She cut off his little goatee beard with a pair of scissors and so inflicted scandal upon his face, which was forced to return to Milan in a state of horrible embarrassment.

'You went too far with Sforza's beard,' Sainctavit told her in irritation. 'The man who is going to revitalize the Italian navy has no need of forced shavings at this point in his career. You should think before you cut off beards. Think of the sub . . .'

But he could not say the word.

Lili explained limply: 'His face was too . . . ordered. I had to adjust it. It needed a dose of sub . . .'

'Don't say it! Don't say that word! I'm going to choose the next one carefully. He will resist any attempt at sub . . .', he caught himself and bit his tongue. 'Don't even try it. He's a civil servant. If you try it he'll report us both to the Gerarchia.'

Simone Pricolo took her to Bordighera and asked her to ride him around the garden with a pair of steel spurs tied to her feet. When his secretary peeped into his bathroom and saw him asleep in the bath covered with cruel circular weals, his imminent disgrace roused Sainctavit to a hysteria of fear and anxiety.

'So, once again! A man close to the central committees ridden with a pair of spurs by a hired whore, subjected to a total sub . . . ah there I go again . . . we know what we are talking about . . . the Premier will intervene and I will be', and he forced out the word with grievous irony, '*restrained.*'

But, to his surprise, he was promoted instead to the editorship of a woman's magazine with a national circulation: *Clara*. So he had been wrong about his myth of nature. She had fuelled his upward propulsion. And lying on top of his Lili who had denied him the further bonus of offspring, though still trying to make her pregnant, he could not help pouring out his praise lyrically into her ear.

'You are the purest green,' he said tenderly. 'You are the green of green, greener than leaves, greener than the greenest of greens. My greenest of green spirits . . .'

But he knew as well as anyone else that the only part of her that was green was her eyes. And even then, they had certainly once been blue.

34

When she was asleep he felt her belly for tumescence. But the Earth Mother was refusing to be anything but sterile.

'You don't seem to understand', he complained gently, 'that the State wants and needs children. Children, did you hear? We have to perform our duties. Are you holding something back? Haven't thought properly about getting yourself pregnant with a miniature Sainctavit? I hope you're not being vain. I'm surprised you think you can live for something else. Imagine all the babies you could produce if you wanted to. Think of the names we'll give them . . . Rafael and Rufio and Benito . . . I would say, my darling, if I could summon up a stern voice: open your legs!'

'But they're always open,' she said calmly.

'Open but not welcoming. Not . . .', his face went sickly green, '. . . co-operative.'

Unsatisfied, he had her examined by one of the city's best doctors.

The gynaecologist pronounced her normal, except that – he pulled at his mouth with embarrassment – it appeared that, how could he say?, her hymen was still in place.

'In other words, she's a virgin.'

Sainctavit laughed.

'Lili?'

'The hymen has not been punctured. It also appears to be extremely tough.'

'It would have had to be,' Sainctavit blurted out and then restrained himself. He mopped his temples. He had not expected this with the hymen.

'But I don't feel anything,' he protested. 'There's nothing tough there. I swear to you . . .'

175

But the doctor insisted: he had touched it with his finger.

'It's impossible,' the editor said. 'She's holding something back.'

'It's possible she doesn't want children, Signor Sainctavit.'

'But that would be contrary to the ethos of the age! She has a secret somewhere.'

'All women have one somewhere,' the doctor echoed, as if he knew.

'But having secrets is also contrary to the ethos of the times. There can be no secrets between husband and wife. I'm going to have to watch her. They're clever with their secrets. I know. I am, you know, something of an expert in their secrets. And when it comes to the womb . . .'

He began to spy on her from that day, although he had to admit to himself that he could not feel any hymen at all – he would have wanted to shine a torch up there just to make sure, but whatever secret she was holding against him he had no desire to treat her with anything but the respect due to the mother. Otherwise she would cease to be 'green'.

In 1928 he bought her a new house in the Brianza hills near the city and supervised the building of it himself. It was a chocolate-coloured Swiss chalet with three floors fitted with electric bells, a spruce bathroom with sauna, an American kitchen and an old Fabergé chrysoprase telephone with bells. The open plan of the structure, developed by its Swedish architect, was designed to put the dweller into spontaneous contact with the changing tempos of nature. On the Art Deco bed – his concession to her taste – he groped around for the hymen inside her and deposited his seed anyway in the hope that the doctor had been hallucinating. Three years passed in the Brianza in these procreative rituals, in the course of which her sterility remained inscrutable. He built a children's room decorated with plastic ducks and frothy cots and every Christmas he made a special effort to deny the existence of her unbreakable hymen. When he failed in all his attempts, he became convinced that she was deliberately denying him a blond boy with a firm chin and a genetically inbuilt Roman salute.

She was taking medications she hadn't let him see.

She was denying the right of the Duce to Lombardic children!

His mind began to spiral into the occult, the only way her will to childlessness might be broken against her own desire.

★

It was strange that a woman should not spontaneously combust into fertility, child-bearing and breast-feeding in the Empire of Green but shortly after he had realized the scale of the abnormality, another abnormality altogether visited him in the form – could it be believed in this healthy and ecologically harmonious environment? – of a small, compressed but virile pustule with a vivid white tip (looking for all the world like a miniature Mount Fuji) on the extremity of his chin.

All his life he had been free from these disgusting entities, cryptic and loathsome signs of a half-disgraceful immaturity. And not only that but the boil which had raised itself on his chin had taken on, mockingly and insolently, the same colour green at its base as the life-giving photosynthesizing leaves that surrounded him in his chosen paradise.

With the properties of a conscious chameleon, it thrust itself into the light of day!

He examined himself in the mirror and touched the carbuncular tip with his forefinger. It resisted the most insistent pressure. It could not be depressed inwards or in any other way modified by touch. It was as hard as a pebble. And beneath its peak of inflamed skin could be seen a sullen lake of pus mustering in the depths of his head.

'I'm becoming an adolescent again,' he said wearily, and thought about lancing it himself. A well-known fascist cannot walk around with a minor carbuncle blazing in the middle of his face. It is vulgar to decline. It is vulgar to decay or regress into adolescence.

Sainctavit quickly realized that the boil expressed in a treacherous way all the vulgarity transmitted from Lili's lips to his heart – and also to her womb. It was as if they had both become children again. And if they were children, naturally she would be infertile and he would have a boil on his chin. It was infuriatingly clear.

At first he resorted to medicine to extricate himself from his accelerating childishness. He summoned a doctor who had once treated his mother for worms, although it was true that he was half Jewish – fortunately only on his father's side.

'It's not that I'm afraid of being laughed at . . . more that . . . that some kind of disaster is going to happen because of it. They are going to ridicule me if it doesn't go away, of course, but I also have reason to believe that', he paused in embarrassment, '. . . that my wife is going to remain infertile because of it.' And he hastily added, 'I mean because she will, naturally, refuse to sleep with me in this condition – and who can blame her? And since the Party has, as you know, declared it a duty of every citizen to reproduce, you can see how important it is that the boil here in question be lanced with or without an anaesthetic.'

'Excuse me?' the doctor said, alarmed.

'Yes, the boil must disappear if the Sainctavit line is to continue and the nation thrive. Besides, I feel stupid . . . I . . .'

The doctor was not so enthusiastic. The carbuncle was a tremendous specimen. It was so (he could not help the word occurring to him) vulgar. Couldn't it be preserved and displayed on his laboratory shelves, bringing students of epitheliology from all over Italy to his feet? This was no ordinary pustule. He trembled with excitement when he touched it. It was like touching a woman's naked leg. He saw what the editor meant.

'But are you sure that it is advisable? A fever may come on.'

'I feel naked. I feel everyone looking at it as if I were exposed. As if I had a smudge of lipstick on my chin. I feel . . . prostituted.'

'. . . !'

'I'm a tart. That's what it's making me. I'm a stupid little tart. My boil is turning me into a tart.'

The doctor broke into a schoolgirlish laugh.

'Don't exaggerate,' he snivelled, 'don't exaggerate. Wrong sex.'

'Sometimes I look in the mirror and I think it's growing into the shape of a . . . of a . . .'

'It's round, like a boil should be.'

'Imagine me at the office. The clerks . . . you know the kind of minds they have. It won't matter what I do or how I'm dressed. All they'll see is the boil. A man with a boil. Horror.'

'Can it be possible', the doctor changed tone circumspectly, 'that your life style is, in some way unknown to you, to blame?'

'What? My life style?' His fascist integrity was suddenly threatened – and by a half-Jew! 'All I try to do is fertilize my bride. Is that to blame for a boil?'

The doctor smirked.

'You mean . . .'

'Sexual infections, my dear boy,' and he touched his nose with his finger in a nudging way. 'You don't know anything.'

'You . . .'

The doctor started tapping his head. And as he tapped Sainctavit heard a small noise inside his own head, an echo within a small military drum.

'It's all', the doctor said while tapping, 'in the head. It's . . . all . . . in . . . the . . . head.'

'The greenness,' Sainctavit said helplessly.

As everyone knew, green was the colour of syphilis.

In the spring edition of *Clara* for April 1931 Lili appeared on the front cover in a bathing suit. The headline next to her short hair: 'The Purple Light of Youth'. Inside, on page thirteen, under a half-page photograph of the Duce sprinting through a field of maize with a squad of plumed generals along a phalanx of saluting hands and another stripped to the waist out-jogging a bunch of air force officers on the beach at Ostia, she appeared again at the opening of a children's home in nearby Varese. 'Mrs Sainctavit the editor's wife and the Prince Massima enjoy a lemonade at the paraplegic children's party.' She is smiling happily, looking far less than her years. The prince, perhaps aware of her age, is admiring the immature glossiness of her skin with a look of astonishment.

There is not a hint of syphilis in her eyes.

She has the same complexion as the children around her.

And seeing this, her husband – who had chosen the photographs himself – touched the tip of his chin and dreamt of lancing, not the pustule at its tip, but the beautiful and swollen mouth that had caused it.

Within a week of the appearance of these two photographs the editor was besieged by written requests from the coquettish and *bella figura* obsessed housewives of the Italian peninsula to explain the powerful attraction – seeming to emanate from the wide lips and the angle of the smile – of that very same mouth. The beauty editors explained in return that this fullness of mouth, simultaneously immature, maternal and insolent, was in all probability the result of a carefully planned, nutritious fascist diet which eschewed all forms of gastronomic eclecticism and foreign imports and relied instead on the wholesome and culturally patriotic staples of rice, pasta and cold-pressed oil.

So, they said, now you know how to achieve the perfect mouth.

Thousands of letters poured in . . .

179

Sainctavit did not know what to say.

His bitterness increased as the greenness of the base of his bubo spread outwards to other parts. His doctors told him his symptoms were those of *Treponoma pallidum* but that the green patches did not – pathologically – fit in. Known chancres did not behave in that way. With the exception, in fact, of two or three normal, though shallow, tumours along his thighs which could be passed off as classical syphiloma, none of his symptoms were predictably syphiloid. And the unfortunate bearer of these medically uncertain stigmata could think of nothing else to do but murder his wife.

There was his jealousy – and the colour of jealousy is green. Syphilis, jealousy, nature. The three joints of his inner structure.

He began to keep a long piece of rope under his bed. He had not planned any exact use for it but its presence reminded him of the possibility of violent exits from his encirclement.

To get in practice, he crept up to her when she was asleep, the rope in his hands, and tied it round her throat. But his readers had voted her Ideal Fascist Woman of 1931! He had to stop himself and unwrap the rope.

The rope was tied and then untied a hundred times.

And how serenely fascist she looked when she was asleep, her black mouth half open and her muscular calves spread at a wide angle underneath him! She was a model black shirt, a *squadrista*, a perpetrator of future *Kristallnachts*!

In the year 1932, as her stomach remained flat and sterile and her hymen refused to move, the pornographic élan of the favourite of the fascist élite assumed for a brief and exhilarating period an international dimension.

35

Anatomy of the kiss II

Forty years later, a member of the Western intelligentsia was heard to remark, 'I've touched the hand which has touched the hand of Fidel Castro!' The tone of the voice was unmistakable: hushed awe, pleasure of self-anointment by vicarious contact with the Supreme Leader's body. But what if the star-struck radical had had to say, 'I've touched the mouth which has touched the mouth of Fidel Castro'? The hand, yes, the cheek perhaps . . . but mouth to mouth?

No, he would not have boasted about that to the comrades.

When the mouth touches the mouth, too many things are exchanged . . .

The kiss is a minefield.

One night, at the house of Prince Borghese (the man who would later terrorise the country at the head of the infamous Decima Mas private army) a certain Amadeo Trabalza, a confidant of the prince and an amateur expert of Japanese *shunga*, placed his mouth against that of one of the female guests, the wife of a magazine editor, and immediately wiped his lips with his sleeve when he felt himself – as a result of this half-drunken intimacy – becoming, in an ineluctable but definite way, pornographic.

He recoiled at once and went upstairs to the bathroom. He looked at himself in the mirror. Yes, his face looked sluttish! He covered his mouth with soap and scrubbed it with a flannel, then descended again, sure that he had wiped away any remaining trace of pornography.

As soon as he was in the garden, however, the guests began tittering.

The prince came over.

'I'm sorry to say it, old man,' he said, 'but your face looks

181

like hell. It looks like a girl's bottom. What's the meaning of it?'

'A . . . you're pulling my leg, Prince. A girl's posterior, Prince?'

'It's an arse all right. Pink and fat.'

Trabalza reached up and touched his face: it was . . . how could it be? . . . rounded, hairless and obscene like a pair of female buttocks. When he moved, it wobbled like a well-developed butt.

'I was sure I'd washed it,' he muttered feebly, retreating in panic. 'So it's still there, is it? A pair of buttocks, eh? I didn't mean to kiss, but now you're pulling my leg . . . all right, if you want me to leave, it's nothing to me . . . I know a face can't be an arse and vice versa. I did science at school!'

Trabalza was shocked. He went home in a taxi and locked himself in his bathroom. He steamed his face all night. His reflection in the mirror was normal, however – the posterial suggestions of his face were a matter purely of the way in which it was viewed. Tilted up or down all might be changed. Then again, a different parting, a spot of grease . . . anything could account for the simulacrum of a female backside.

At dawn he went outside on to the deserted streets. He wanted to test his steam technique on powerless individuals rather than on menacing crowds. Carefully and fearfully, he crept down to the Galleria and stopped at the Café Beffi. It was deserted, the waiters setting out the first tables of the day. But as he continued down the arcade a figure approached from the opposite direction. It was a tramp staggering home from a night on the bottle.

They came to within a few yards of each other, Trabalza nervous to see what the hobo's reaction to his face would be and the tramp oblivious until the last moment when, within inches of the art historian, he gave a start, recoiled, swayed and wiped his mouth.

Amazement was written on the down and out's face.

Louche spasms shot through it.

'It can't be . . .', he mumbled, wiping his mouth a second time. 'At last, my lucky day! At dawn, too, in the Galleria . . .'

Trabalza stood right in front of him.

The tramp chuckled deliriously.

'Aren't you cold, honey?' he cooed.

'Cold?'

'I know what you want. Let me tell you, sister, you came to the right person. But shouldn't we . . . er . . . we . . .'

He winked and cocked his head.

'Shouldn't we . . . eh?'

Trabalza frowned. The tramp took a step forward, squinting uncertainly, as if what he saw couldn't be real . . . no, not just a woman, in the flesh alone with him at dawn, not just a woman, but a naked one too.

'I warn you,' he burbled playfully, 'I'm going to pinch you, yes I am, I'm going to make you black and blue, I'm . . .'

Trabalza stepped to the right; the tramp stepped to the right with him; Trabalza stepped to the left; the tramp imitated.

'Now, now, stop trying to get away . . . you took your panties off in front of me, not the other way round. No time for dishonesty.'

And lurching forward he planted a hot alcoholic kiss on Trabalza's mouth.

The historian retched with disgust, retreated and spat. And yet as soon as he had been kissed he felt a burden leaving his face. It felt lighter and more natural. He touched it to find that it was once more a man's face, reasonably formed and furnished with stubble.

'I've passed it on,' he thought to himself, looking over at the varicose face of the tramp and suddenly seeing the female backside he had formerly felt attached to his own face.

The tramp, too, saw the change. The 'backside' vanished and in its place stood the tall, haggard art historian, peering at him.

'Where's she gone?' he murmured. 'The naked tart . . . ?'

'You've made a mistake, sir.' Trabalza relished his cruel superiority achieved with a single kiss. 'The naked tart is you.'

'Me?'

He took a look at himself in a shop window.

'That's not me,' he whispered, incredulous. 'I'm still pissed. I'm going home.'

And turning on his heel, he staggered off.

It seemed, then, as if the kiss had acquired a life and objective existence of its own. It flew from mouth to mouth, adhered to faces in the form of a scatological illusion and exchanged host bodies through the momentary synapse of an embrace.

The tramp too went home under a bridge, lay down and fell asleep, unsure how real the ugly feeling of his face was.

A day and a night passed.

When he woke he found himself surrounded by leering schoolboys. They had found him dozing in his sheets of newspaper and took him for something else altogether.

Their lecherous and pimply schoolboy consciences were stimulated to the point of abuse by the pair of firm and uncovered buttocks that they had stumbled across so luckily spread out in a bale of newspaper.

'You go first,' one of them sneered.

'No, you go first.'

'What's the matter, never seen one before?'

'I saw one in the swimming pool cubicles.'

'Not as good as this one.'

'Nah. This one's a real cracker.'

'The one I saw was rounder.'

'But this one's all alone.'

They stared at it in fascination.

But at this point the tramp woke up and yawned, rubbing his chin with his elbow. Seeing the schoolboys all around him he scowled and got up.

'Twenty lire,' the boys said.

'What?'

'Twenty lire for a hand job.'

'You . . . twenty?'

The unacceptable truth dawned upon him. He raised his fist and lashed out. The boys scattered laughing and hurled stones at him. He chased them into a large street. And the passers by, to their disgust, saw only a naked female anatomy chasing a handful of jeering schoolboys. They called on the police to arrest her.

Passengers in a passing tram cheered.

'Keep them off!'

The tramp reeled, unable to grasp his situation. Covering his face with his hands he left the street in tumult and made his way to a hostel he knew and forced his way in, despite its being an all-male establishment. The nuns who ran it came chasing after him. 'Get out of here, Satan!' they shrieked.

Running to the rear of the building, which he knew intimately, he exited by a back window and made his way along a precarious ledge overlooking a municipal cistern filled with a foot of green water.

His despair had reached intolerable proportions.

'I'm already dead,' he said to the sisters as they appealed for him to come down. 'It happened in the Galleria. I would have been happy reincarnated as a dog. But no, I must have done something worse than I remember . . . I came back as a woman! But now I know what death's like, I can do it twice.'

And so saying, he jumped off the wall.

As he hit the concrete base of the cistern the sisters had run shouting into the street. They flagged down a taxi. In the taxi was a world-famous American swimmer named Arnold Wangler.

'A tramp has fallen in the cistern', they yelled, 'and has to be resuscitated.'

Wangler jumped out of the taxi, ran to the window, tied four sheets together and let himself down to the cistern. The tramp was moaning. It was case of immediate mouth-to-mouth resuscitation.

But as Wangler pressed his mouth knowledgeably against the tramp's, he suddenly forgot about the latter's pale but slowly reviving face. He was more concerned with his own. It was changing shape. In disgust, he wiped his lips. But too late.

When he re-entered the taxi, he did so with smile that was nothing if not whorish.

By means of the immaculate physique of the champion Wangler, the kiss was soon able to leave its country of origin and begin a gradual circumnavigation of the globe, for the swimmer was already booked on to a ship for his return home and within a week was half-way across the Atlantic. But the kiss did not manifest itself immediately. The strength of the American's face subdued it. It lay dormant in his lips ready to infect the mouth it would kiss.

Wangler had a fiancée. He dreamt about her every night. She was everything he wanted: oh, the rosebud lips! Oh, the blossoming virginity! Oh, the intact thighs imbued with the soft and yielding wifeliness of apple pies!

Oh, June was a perfect fiancée, a rich father and a facility with the gymnastic horse, a good top spin on her nevertheless submissive and charmingly losing serve, a little compact bun on her head, mobile and moist eyelids, a popinjay of a tongue and an abacus head for figures. June, June, June! Pulpy, mild, soapy, ovary-filled June with her pockets filled with tablets of chewing gum and some limey scent in her armpits. What more could he want? What more could he ask to kiss? Her lips . . . his lips . . . lips all round, kisses, kisses and more kisses until kisses made Wangler juniors.

She was waiting for him on the harbour front at New York. They ran to greet each other. Her blonde bun was down in tresses. A golden vision. June filled with microscopic babies waiting to be activated by kisses. And so, falling with chirps and sighs and blubbers into each other's arms, they kissed.

But as he kissed her mouth, his beloved fiancée disappeared before his very eyes.

He took a step back to get a look at her.

He frowned.

'What've you done to your hair, sweetheart?'

She was taken aback.

'Why nothing. I thought you liked it like this.'

'It must be the hair, but . . .'

He fell deep in thought.

'I can put it back if you want.'

'Perhaps it's not the hair after all.'

Plunged into a bad mood, he sulked all the way into the city. The more he looked at her the more . . . cheap she looked. Her charm had evaporated. This was not how he had remembered her at all. It couldn't be. He studied her in amazement: she was a tart, a tart, his June, his tennis partner, his portable ovaries, his pumping womb.

Furiously, he called off the engagement.

She must have been seeing other men!

'Or else', he suggested subtly, 'you had some homosexual surgeon do something to your mouth. It looks all wrong.'

The formidable athlete was quoted in the newspapers.

His golden vision had dimmed . . . her mouth had gone haywire.

'You know me, guys,' he said to the reporters (sighing and raising his eyebrows), 'I wouldn't marry anything less than perfect.'

Thinking of her face, he could not bring himself to use the word 'anyone'.

And the vestal June, realizing her husband-to-be considered her face inferior to his, began drinking heavily and sleeping in the street.

Six months passed.

She deteriorated and ended up homeless.

Wherever she went, men asked her 'how much it was'. Her father lost all trace of her. She lived in a Salvation Army hostel and felt herself gravitating towards everything her future husband had accused her of being.

Then one night, as she was walking in the Bowery an old blind man with a white tin cup and a grotesque sore on his forehead, feeling her slip past him, caught hold of her wrist and asked her for a kiss in exchange for the dime he had just earned.

The blind man's face was split open on one side by a two-inch scar. He came up only to her shoulder. Taking pity, and needing the dime, she bent down and kissed him on the lips.

Carried in the improbable form of a blind man's mouth, Lili's kiss made its way from there to the mouth of a small girl by the name of Teresa de Trentville who, out for a walk in Central Park with her mother, mistook him for a shaved, naked poodle only realizing at the last moment – as her mother impatiently slapped her wrist – that the soft pink thing she so much wanted to kiss was in fact the buttock of an exposed woman begging for dimes on a park bench.

'I've told you not to go near those kinds of woman,' her mother scolded. 'Especially when they're exposed.'

But the child had apparently already been corrupted.

Why, she looked like a piece of thigh herself!

The mother raced her home at once, tucked her in bed and called the doctor.

'What are the symptoms?' the doctor enquired when he arrived.

The mother was wrongfooted.

'Well, I can't say exactly. You see she went up to this naked whore in the park and kissed her backside, God knows why, I can't think what she was doing unless . . .'

A vision of lesbian communion.

'At such a young age, it can be stopped, can't it – they have a new drug in Switzerland don't they . . . made with green clay?'

'But why is she sick?'

'Look at her yourself, doctor.'

The doctor peered through the door. He saw a voluptuous female behind nestling on a frilled child's pillow.

'I see. Is she doing it deliberately?'

'She's sick, doctor. That backside gave her a virus. Can't you give a shot of penicillin?'

'I have no idea . . . it's incredible.'

'And what's her father going to say?'

Her father, a wealthy surgeon with a healthy dislike for the female anatomy and its ramifications, prided himself on the vacant girlishness of his one and only daughter and when he returned home from work he liked nothing better than to creep into her room, bend down in the dark, and steal a father's kiss from his sleeping princess.

The light had been left off that night and so his kiss took place as usual while the trembling mother waited in the next room. But when he emerged he was everything that his daughter had been moments before.

A vicious pornography flowed from his lips.

'She seemed a little hot,' he said. 'Was anything wrong?'

'It's nothing,' the disorientated mother whispered before she fainted.

'There's been an epidemic of backsides in the neighbourhood.'

'What crazy minds women have,' de Trentville mused as he took a taxi that night to the airport. He was flying to Hawaii to perform a facial lift on a wealthy islander. And yet the reflection of his face in the plane's washroom mirror had – to his consternation – ceased to be American. It was a face that was normally cemented together by a national physiognomic integrity, but since he had left his wife and child, perhaps since he had been in the bedroom with his daughter, it had succumbed to a traitorous anti-Americanism. De Trentville of New York with an unAmerican face, a face ludicrous, exhibitionist and – if it could be put that way – decked out in stockings and suspenders?

'An epidemic of backsides.'

He repeated his wife's peculiar phrase to himself.

As a surgeon he considered the possibility in rational terms.

To begin with the face is not part of the body like any other. It is, for example, far more elusive than the brain. It is possible

188

to weigh the brain so we can say, 'The average brain weighs between 1,200 and 1,400 grammes.' We can also say that Anatole France had a cerebral organ weighing one kilogramme while Ivan Turgenev had one weighing half a kilogramme. We can separate – physiologically – a talented brain from an ordinary brain. The brain, contrary to myth, is relatively simple to quantify, or will be with time and the astonishing progress of that branch of science which was once known as phrenology. But take the face: how much does a face 'weigh'? What does a face consist of? The face is the result of ceaseless interpretation, it has no physical reality at all. And if this is true of the face why should it not also be true of the backside? The backside, like the face, is the product of ceaseless interpretation. And to go further . . . if we grant this, is it not also undeniable that faces and backsides are interchangeable, that a backside can replace or be mistaken for a face and vice versa without the intervention of any medico-physical disaster? Why is it so surprising that the order of a face should be dissolved by a kiss and replaced with the corollary order of a displaced backside?

And, the surgeon thought, if my face is patriotic, American and harmonious with the stars and stripes, it is also true that nothing guarantees that it should remain patriotic, American and harmonious to the star-spangled banner. It could change sex, nationality, race . . . or turn itself into a backside. And why not a black, female, Puerto Rican backside? It could be any backside, it could be a compendium of backsides. It could simply insinuate a backside.

And as a backside it could do everything that a face does, except that the normal order of the personality would dislike its unaccustomed position on top of it instead of below it.

De Trentville thus came to the admirable conclusion that epidemics of backsides are possible and indeed frequent enough. He came to terms with the backside/face inversion and landed in Hawaii with peace of mind.

He performed the operation on his client and then, at a hotel reception ceremony complete with plump dancers in straw skirts, transmitted the vagrant kiss to one of them before flying home the next morning. And from the dancer, who carried the kiss with a certain gravitas, it made its way to the mouth of a Filipino sailor, who took it to Hong Kong, where it changed hands several times in the red light district before finding passage on a banana ship steaming back to Mogadishu. And from Mogadishu, flying from labourers to 'port wives' to cocoa company clerks to colonial officials, it made its way through Africa spreading chaos, revolution and confusion in its wake until it came to Alexandria and from Alexandria, winging its way across the Mediterranean in an Italian warship it arrived back in the land of its birth, flew up the excellent motorway system and made a triumphal entry back in Milan, where it took less than three days to re-alight upon the mouth of Lili Dorziat, who welcomed it back and there and then made a resolution not to let it out of her sight again, even if Prince Borghese himself, the future leader of the infamous Decima Mas private army, abandoned all principle and asked her personally to lend it to him for a while.

In the end, she said to herself correctly, a kiss belongs with the mouth that gave birth to it.

In this way, for the sake of convenience, modesty, an efficient economy and the overall greater happiness of the human race, the conversion of faces into backsides can be avoided . . .

36

The summer of 1932 was a hot one. A climate of physical fitness and hygienic nudity descended upon the provinces. In the calm and blue days of May the local Party at Monza received a letter from the Ministry of the Interior in Rome. It read: 'Please expect Chief Ideology Officer Prof. M. Tasso for a lecture on "Physical Integrity and the Self-sufficiency of the Masses" on the 23rd at eight o'clock. We expect accommodation for the professor and his wife and five assistants. You will also be expected to provide an acceptable public venue equipped with slide projector and blackboard and to ensure a good attendance from the local population. All uniforms to be worn as usual. *Viva il Duce!*"

Sainctavit was thrown into simultaneous bliss and electrification. Matteo Tasso was author of *Roman Youth* and the monograph *Mars and His Children* and inventor of the Higher Duty: Sainctavit had read everything, he had them all in his domestic library, he had soaked up every exclamation mark. Tasso's photograph appeared often in the pages of *Il Popolo*, a fox-like head with steel-rimmed glasses and a spade-shaped white beard. Hearing the news of his imminent arrival the following week, Sainctavit drove home and locked himself up with the professor's works, four two-inch volumes in all, ranging from articles on the destiny of Aosta (a subject dear to the Duce's heart) to the Mesoamerican indian origin of syphilis.

He came out refreshed and invigorated.

'The body is a temple in the grove of Mars,' the professor wrote, in high-fascist style, 'and if its altars are not kept burning, faith in its virginal beauty will fade as surely as winter comes.'

Such sublime and chaste poetry!

Such moist and patriotic dithyrambs!

Sainctavit regretted that he had not had a gym built into his ideal house. The greenness of nature should properly be complemented by the ellipsoid shape of Roman arm muscles. The professor urged the urban dregs to launch themselves into heroic self-immolations of collective agrarian endeavour, marathons of reaping and semi-mechanical threshing which would both feed the bulging pregnant peasant girls who were the nation's 'spinal column' and send a disinfected broom crashing healthily through the fetid brains of all smoke-stack intellectuals and partisans who had not yet availed themselves of the Duce's fraternal advice to get their backsides out of café chairs and into leather tractor seats.

Above all, Tasso's notion of the Higher Duty held that the instant readiness to sacrifice one's physical comfort or survival to the Party, which constituted the most valuable form and expression of the Higher Duty, could be read in the physiognomy of the true acolyte. His face would immediately reveal his readiness or his lack of it. Faces were either 'pure, direct and undistorted' or 'vaguely reminiscent of the cunning of Moses'.

But did mirrors tell the truth?

Sainctavit was convinced that overall his face conformed to the professor's desideratum, or at least the mirror told him so. There was only one problem, but a terrible one: the boil.

He backtracked through Tasso's texts to find any mention of skin blemishes but none could be found. What, then, was the Party line on carbuncles? The professor didn't even raise the possibility of the existence of such defects in the ideal martial face. It could only be inferred that these phenomena were alien to the 'pure, direct and undistorted face'. In other words they could not be accommodated within the ideological context of modern reality. And since in this case the green base of the pustule gave hints of wider disorders, the urgency of its removal was much greater.

There was no prospect of lancing it, which in any case at such short notice would leave ugly scars. Make-up could not hide it either. If they had given him more notice he could have grown a beard, but all he would have after a week would be a wretched shadow of half-baked bristles unable to cover the outermost tip of the boil. In short, there was only one solution. He would have to invent an excuse for an elaborate poultice.

He soaked the poultice in camphor and coffee and attached it by means of two pieces of surgical plaster. Suddenly the feeling of nudity that had plagued him for so many weeks disappeared. He felt 'dressed' once more. The square of white linen certainly disrupted the masculine lines of his face, but it did so in a way that was untainted by nudity. Immensely relieved, he wrote back to the Ministry in Rome: 'All arrangements made, await with fervour and anticipation the arrival of our distinguished visitor.'

And to Lili he said: 'Keep that mouth of yours under control. No flirting with the guest. No overtures,' he rolled the vowels contemptuously. 'Remember the professor is a stern customer. The inventor of the Higher Duty will not appreciate a wanton mouth . . . I mean, a face that is not organized and well in control of itself.'

'But', she said, 'can you really be talking about a face?'

And burst out laughing.

'It may seem absurd to you,' Sainctavit exploded, 'but let me assure you that for Professore Matteo Tasso faces are not a laughing matter. In this country now the wrong kind of face can get you sent to the concentration camp.'

And with a twinge he touched the sensitive tip of his boil under its swathing of perforated cotton and linen. With dismay he noticed that every two hours or so a kind of yellow stain appeared at the centre of the dressing, indicating that the infernal thing was leaking in some way, spoiling its disguise with traces of serum. There was nothing to be done but change it ceaselessly and punctually. Hence the emergence of a damp patch had to be verified every now and then with his finger. Only when the dressing had been changed and the boil swabbed with iodine did he feel that his 'clothes' had been laundered and that he was once more presentable.

When the morning of the professor's arrival came he dressed up for the first time in months in his immaculate black uniform with a felt beret carrying a metal eagle badge and a leather strap crossing his torso diagonally and his dressing neatly held in position by two gleaming strips of plaster, around which he had shaved that morning with extraordinary skill and daring. As the morning train from Rome pulled in he catapulted himself forcefully through the billows of steam in order to be the first at the bottom of the small wooden steps that a committee member carried before him. He had organized the welcoming band himself, and its assorted dented tubas and trumpets started up with a rousing rendition of the famous *squadristi* song which the assembled Party members filled in with robust voices:

Siamo i fascisti
Il terrore dei communisti!

The train stopped, the band rose to a crescendo and the door was flung open to reveal a grubby little man in a stained suit peering drily out at the crowded platform. The wooden steps were placed under his feet. Sainctavit saluted so violently he pulled a muscle in his triceps and the face of Professor Tasso – smaller and even more fox-like behind its steel-rimmed spectacles – cast a half-mocking look over his face.

'Welcome, Professore, your always avid readers and admirers are honoured.'

'Viva il Duce!'

'The steps, Professore . . .'

Tasso looked down and remembered his feet. He descended anxiously, wobbling and cursing. An assistant carried a beaten-up old briefcase behind him. The professor seemed displeased. Sainctavit touched his dressing, but found that it was in order. The official car drove them back to the Party HQ, where the severe visitor poured himself a glass of mineral water and wiped the insides of his glasses with his elbow. Sainctavit could not help his disappointment: Tasso had all the mannerisms of Italian academics of the 1920s, beards, steel rims, grey suits, insufferable endless quotations, tobacco-stained fingertips, an unbearable armoury of physical and mental pedantry, a pedantry so dense, impenetrable and solid that it sank every five minutes under its own weight. He went home and asked Lili to wear a veil.

For weeks beforehand the Party members had been rallying the masses and so the improvised lecture hall was filled to capacity to hear the disquisition of Matteo Tasso on the integrity of the faithful fascist body. He stood up on the podium elevated (though the propaganda instincts of the members had made it impossible to perceive) on three volumes of Carducci. A cold, fleshless light burned in the hall. The men had dragged along their wives and here and there the monotony of intent faces was broken up by a splash of lipstick. But on the front row, faithfully seated next to her husband, Lili – all in black, and a veil draped over her face – caught the professor's eyes again and again. Her mouth, uncoloured but nevertheless brilliant, would not be screened by the simple fold of net. He considered stopping the lecture and asking for it to be removed but, realizing the absurdity of such a request, restrained himself, averted his eyes to the flags draped at the back of the room and opened his three-hour lecture with a quote from the Duce's excellent work on the Aosta problem, in which there is some discussion of the matter close to Tasso's heart: the coherence of the race.

'Although', he said, 'our leader makes no specific mention of the question of physique and racial features in general, it is beyond question that these matters were to the fore in his mind at the time of writing, and indeed ever since. With unwavering logic and consistency he has insisted that the purity and regularity of the face and of the body is the foundation of the healthy and self-sustaining State such as we wish it to be in this age. How is it possible to imagine the faces of our youth riddled with foreign elements . . . protruding brows . . . narrow eyes . . . over-prominent jaws,' the audience began affectedly wincing and uttering mutters of disapproval, '. . . thick lips . . . enlarged craniums or abnormally salient noses? How could we sit by and watch the intrusion of such disturbing elements without reacting violently, indignantly, morally? How could we watch impassively the growing domination of suspect traits over our own faces? Is it not true that a people who cannot determine their own faces are irrevocably lost?' He paused for a drink and watched the faces in front of him flinching with expressions of unmentionable horror. 'When each child is born his parents naturally and understandably wonder about his or her face. What do they wish? For a proper face, a true face, an integral face. A face wholesome and clean. A face devoid of scars, blemishes, warts or signs of degeneracy. Not just any face for our children, comrades . . . we want and demand the faces of our deepest desires and ideals, the faces of our fondest dreams. And who is to say that we, the arbiters of society and the State, do not have a sacred duty to maintain the lineage of comely, noble and uncosmopolitan faces upon which our nation's future depends and without which we will inevitably be little more than a scavenging horde of bastardized mongrels? I leave it to your imaginations . . . what will the future be like

195

when the face of a Yugoslavian is indistinguishable from the face of an Italian?'

The audience laughed, stamped its feet and finally wept with rage. The professor moistened his throat and continued, touching now upon the relation – proved by the latest findings of teams of geneticists and nutrition experts working secretly in the Alps – between pasta, genes and gymnastic horses, now upon faces and the soil, faces and manual toil and faces and sexual abstinence, and the more he talked the more a bloodless colour came into his knuckles and the rim of his forehead, giving him the blush of a sprig of mimosa.

Sainctavit was enraptured. He had suspected it all along. The noses of Roman emperors seen sideways on their coins! The imperial form of the nose! He touched his dressing and dared to stick out his chin proudly. He was hoping that the professor would notice the resilience of his facial profile and go back to Rome singing its praises . . .

But as the professor moved into the last third of his lecture (purity of skin, procreation and brown bread) and Sainctavit forgot about his small cosmetic problem, the professor's eye became progressively engaged by what appeared to him as a malfunction in his vision. He blinked and paused for a second. It really did seem as if the leading, stout fascist in the front row . . . as if his chin . . . as if there was something appearing on his chin, as if a displacement in the tidy order of things were uncovering a shameful secret. For, unknown to the faithful Party member firmly grasping his wife's hand and hoping that – beneath the heavy veil – her mouth was not up to unforgivable tricks, the two strips of adhesive tape holding his dressing in place had slipped out of joint, disengaged themselves from the smooth underside of the jaw and were beginning to hang limply down on either side not of the antiseptic dressing but of the most monstrous, the most offensive boil the academic had ever seen. And for the first time the skin at the tip had broken, the base had swollen to terrifying proportions and the suppurating volcano was discharging a hideous liquid in all directions.

The professor swooned, held a handkerchief to his mouth and teetered slightly. He could not take his eyes from it. Could anything so appalling exist in nature? Could anything so profoundly anti-social exist in the subdued empire of the Duce? He felt shaken.

Curtailing his lecture abruptly, though to clamorous applause, he left the podium shaking his head and asking for a whiff of smelling salts to stop himself fainting.

The meeting disbanded, Sainctavit chased after his guru. But the professor had changed his plans. Running directly to the street he ordered the Party officials to provide him with a car: he was going directly back to Rome.

'I would never have believed it', he murmured angrily as if to himself, 'if I hadn't seen it with my own eyes . . .'

'Professor,' the Party secretary, who happened to be the same Prince Massima whose photograph had appeared in Sainctavit's publication, 'we trust that you are not unfavourably impressed by your audience's reaction. I can assure you that they . . .'

'What? The audience . . . reaction? Ah no, I didn't hear a thing. It was the fellow on the front row. The one with the pretty wife. His dressing . . . I mean, the thing on his face . . .'

'We can explain. The doctors have said that Signor Sainctavit has been suffering excessive strain and nervous tension, a situation which often . . .'

'Strain? Tension? Rubbish! A thing like that is the sign of corruption! And in front of all the local youth! It's abominable!'

In short, the professor hurried back to the Ministry of the Interior, where he called a meeting with Tommaso de Gesu, the senior officer with jurisdiction over local Party matters.

'I've just returned from Monza,' he said coldly, 'where I saw for myself the concrete danger facing the Fatherland. One of the Party members there has allowed a hideous deformation to scar his face, despite the fact that the local population looks up to him as a prominent representative of our programme. Would you believe it, he has the largest boil in Italy on his chin! He looks diseased. Even a Jew couldn't look worse. People are going to start talking. What kind of a man, they are going to say, sports a boil like that on his face? He probably runs a child pornography ring!'

'Well now,' the suave de Gesu considered, stroking his chin. 'We can't have a boil harming our reputation in the Monza district. Did you suggest an operation?'

'But this is a criminal act. It's subversion. It's not a matter of persuasion. He has to be punished.'

'But', de Gesu objected thoughtfully, 'it is not sufficient to

197

punish him, it is his boil which must also be punished. That is, it has to be made to disappear. If we punished him and the boil survived and continued displaying itself on his face, then the punishment will have been in vain. Is that not so?'

'That is exactly so.'

The professor clucked his tongue.

'That is why an operation is preferable.'

'But risky.'

'True. Firstly, it might not work. Secondly, it makes a mockery of us.'

'It would be infinitely preferable . . .'

'Regrettable in the circumstances . . .'

'But justified by the logic of the situation and the interests of the Party . . .'

'. . . and commendable in the eyes of the leader, who wouldn't hesitate to do the same if so asked . . .'

'Much tidier.'

'Neater.'

'As it were, surgical.'

They shared a gentlemanly laugh.

The professor was profoundly anxious to have the boil arrested.

He kept gesturing towards the telephone.

'It could be done tonight. I would say that every minute it is exposed to our people, the greater the danger is.'

'Oh, you really are very thorough are you not, Signor Tasso?'

The ironic de Gesu picked up the phone.

'Make up a warrant for a Paolo Sainctavit, Monza Party, and bring it in immediately. I'll sign it as soon as it's done. There.'

He put down the receiver and took a toothpick from the rack on his desk. 'A whisky, Professore Tasso?'

The professor slumped with relief. The memory of the boil still left a bad taste in his mouth.

'With pleasure, Signor de Gesu. I must admit I'm exhausted.'

'Vigilance is an exhausting vocation, Professore Tasso. Soda and ice?'

As soon as he saw the professor making for his car with an air of consternation, Sainctavit himself had guessed the cause. When he felt the liquid seeping from the boil and the dressing dangling out of joint he knew Tasso had seen his appalling defect. Rushing home, he took off his uniform in shame and decided to execute himself, a sentence which honour would in any case dictate.

The fragrant night out in the hills did nothing to calm him.

'Stay down here,' he ordered Lili. 'They're going to arrest me but I'm going to do what they're going to do before they do . . .'

'It's only a boil,' she said quietly.

'Typical of a woman: no understanding of ideology . . . What's the use? The militia will be here before dawn.'

He went up to his room and closed the door. In the bathroom he turned on all the lights and looked at the carbuncle in the mirror. He understood exactly why the professor had been so shaken. Naked under the overhead electric light it possessed the pornographic vitality of a nude leg. And simply because the skin had broken and a stream of yellowish fluid was flowing downwards from its crater.

It's all down to her, he thought. It's her boil, not mine. She is the originator of the nation's largest pustule, and no other. But no one would believe him; the tribune would laugh his explanations out of court.

Going to the wardrobe he dragged out the silk belt from one of his dressing gowns and, knocking over his drugs cabinet as he crashed across the room, went back into the bathroom. A long brass rail ran above the bath bearing unused curtain rings. He threw the belt over the rail, constructed a crude noose with one end, slipped it over his head and climbed laboriously on to the rim of the bath. Wiping the tears from his mouth, and uttering a hoarse cry of 'The Higher Duty!' he launched himself into space.

He had forgotten, however, his recent weight recorded on the new American automatic machine in the bedroom. The belt snapped as it bit into his neck, and the rail buckled and snapped out of its brackets at the same moment and the tragic mass of the former pimp, puppet seller and servant of the Higher Duty plunged earthwards in a flurry of flying soap and scattered brushes, the upper part of the nape striking the edge of the bath just as the left foot shattered a porcelain towel rail under the window. The light bulb was hit by a flying curtain ring, cracked and went out and the music of anguish and humiliation that raged in his head was silenced as he drifted in slow motion towards a plastic potty he had bought in the hope of inspiring maternal impulses in his infertile wife. A blue haze of starlight came through the window-pane broken by a piece of the ruptured rail.

And the worst of it was that, as he glumly perceived in mid-flight from the corner of his eye, the plastic potty was pink.

37

The Sainctavit dossier, delivered express by a sombre boy, arrived on the desk of the great ideologue Galeazzo Ciano, who as the Leader's son-in-law would soon fly in a plane over the Ethiopian town of Adowa with malice in his eye. The newly appointed propaganda chief opened the dossier bound with red strings, cast an eye over it in a hurry and convened a short meeting with the Monza Party chiefs, de Gesu and Tasso. 'It seems to me', he said circumspectly, 'that the Sainctavit woman should be married off as quickly as possible, and preferably to someone inside the Party. After all, she's normal: no trace of fununculosis on *her* chin!'

De Gesu: 'Quite correct, sir, absolutely correct, we don't want ugly noises being made by a widow.'

'So we need . . .'

'A victim.'

'So that's how you see it, do you, de Gesu?'

De Gesu shrugged and picked his teeth.

The Party chiefs looked round at each other.

'If', Tasso said coolly, 'it is anyone remotely eligible, sir, tongues will wag. We need a stooge.'

'Someone with an estate', Ciano mused, 'big enough to shut her up.'

'Turn her into a housewife.'

'Get her producing.'

'Making bales . . .'

'. . . and *bambini!*'

'A containment operation, gentlemen.'

Tasso looked into space; then clucked his lips.

'There is only one choice,' he said. 'Prince Massima.'

'Massima?'

Ciano looked doubtful.

He couldn't disguise his hatred for aristocrats.

'I hear he shoots his peasants,' de Gesu put in. 'For insubordination.'

'Ha ha, does he now? Does he now?'

Massima became more attractive . . .

'I didn't think they did that any more. What a character.'

'He also keeps a whip handy,' Tasso said, suppressing a yawn.

Ciano clapped and rubbed his hands.

'It's decided, then. Call him in and debrief him. Tell him . . . tell him we need kids and . . . and obedience and . . . bales . . . fresh eggs for the workers, you know . . . in a word husbandry.'

'Husbandry, sir.'

'Yes, husbandry is the word.'

'In the name of husbandry . . .'

'He's come over, sir. He'll see the morality of husbandry.'

Tasso finally yawned and in so doing revealed a lonely and sinister gold tooth.

Ciano lit a cigarette and crossed his boots.

'Now – can we arrange a ceremony without delay?'

The Party deputy secretary raised a hand like a schoolboy.

'If the prince is agreeable, sir, it can be done before the end of next month.'

'The perfect solution.'

Tasso wiped his glasses.

'If there are any loose ends . . . ?'

'No . . .'

Ciano considered for a moment, then snapped the dossier shut and tied up the red strings.

Three days later Tasso and de Gesu sat before Prince Massima and made their proposition, making clear also that he was in no position to refuse it. The prince, who was dishevelled and vague, scratched his mop of greying hair and scowled.

'But I don't want a wife,' he whined. 'I never did want one.'

Whereupon the frightening Tasso: 'Prince, the Duce has pronounced on this matter. Think of the consequences of letting this woman on the loose. Absolutely not, prince, absolutely not. Besides, you know that we need children. And increased agricultural productivity. You understand.'

'Well, I . . .'

'Did you hear that, de Gesu . . . the voice of a patriot.'

They offered him a glass of *vin santo*.

'And remember, prince, remember to be kind. Treat her with care . . . and multiply!'

The heads roared with laughter.

They nudged each other violently.

They had all seen that mouth of hers . . . a ripe strawberry, or some other brightly dyed fruit.

But the prince blushed and the meeting was adjourned.

As he travelled back to his estate, he found his hand fidgeting coldly with his leg as it never had before. He had never expected a wife. After a lifetime of rural solitude his image of woman was closely tied to that of gestating cows, chickens and ewes. The vast estate . . . the disorderly estate . . . the crumbling moist villas filled with snakes . . . the shit-filled outhouses smelling of mould-infested bags of compost . . . no, she was going to revolt against him . . . the spiders, the spiders were going to be a problem, and the scorpions, the moths, the peasants.

He ground his fist into his leg.

'I don't want a shitty little woman on my land!' he groaned, clenching his teeth. 'I want more cows and they send me a woman! They've been waiting to get me for years, the suburban bank clerks cum black shirts . . . they've been waiting to demote me in the Party and load me up with a cow of a wife. And all the money I'll have to spend, the shitty money, the money . . .'

Yes, new pipes for the lavatories, proper movable curtains, bed warmers, heaters on castors, china basins, insect repellents, carpets, electric lights, laundry machinery, contraceptives, knives with apostle handles, atomizers, radio sets . . . ice . . .

A tragic exertion of previous forces.

And then the peasants, the peasants, no you couldn't forget the peasants, the peasants were always there like an immovable background waiting to be set on fire by a woman, by a change in the order. Heavy with foreboding, he steeled himself for stormy seas. And then he remembered the money again and hit his leg so hard with his fist that it bruised. The money was going to wound.

At the marriage in the church of Santa Agata, the confetti

touched her lips and stuck there like the petals of a flower shaken over her body by an omen-throwing spirit. The prince leant down and kissed them by accident. And as he felt the thickness of her lips lined with saliva and paper and burning with a nameless kitsch, he felt his foreboding explode into terror.

VIII

VIII

38

The Belle Époque writer Paul Morand, describing the clash of opposing social interests, uses the phrase: 'C'était la guerre du monocle contre le pince-nez.'

And if this analogy is to be forced upon our heroine's marriage to Prince Massima, it would be modified to: 'The war of the female mouth against the male whip.'

The prince was:

1 Miser
2 Amateur violinist
3 Prohibitor of pesticides
4 Prohibitor of machinery
5 Mystic of the Land
6 Advocate of the manhunt
7 User of wooden plates

He professed admiration for:

1 Nero
2 Marconi (mistaken identity)
3 Vittorio Emmanuele
4 Sobieski of Poland

He dressed in filthy Oxford tweeds inherited from his father. From time to time he exhibited the sly and dangerous *morbidezza* of the peripheral European aristocracy and uttered pointless interjections such as 'Geronimo!' and *'avaler des couleuvres'*.

If the mooing of a cow that had been unfed for three weeks

interrupted his playing of the violin, he would ask some grovelling menial to stick a hot brand up its backside.

If his boredom got the better of him he would retire muttering to his philistine library and study, with its stench of turpentine, and write gigantic jeremiads against combine harvesters.

As for Lili, there was nothing to do but shut her up in a wing of the main house, giving her the keys of course, but telling her not to speak to the peasants or travel outside without his permission.

And so, confined to a series of peeling, ochre rooms, she paced up and down for weeks on end, biting her lips, twisting her fingers, turning her unhappiness and bitterness over and over in her entrails until they became habitual.

They ate together in the evenings in a whitewashed hall corroded by bacteria: transparent soups and plates of noodles served by grinning automata.

Moved by obscure desires, he sometimes enveloped her in mystic embraces. But the smell of his lips drove her off.

At other times he climbed up to her rooms, tapped feebly on the door and waited crouching like a naughty child until her refusal to reply compelled him to go away. And never once was this ritual discussed.

Years passed executing these shadow dances.

She ordered her calendars from Monza and marked the days with black inverted crosses.

'Ah, the rhythms of the Land,' her husband lectured on the rare days he took a spade and waved it around uselessly in some field of failed vetches or other. 'What need do we have of electric light switches and tooth brushes when we have spades to wield, vetches to manure and peasants to flagellate?'

But with the passing of time, his worship of the Emperor Nero took on the form of an imitation deriving perhaps from the same hidden lesions of the brain. For in the first months of 1938 he began mistaking salt cellars for servants and automobiles for horses. A gradual elision of objects took place in his mind – but could it not also be said that this was the result, not of the growing tumour in the right side of his brain which the neurologist would quickly identify, but of the growing force of vulgarity that his bride was implanting in those same occipital lobes by means of the rare and ceremonial kisses that she bestowed upon his head?

It began, simply enough, with the salt cellar.

One night, as they were eating alone, he began to stare at it intensely. His head rolled to one side. He stopped masticating. Squinting and then twitching, he stared at it wonderingly and then menacingly.

A snarl came to his lips.

'To the right!' he said.

'Excuse me?'

'Not you. The servant.'

He wiped his mouth and laid his napkin to rest.

'To the right!' he repeated. 'One step to the right. Are you deaf?'

'Teodoro . . .'

'Shut up. I'm talking to the servant.'

He clenched his fist.

'To the right. One step to the right.'

Silence. The trees creaked outside.

The salt cellar was 'disobeying' him.

'You'll be punished,' he tittered. 'I'll fire you without comp-ensation . . .'

He turned to Lili.

'You see. That's what happens when you let them read. They become Marxists!'

'Teodoro . . .'

'No, no, don't plead with me on their behalf. You should know better. Everything here belongs to me. My objects. Look at him. He's cocking a snoot, *sapristi*! He thinks he's Victor Hugo!'

He leaned over and put his face against the cellar.

'One step to the right or you're out!'

Waving his fork, he turned to Lili again.

'You see, he thinks he can outface me. Let this be a lesson for you. One has to know how to deal with one's possessions. Especially the servants. When they get ideas into their heads they think . . .'

At this point, hearing the shouting, a servant came into the room. Massima stopped dead in the middle of his flow and froze. The servant froze (the master wasn't well by the looks of things). Massima went pale. The servant went pale. Massima looked at the salt cellar, then at the servant, then back to the salt cellar and then once more to the servant.

'I'll be damned,' he whispered to Lili. 'Do you see what I see?

A salt cellar has just come into the room on its own! It's moving on its own, I swear. I'll be damned if I ever saw such a thing!'

'Sir?' the servant squeaked.

Massima jumped up in amazement.

'It talked!'

He sat down and they froze again.

He stared vengefully at the salt cellar as if to say: I'll catch up with you later.

Lili now rose herself and excused herself.

'What's the matter, my pet?' Massima exclaimed. 'I know it's a bit odd what with this salt cellar moving around on its own, but there's a scientific explanation for everything – it's no excuse to abscond.'

'I have a headache.'

She left the table and went to her room.

It was impossible to explain his behaviour. It was true that it was not the first time he had mistaken one key for another or a pool of water for a dry ditch or a white cloud for a black cloud, but up until now his lapses had been small and simple slip ups, malfunctionings that needed no severe explanation. But she had seen the salt cellar and the servant, the mutual freezing and incomprehension. If he was going mad, what spirit of symmetry and inversion was this madness going to uphold? She was alone with him in the building with the servants. There was no one but them and the servants. Either she broke ranks with her adopted class and joined the indubitably sane servants or she stuck with it and preserved her position, complete with Rolls-Royce and electric curling tongs. On the other hand, she could wait until the prince attracted the indignation of his brother fascists and was locked up in the Monza lunatic asylum or the tumour that might be lodged dangerously in his right hemisphere touched a vital nerve and killed him outright . . . in which case she would add to her capital assets.

She kept catching sight of her face in the strange hexagonal mirror fixed into the dressing table which his mother had used. The two lines on either side of her face were unmistakable. They formed two elongated Ss around her lips like the holes in a violin around the strings.

They were spreading up towards the wings of her nose.

In a year, in a month, in a week . . . in a second, perhaps, she would be old.

If she joined the servants it was possible they would skewer them both on pitchforks. If she supported Massima it was equally possible that he would mistake her for a bale of hay and skewer her on a pitchfork. As she heard him coming up the stairs after her she prevaricated over locking the door. But if she locked the door he might be assailed by a moment of lucidity, a moment which might destroy everything . . .

He padded along the corridors talking to the doors.

'I thought I told you all to go to bed. You're hanging around waiting for a scene, aren't you? I know how your microscopic intelligences work. You like it when the masters make a scene. But orders are orders – get back to bed at once!'

He entered the room quietly and respectfully.

Stealing up behind her, he put his arms around her.

'I know it seems severe,' he whispered tenderly into her ear, 'but without severity a house cannot be governed. It may be difficult for you. But you have to learn. Otherwise it is *avaler des couleuvres*. Everything as far as you can see', and he gestured vaguely out of the window, through which a low red horizon studded with tiled barns and stooks could be seen, 'is yours and mine. Every insect. Every stone. Every living thing. Well, if that's so, you have to know how to govern them. The estate is a system. In the system every thing has its place. You can move the objects around as you would pieces around a chess board – they don't mind, it's their function to be moved around according to your will. And if they do mind they have to be curbed. Yes, they have to be curbed,' he liked this word, and practised it a few times. 'Without being curbed they would ruin the system. They would turn us into sausagemeat. Yes, they would turn us into sauerkraut and sausage, *sapristi*, imagine that!'

And he burst out laughing.

The next, while out walking with his foremen looking for poachers, he mistook a cow for a pheasant-bagger, unslung his double-barrelled shotgun and blew a hole through the centre of its forehead, equidistant from either horn. The foremen, terrified at the thought of adverse reactions, applauded loudly and declared they had never seen a fatter more vicious-looking poacher than the one he had just shot – and how rightly, all things considered.

He helped load the carcass himself on to a lorry. As he touched the limp head his hands were covered with blood.

He looked down at them in fascination.

'Why look at that,' he murmured to the foremen. 'It looks like cow's blood. Now I know what I always suspected, gentlemen – that all human blood, *par dieu*, is not the same!'

39

From salt cellars and cows, the prince's failure to decipher the organization of objects and organisms that lay around him extended to windows, radio sets, dolls, wardrobes, swords, fish and plates of jellied eels. A violent spirit of inversion seized him. The eels were grenades. The radio set was a sneering farmhand. The wardrobe was a giant red flag emblazoned with the words, 'Massima's head for fish bait!' Everywhere he turned the world was mined with subtle and traitorous traps. The brass taps installed in his bedroom wash-basin were no longer taps: they were coils of electrified barbed wire stolen from the cattle sheds by the ingenious proles and wired up from a generator to his basin to give his noble fingers a lethal shock as he washed himself. And conversely, when he suddenly came face to face with the decreasing numbers of workers and peasants who crossed the fields and occasionally ventured as far as the house he had to squint, look hard and pinch himself to make sure they were not ambulating chickens, bushes or tractors filled with a miraculous anima of revolution. The sea of nature was squirming under his feet, one half of it meticulously obedient, the other corrupted by leftist propaganda, ready to rise like a snake and deliver a nasty bite to the neck.

More and more, he felt unsafe in the fields. He retired to the house and delivered orders to the foremen, who assembled in the courtyard, by means of notes scribbled on pieces of paper.

The orders, however, could not be fulfilled.

'Take the peasants loitering on the horizon in a north-easterly direction and who are disguising themselves by assuming the form of trees and give them four hundred blows with a cane each to the lumbar region!'

'Any peasant impersonating a bale will be shot!'

'Dogs are forbidden to be servants and vice versa!'

His disorder progressed as the Monza Party became increasingly suspicious. A policeman with a monocle and a baton arrived to inspect his face.

'Sir, it has been suggested by the Party that you should spend a comfortable night in hospital.'

He looked straight into the prince's cold blue eyes.

'Boys, boys, it's talking! Where's the net?'

'Prince . . .'

'Shoo – whineey! Back in the pen, cluck cluck. No, he won't. He's a stubborn one. We'll have to get him by the neck, boys.'

The policeman took a step back.

'You refuse?'

'Ha ha ha, you witty little bird! I'll cook you with chestnuts and sea salt. He's a cunning rogue, this one.'

The farmhands, the prince and his foreman gave chase to the policeman, who reached the gates and dived into the car. He fired a shot over their heads. When he got back to Monza he told the dismal story of the chase. The council raised its eyebrows. Astounding! Two fascists round the bend and a piece of mouth in common between them. Had the marriage backfired? They sent a note to the unstable prince.

Dear Prince, a specialist in ambiguous tumours arrives tomorrow from Milan, by the name of Hermann. He is at your disposal, in a spirit of irreproachable comradeship. Yours, the Council.

The prince was not impressed.

'We're about to fight the ultimate war against the pullulating microbes of democracy and they're complaining that I maintain discipline at home, resisting the universal impulse towards anarchy and disrespect, enforcing the natural right to govern and squash! Have they forgotten the ethos of the eagle which we wear on our proud caps? Have they forgotten the memory of the Sforza, and their anal stakes? Once the spirit of cruelty is dead, the world is nothing more than a brothel filled with copulating monkeys! There'll be nothing left to do but *avaler des couleuvres*.'

He picked his nose with disgust and decided on an appropriate measure of self-assertion. Gathering all the salt cellars, pepper pots, knives, forks, casseroles and slotted spoons – every kitchen utensil he could find – he piled them up in the compost heap behind the kitchen (from where the kitchen workers had fled in terror) and covered them with methylated spirits. He then set fire to the heap and stepped back.

Lili saw the smoke. She leaned out of a window.

'Look,' the dictator said, 'I'm burning my servants *en masse* since they refused to obey me in the manner to which I am accustomed. Don't worry – they breed like flies. There are hundreds more out there.'

The assorted metal shapes twisted in the heat, softened and curled, turned white and then blue-black. When the fire died there was nothing but a smoking pile of distorted fragments.

When Massima saw the mutilated bodies of his mutinous servants, he let out a howl of joy and picked up his violin.

As his bow scraped across the strings, Czechoslovakia disappeared quietly from the map.

40

He came up at night to knock tamely on the door hoping for a chance of an occasional mating, for of everything left to him she was the only one that remained undistorted in his field of vision.

True, he sometimes momentarily mistook her for a coat stand or the walnut lamp in their bedroom. But if he did he identified her immediately by her mouth. Like his own reflection, it did not change.

One day he was eating a chicken with his wife in the white-washed hall. He ate greedily, snapping the bones with his teeth. From time to time he spat one out, left it where it lay on the floor and carried on crunching, humming inanely as he did and leaving piles of skin to one side of the plate. Then suddenly he stopped, leaned forward slightly and went red in the face. His cheeks billowed out; his eyes popped.

A bone was stuck in his throat.

He rose and performed a semi-circular motion, beckoning at the same time to his throat.

Lili rose as well and hit him violently on the back.

He coughed, spat and cleared his voice. He was able to speak since the main part of the bone had been ejected and hurled across the table, but a splinter had broken and remained stuck half-way down the trachea.

Induced regurgitation failed to dislodge it.

'You'll never believe it,' he said, breathing with difficulty and still pointing unnecessarily to his throat, 'and I would never have believed it myself if I hadn't seen it. Just as I was putting that breast into my mouth, a servant – who must have been hiding under it all this time – jumped up and flew into my mouth, and so quickly I must have missed him . . . and now he's tried to strangle me by sticking in my throat. I can feel his heels digging in. How can I get him out? You see . . . they're completely mutinous now. Uncontrollable. I know what I'll have to do: I'll have to make an example of one of them and make his comrade', he used the word with anguish, 'come out and face the music.'

For days the bone remained.

It tortured him, not because of the pain it inflicted upon his throat, but because it practised insubordination in such a matter-of-fact way.

For every waking minute it reminded him of his loss of control over his estate.

Hauling his meagre furniture into the salon he berated it while prodding it viciously with a pitchfork.

'All right, comrades,' he sneered. 'One of you got into my throat. But you needn't think your little piss-pot revolution is going anywhere. I have even your chicken-bone compatriot under control. Tonight I'll stand on my head and flush him out with an emetic. You'll see how wretched he looks when he comes out, too. Thought you'd stick in your master's throat, did you? Choke him on the sly with his chicken?'

When the emetic and yoga failed, he resorted to opera exercises. Still the bone bit into his windpipe. When he lay down he had passing feelings of nausea and suffocation. The revolution of the household objects posing as servants might have been more successful than he had supposed.

With every day that passed with the bone half blocking the passage of air, his realm became more insubstantial.

'I'd like you to look at it with a mirror,' he told his wife. 'Talk to it. Be commanding. Tell it to do as it's told. Tell it to remember its duty to lord and master. Tell it to forget all the propaganda. Tell it . . .'

But he could not think what would persuade it to surrender.

And even worse, the rebellious element was now inside him.

'Talk about *avaler des couleuvres*,' he said darkly.

When he was asleep, however, he held dialogues with it. He tried to inflict dialectics on it. He pointed out the futility of its political demands, the uselessness of its imported Germano-Judaic ideology, the vulgarity of its derivative vocabulary. He pointed out that his family, whoever they were, had lived for five generations on his family's land and had always worked for his ancestors.

In short, he refuted its revolutionary spirit.

'You may cause me momentary discomfort,' he told it every night before dropping off, 'but we'll see who has the stamina of social commitment!'

Two months passed and still the bone resisted him.

He began to despair.

Perhaps nobility was done for after all.

The world of objects, having now reduced itself essentially to a servant-bone stuck in his throat, was eluding him.

He locked himself in the house and barred the windows. The objects, the servants were out there, and he admitted that they had successfully gained independence.

'They are out-playing me,' he said thoughtfully. 'They are waltzing around me. Inside out: that's what they are . . . inside out. And how can I out-manoeuvre them without making myself more inside out than they are? If they pretend to be what they are not, I too will pretend to be what I am not. I will cancel out their inside outness!'

One morning in the following week, Lili returned from a visit to Monza to find the prince alone in his mother's bedroom dressed from head to foot in his grandmother's ball gown. His face was extravagantly painted. His hair was done up in a gigantic chignon studded with Indian Ocean pearls. And as he sat there contemplating himself in the mirror, he talked softly to the chicken bone.

'You've been outsmarted,' he said happily. 'You're a chicken bone, are you? Fine. In that case I am the sugar plum fairy.'

Real servants were huddled around the doorway, peering in with amazement and terror. The master in a lilac and net dress prancing round his mother's bedroom holding forth to a chicken bone stuck in his throat! The lord of the great Massima estate magically and unexpectedly transformed into a transvestite! Revolution in the form of a sodomite perversion! Their mouths hung open. What would the Holy Virgin do next?

But as Lili approached the room unable to suppress her smile of satisfaction, a gardener who had always mistrusted her pushed forward and pushed his black thumb contemptuously into her sternum.

218

'I knows what yer are,' he said, with red eyes. 'Yer made the marster like what he is in there. Yer made 'im a pansy, yer did. Yer git yer fancy arse outer our estate, if yer please, or we'll cut yer up with this.'

He showed a short machete.

The others edged forward, too.

'The beloved marster,' they growled, 'the kind and generous marster!'

From within the master's voice ascended in strange scales and arpeggios.

'She done in the marster,' a hag cried. 'She done 'im in with a chicken bone.'

'A chicken bone what's turned 'im pansy.'

'Oh the poor marster, the unfortunate marster!'

'A marster can't eat no chicken bone. His throat ain't made for no chicken bones.'

'She's a witch!'

They crooned ensemble at this word.

Their eyes rolled.

They took out their weapons.

'What's the marster to do now with his chicken bone?'

'It can't be moved!'

'It's a bewitched chicken bone!'

More croons.

'He's as good as dead.'

'That's what they call a "Transylvanian".'

'A foren chicken bone.'

And they lamented in chorus, beating their breasts.

'The marster! The marster! Since he was a little boy!'

'Sucked our breasts . . .'

'Rode our 'orses . . .'

'Played our skittles . . .'

'Ate our noodles . . .'

'Since he was a little boy!'

Lili retreated at the first opportunity. A light snow was falling outside. The air of freedom was cold and white.

As she ran skipping down the frozen mud path to the outer gates she heard from time to time the scratching of a violin, the mooing of a cow, the clank of a poker. A pale moon was rising. The chicken bone was talking back.

A servant had meanwhile picked up a telephone and called the fascist militia in a panic.

They were informed of a crime against 'the marster'.

'According to our best information,' the Party secretary informed the council, 'our former companion Prince Massima has been forcibly turned into a transvestite. The peasants are accusing the wife.'

'They mean the same one?' they asked, incredulous.

'The same one.'

De Gesu rose.

'It may well be gibberish from those apes, but it is not impossible, brothers, that psychological pressure, extortion and manipulation – and we all know how a woman can use her body! – could in fact amount to exactly the same thing. I suggest the militia pick her up and bring her in. She's clearly a . . .'

He wasn't sure what he was going to say – 'menace'? But that was idiotic. He paused, then let his sentence trail off unfinished. He sat down, shaking his head.

The council smirked and also shook their heads.

Of what could she be accused?

How was it possible to try a mouth in court?

For they all knew, with the instincts of their testicles, that only the vulgarity of that particular organ – and never a mere chicken bone – could have reduced the masculine Prince Massima to a state of paradoxical transvestitism.

IX

41

Lili Dorziat was never tried by the fascist courts. At this delicate junction in her life the Duce discreetly intervened. A trial would re-awaken memories of long-forgotten scandals. It would impede the war effort.

'And finally', he advised the Gerarchia, to whose attention this infamous case had come, 'she's just a tart. Nothing more or less. Are we going to shoot ourselves in the foot over a tart who didn't know how to behave herself? And the judgement, of course, will be the same. We ought to remember that the American press is always ready to use tart stories. They don't mind getting their hands dirty. But I see no reason why they should be helped. The best thing, gentlemen, is to make the offending party disappear.' And he added after a pause, 'Besides, I take it that it's very unlikely that she'll be bearing any children for the nation!'

But even as he was saying this, the ladies' man was thinking to himself that it was a shame that he had never met her. They would have got on like a house on fire. Providing, of course, that she didn't give him syphilis.

The Duce's prognostic wisdom condemned her to an asylum. Close to the seaside town of Torre Marina near Foggia, the asylum of Santa Anna answered his demands for isolation and secrecy.

42

An oval window looked out over a dark and nostalgic sea. Dolphins danced in the ocean and submarines, putting up their periscopes, wondered at the sudden 'fragrance' (they had no other way of putting it) that they detected in a high window of the high-security asylum on the tip of the promontory they regularly passed in the hope of seeing naked women dancing on the roof tops.

If they had been able to focus in greater detail, they would have seen a shaved head standing by the window with the perfect ovoid shape of one of Piero della Francesca's mystic eggs.

But what was Piero della Francesca to them?

And what did they care about eggs unless they were edible with a pinch of salt?

How could they imagine the arc of a celestial compass descending to design a mere human head?

They passed by wondering if the mad cows were now setting fire to themselves in their spare time.

The asylum director, D'Agata, wearing a strange lanital suit to promote the nation's latest artificial textile, made a personal call as soon as he heard that her name was, as it were, elevated to the nobility.

The barber's scratches were fresh on his face and behind him stood a shy teenage boy in a dirty white apron.

The director ostentatiously laid a clementine on the table.

And as he did so, he looked wistfully at her privileged nails.

A woman in her late thirties, he mused to himself, but still worth a bit of attention by means of otherwise unobtainable clementines.

'A regrettable posting' he said of himself, 'and one I would have otherwise refused. But – *Roma è Roma*.'

This phrase meant nothing but he kept repeating it, as if it explained everything about everything.

He then brought forward the trembling youth, who had his hands buried in the apron. A red, inflamed, acne'd face . . . a pair of awkward legs.

The teenager bowed.

'Always bow,' the director reminded him, and kicked him hard in the shins. 'Don't be afraid to kick him in the shins,' he then said to Lili. 'This is your factotum . . . that is to say, I'm presenting him to you, to show my respect. No, no, madame, I insist . . . how could I do otherwise?'

Lili held out her hand to the factotum, who did nothing.

'Oh, madame, I see you're still a little naive, if I may say . . .'

And he whacked the shins again.

'His name's Topolo, a country boy and really a mouse with it.'

The teenager suddenly grinned stupidly.

'Don't be too genteel with him, Princess. These orderlies', and he whispered, '. . . Greeks.'

By which he meant southerners.

The teenager bowed again.

'It's the best we can do. Low IQ and . . . but why complain? We know where we are, Princess, don't we? . . . if I may be so bold as to say "we"!'

He was tempted to stay longer: her mouth was truly . . .

But submitting to duty and turning on his heel, he winked and clattered out.

She was alone with the boy, whose fingers quivered as he held the hem of the apron. His name was Enzo.

Looking up warily, he too caught sight of her mouth. It made his fingers sweat. His family had sent him to Bari for work and he had ended up in the loonie bin against his will.

Dividing the clementine, she gave him half.

'It's better than the army,' she said.

'No clementines in the army, miss.'

'The clementine is here because of me.'

'I know, miss.'

'You'd rather eat clementines than kill Albanians, wouldn't you, Enzo?'

225

'Yes, miss.'

'Then we've both landed on our feet, haven't we, Enzolino?'

He shrugged.

'There's only one other thing I want: I want flowers.'

'Yes, miss. I'll steal them for you.'

'Every day, Enzo. I want them every day.'

'Yes, miss.'

'Red ones and yellow ones . . .'

'Yes . . .'

Every day the boy brought the flowers.

The floral smell became so intense that the guards came running up the stairs, intoxicated but holding their noses. D'Agata, climbing the stairs after them, peered through the hole in the door.

'It might be unchivalrous', he murmured to them, 'but the flowers are not from me – get rid of them.'

But however much they carted out the bushels of flowers, the cell stank with decomposing petals.

Lili did nothing with her days. She sat by the window and looked out to sea. From time to time she took out one of the flowers she had saved, parted the corolla with her fingers and buried her face in it.

Before long, she forgot what year it was or where she was on the surface of the globe. In the distance, reassuring and melodic, she heard the graceful singing of torpedoes.

43

She passed the days playing solitaire. She taught Enzo how to play and later taught him German as well. Devoted and unquestioning, he ran up and down the stairs like a willing dog.

'When will three queens turn up?' he asked.

'When I decide on an appropriate gamble.'

'What will you gamble?'

'When two queens turn up,' she said, 'I'll ask you to go downstairs and steal a pistol. The gamble will be myself.'

'That's an aristo joke.'

'I'm not an aristo and I've never made an aristo joke in my life.'

Her head, as he saw it, was segmented into parts, so that he could say to himself, 'The nose is older than the mouth and the ear is younger than the jaw.'

The oldest part of it was ancient.

The youngest part was infantile.

He waited for the queens to arrive in their sinister row, but weeks passed without any sign of them.

But what if they did come? She made him promise he would 'execute' her.

And the more he obeyed her in canine fashion, lacking only a tail to wag, the more he was permeated by the spirit of her mouth. It 'imprinted' its shape upon him.

If he had to kill it, he would be simultaneously killing himself.

When D'Agata peeped through the keyhole he saw them together concentrated on their card games, holding hands, murmuring together in the corner. He didn't like it. A farmer boy consorting with a princess. It didn't gel. And why was she there? A furious council up north, gossip about a transvestite and a boil . . . the crocodile pormanteau . . . the flowers. Her disdain for lanitel . . . the division of the clementine (oh yes, he'd noticed!). He began to write a pretentious and politically motivated diary. And yet . . . he was jealous.

Jealous of the farmer boy!

But Lili's gambling career was about to deliver her from the possibility of love from D'Agata the diarist.

For one day she flipped over two queens in a row.

Turning to Enzo solemnly, she said: 'Go downstairs.'

The farmboy was dumbfounded.

'But this is stupid! Who's going to do it?'

He wrung his hands and the fingers dangled and twisted hysterically.

'They'll cut my head off!'

'You're going to do it, Enzo. You have nice hands for an executioner.'

He ran down to the guardroom, empty because it was lunchtime and the guards were examining a crate of cherries in the courtyard, and took a pistol from the drawer by the heater. It was fully loaded, with a greasy butt. He walked slowly back to the cell, gradually shedding the gloss of sweat on his back and forearms. He was acclimatizing.

'Shall we guess what card it's going to be?'

He sat down on the opposite side of the table and laid the pistol between them.

She turned the card: four of hearts.

'Poor little Enzo. Go to America. Make your way. Manufacture something useful for the masses. Why not disposable plungers or coat hangers? I have a theory about coat hangers. If they were in the shape of a female mouth, they would sell in their millions. An unconscious desire for coat hangers would enter the collective brain. Every time a man opened his wardrobe and saw his array of coat hangers – tinselled hangers, aluminium hangers, velvet-wrapped burgundy hangers, fishnet hangers, lace-frilled hangers – he would be filled with desire for mouths and so, triggered by the insidious suggestion of the mouth-shaped hangers he already had, he would rush out and buy more so that he could be surrounded by the divine form of the mouth, the mouth that fills his dreams, the mouth that gives birth to his vulgar habits.

The mouth, Enzo, is the midwife of man's madness. I could think of nothing better than the gradual but inexorable spread of its influence to all corners of the earth. And lodged so innocently in a man's most private recess . . . his wardrobe! Without even knowing it he would be exposed to it night and day, he would fall under its influence without any ready antidote to hand, with no cure but a puritanism he no longer believed in to save him. Take my advice, little Enzo Topolo: the era of the coat hanger is only just beginning and it will run parallel with the era of the female mouth. Our mouth will be our revenge and the humble coat hanger will take on a life of its own. New and terrible millionaires will be created in the process. Kitchen sinks, ashtrays, bidets, automobiles, waste disposal units, telephones, flag insignia, underwear, lavatory seats, double-breasted suits, can openers, television screens, gramophone horns, airships, transatlantic liners, soap boxes, dog kennels, iced biscuits, pecorino cheeses, coffee machines, aerials, sandwiches, shoehorns, pencil sharpeners, nail cutters, curling tongs and coat hangers . . . they are all going to to be impregnated with the colossal spirit of the mouth. The melodic line of the mouth will run through all of them and as it does so that magnificent organ of consumption will be more worshipped than at any time in its short four-million-year history! You are going to profit from it, Enzo Topolo, you are going to be a sage and worldly parasite! Only, don't forget – and she pouted, opening her mouth and thrusting it towards him – don't forget what you already love!'

The stupefied Enzo had not heard a thing. He waited for her to turn the card.

'What an exciting game of solitaire!' she sighed.

Enzo flinched as she flipped the fourth card over.

Queen of hearts.

He groaned and felt faint.

'I thought you promised,' she said softly. 'Perhaps you didn't say but you meant it. Pick up the pistol.'

He took the butt of the pistol into the palm of his hand, felt it sag towards his knee and then brought it level with her mouth. The slime on his forearms had come back. What had she been jabbering about coat hangers, mouths and lavatory seats?

She formed her lips into an oval.

'Put it in it,' she ordered.

'But it was only a joke with the queen.'

But disobeying himself he poked the barrel into the hole between the lips. Her eyes flared, black and purple, and looked into his own. The left eye winked. Sweat poured through his fingers, but the trigger was stable under the pressure of his index. The eye winked twice. The three queens looked up at him accusingly, dancing between them.

As the room turned white and the window exploded he closed his eyes and left the winking eye and the mouth far behind.

A spurt of blood hit the deck of cards and rocketed backward from the back of her head, spattering the white door behind them.

The head remained still. And as it did so he pulled the trigger.

44

On 23 July 1946, as he was passing through the straits of Gilbraltar carrying nothing but a four-inch potato knife and a crocodile portmanteau on his way to Philadelphia, the twenty-year-old Enzo Topolo – hearing the sound of jaws masticating pheasant wings and boar steaks in the emerald and butter dining room of the *Prince George*, under whose ovular opened windows he was sleeping on an oilskin – had a dream of a woman he had once shot through the mouth.

They were sitting around a roulette table. The woman was dressed in a cluster of giant feathers. Behind her stood a small group of servants in simple check suits, all holding their hands schoolboyishly in front of their knees. One of them had a mutilated ear, incompetently disguised by a tattered bandage. The fattest one, scowling in the shadows at having to obey orders from a female, wore a pair of Moroccan carpet slippers embroidered with tiny silver discs and kept one hand glued to a vulnerable zone of his forehead. Another tittered in the background, bending his knees like an infant and continually shuffling a pack of cards. A fourth had a violin string wound around his little finger and a lead soldier peeping out of a pocket. The fifth, the saddest and the most proud, nursed a huge boil on the end of his chin, which suppurated embarrassingly on to the fingernail that coaxed it. The five of them sulked and cracked unpleasant jokes as the mistress played, but as soon as she turned round with a steel gaze they subsided into silence and cracked their fingers nervously.

Her face was brilliantly lit under the overhead lamps hung low on thick rubber cables. A white face, with a huge mouth swinging in and out of the light, the corners flecked with dried blood. And he dreamt he was beating her at craps, while the five wretched

231

servants sniggered and the cracked corners of the mouth flirted with his own mouth across the table.

Finally, unable to contain his curiosity, he asked her who the servants were, where they were going and where she had got them.

'They're my souls,' she said charmingly, 'and I'm taking them back to Hell!'

When he woke up, he felt a light pressure on his bowels making him throw up over the side of the ship. He swore to himself he would never open the crocodile portmanteau. What a crazy thing for her to say! What a load of mad horse shit! He laughed all the way to Oklahoma, though. And he never forgot her expression as she said the word 'Hell', as if she knew exactly what it meant, a word that means nothing at all.

A NOTE ON THE AUTHOR

Lawrence Osborne is the author of a novel, *Ania Malina*, and a work of non-fiction, *Paris Dreambook*. He has lived in Paris for many years.